Cover Licence provided by
selfpubbookcovers.com;
Copyright © AmberCovers 2015

Paperback First Edition 2016

Published By:
Alternative Fiction,
Waterford, Ireland.
Publisher's ISBN: 978-0-9934247

Printed & Bound By:
IngramSpark,
La Vergne,
Tennessee,
America.

ISBN-13: 978-0-9934247-0-0

For John and Emmet

CHAPTER ONE

"Here's another weird piece of shit for you, Inspector," the man in the dark suit announced scornfully, throwing the stapled four page document across the desk of the seated man, nearly spilling his hot coffee in its plastic cup.

Detective Inspector Albert Maher looked up at his superior, Detective Chief Inspector Richard Bellings of New Scotland Yard with a sneer. Bellings always referred to him as 'Inspector' and not by name, preferring to maintain an impersonal relationship and a constant reminder to his insubordinate of his authority. Christ, Albert pondered, the DCI even had a poster of Robert the Bruce in his secluded office at the end of the building, remarking often of his direct ancestral link to the Scottish king. But rather everyone knew he spent most of his time there viewing pay-site Asian porn and dating websites, keeping his underpaid secretary busy ferrying him disposable handkerchiefs.

"Let me guess," Detective Maher sighed. "Some kid lost his favourite hamster at a neighbour's party."

"Don't be obtuse," Bellings snarled. "Read the file. The man was allegedly mugged and is currently under observation until six pm tonight in St. Thomas Hospital. MI5 have cleared him of any link to Al Qaeda, but his identity papers are proving much confusion. His apartment has also been burgled."

"Hasn't had much luck has he," Maher laughed, flicking through the report. "Says here the only witness to the assault was a wino. Great, that should clear things up." Albert shook his head and then stopped. "Wait a second…is this for real? Witness declares the victim punched his assailant in the chest, sending him a distance of over one hundred metres?" Maher stuttered in astonishment. "An Olympic weightlifter isn't that strong!"

"Like I said, a case right up your street." Bellings smiled. "Washington is sending a CIA agent over to investigate. Apparently the man might have worked for them in the past. They said he matched the description of an operative who did some undercover work in Cambodia in 1970."

"The Central Intelligence Agency is not that blind or stupid. My three year old nephew could tell this man by his picture is barely thirty five years old!"

"Just check it out," his superior snarled. "Last thing I need is the Prime Minister on the phone screaming at my ear because the Director of the CIA is being denied access to one of their agents." Bellings sighed. "I need confirmation of his identity."

Albert turned to the adjacent desk where sat his partner, Detective Sean Neilson, smiling into his coffee, knowing all too well of his friend's hatred of their superior.

"Oh no," Sean laughed. "You're on your own with this one. I'm off in five minutes to an early lunch and then home. My wife promises something special for our anniversary and she said not to be late."

"For fuck's sake, Sean," Albert said, gritting his teeth. "Everyone knows your wife hates your guts. You know there's not a chance of getting laid tonight. Special probably means your bags are packed and she's now dating your balder but more successful brother."

"She just likes to play hard to get," Detective Neilson smiled. "Besides I know your fondness for crap cases. Have fun interviewing the wino." Sean said, rising from his seat and made for the elevator.

"Thanks," Albert shouted, collecting his coat from the back of the chair.

A long car journey through London's afternoon traffic and Albert Maher arrived at St. Thomas Hospital. He hated the sterile smell of hospitals, overworked nurses performing mundane tasks without complaint, the procession of terminal patients whose only joy was three cigarettes quickly smoked in ten minutes at the entrance.

Two floors up and several corridors later he found the private room. The patient was sitting up reading The Sun, a tabloid newspaper of vacuous celebrities and airbrushed topless models. A bit lowbrow for someone who once worked for the secret intelligence community, Albert pondered. The man appeared as in his file to be in his mid-thirties, curly jet black hair barely touching the shoulders and having the skin complexion consistent with someone of Middle-Eastern origin. The patient was handsome, ensuring better service with the young nurses who catered to his every whim. The report said his name was Sam Philips, an Information Technology Consultant for a large computer firm in central London, responsible for the maintenance and upgrading of servers for banks and government departments. The Secrecy Act prohibited all further investigation into his employment history and working operations. A perfect cover for someone who wanted to remain anonymous.

The patient looked over the top of the newspaper at his visitor. An aging detective in a £200 dark suit and badly matching tie stood before him. The policeman to his eyes appeared to be in his early fifties, balding grey hair and neatly trimmed white beard. The air of twenty year apathy was all about him, a detective downtrodden by perpetual bureaucracy and arrogant superiors with their vision solely fixed on being Chief Constable by their fiftieth birthday.

"Take a seat, Inspector." Sam Philips announced.

"How did you know I was an Inspector?" Enquired Maher, placing his tired body on the uncomfortable plastic chair.

The patient smiled. "I surmised New Scotland Yard discovered my background in the Central Intelligence Agency. Besides I already gave my victim statement to two uniformed constables. It was only a matter of time before they sent someone higher up the food chain to interview me."

"You're proving to be quite the quandary at the office, Mr. Philips." Albert declared. "We can find no social security number for you, no education history and no trace of employment before your current one. You are a ghost."

Sam laughed. "I have been called many things, but never a spectre. However, there have been many over the years who would have liked me to depart the mortal plane."

"Of that I have no doubt," Maher nodded. "Your recent assault is proof of that. What exactly happened last night?"

"I received a blow to the head and was dazed when the paramedics discovered me," the patient said, shrugging his shoulders. "The exact details escape me."

Albert revealed the file and flicked through the document. "Witness declares the man, that being you Mr. Philips, entered the alley just before midnight. He knows the approximate time because he had just purchased a bottle of whiskey from the nearby off-licence just before closing time."

"A reliable witness is always good, detective," the patient said and burst into laughter.

Maher continued without responding. "Witness says a black van pulled up alongside and three men jumped out and tried to bundle the victim into the vehicle. Mr. Philips punched one assailant in the chest sending him flying through the air a distance of one hundred and ten metres and pushed the other two men to the ground. Any of this sounding familiar?"

Sam shook his head. "Can't say it does, copper," the patient replied. "But you know what a knock to the skull does for memory."

"Speaking of blows, do you work out in the gym as part of your employment, Mr. Philips?"

"You know I can't talk about my job, detective." Sam retorted sharply.

"The witness said you then ran off to a nearby wall which you tried to scale but which collapsed, covering you in rubble. The wino then went for help. Paramedics discovered you unconscious but without any injury. Remarkable, Mr. Philips."

Sam smiled. "Just lucky, I guess."

"You were covered in blood, none of it yours." Albert said, rising from the seat.

"Furthermore, we could find no trace of the men and all cameras in the streets leading to the alley had been disabled. Quite professional for a mugging."

"You should head for the docks with all this fishing, Inspector."

"Too professional to make it some random racist attack, drunken soldiers angry at fallen comrades in Afghanistan. The CIA believe you match an operative that did work for them in Cambodia during the Vietnam War. But that was over forty years ago."

"Can't be me then," Sam replied. "Though my chemist does recommended the best anti-aging cream in London."

"Your apartment has also been broken into, quite a mess they made but apart from a laptop nothing else appeared to have been taken. Cash was left on the kitchen worktop. The computer shop which sold the computer said it was only a cheap laptop, one of their lower range used for simple word-processing and internet access. Not really worth their trouble unless they thought there might be valuable information stored on the hard drive."

"Maybe they heard about my fetish for women with large asses, I had built up quite a collection, some movies too." Sam laughed.

"Neighbours said you lived alone, no girlfriend and even no friends ever called." Maher stated. "Any family we can contact for you, Mr. Philips?"

"My parents and my brothers are long gone, detective."

"That's an interesting tattoo you have," Albert declared, pointing to Sam's chest where a large marking could just be made out from the top of the opened pyjama shirt. "Doctors said they have never seen anything like it, appears to extend deep below the skin, even into the ribcage itself. They said it looks like some form of writing, but not a language they recognise."

"It's Sumerian, the ancient words of Mesopotamia, the northern mountain region to be exact." Sam replied sharply. "It means 'Firstborn.' It was a gift, among other things from the Father of my father as recognition of me being the first child born into the family."

"Your grandfather had incredible skill, he must have been popular. I'll bet he always had some wise words for every passing traveller." Maher grinned.

Sam sighed. "Indeed. But he stopped talking when people no longer listened. However, he was not my grandfather, it's complicated."

"Everything about you is complex, Mr. Philips." Albert said. "The only reference we can find to a Sam Philips is a baby who died stillborn and is in the cemetery." Inspector Maher declared. "Where is Mesopotamia anyway?"

"Iraq." Sam replied flatly.

"At least that might go some way to explaining the confusion over your identity. Your papers were probably lost in the war. I believe the Interior Ministry suffered damage," Maher stated.

"That was probably it," Sam smiled.

"You are some bullshitter, Mr. Philips," Albert snarled. "However, I can neither arrest nor detain you, and any further questioning appears pointless. But don't leave Britain without notifying me, or I will have Interpol drag you back here and I don't care who from the CIA tries to bust my balls."

"Goodbye, Inspector." Sam laughed and watched DI Maher leave before calling the nurse to bring his clothes and prepare the discharge papers.

CHAPTER TWO

"To order, gentlemen, please," Grandmaster Samuel Carson shouted, drowning out the noise of the men who filled the hallway and entrance of the forty bedroom mansion, situated just outside London on a sprawling estate, the nearest neighbour two miles away in the village.

The fifty-five year old glanced over the congregation, membership in the English wing of the Illuminati being exclusively male. Over a hundred men from privileged backgrounds thronged the large building. Eight representatives of Parliament, seven of which Conservative including one Minister congratulated themselves. Also present was the Chief Constable chatting to his nominated lieutenants, hungry and waiting for their own moment to shine. Other associates included the current Lord Mayor of London and five billionaires made from company directors. No lottery winners would be found here, no amount of money could buy membership into such exclusive company. No working class slobs who considered themselves fortunate to live a daytime life of drunken debauchery to match their already soulless nights would find place here, Samuel pondered. Historians wrongfully believed the Illuminati were Satanists, but the truth is representatives of such an elite order were too consumed in self-worship to bother glorifying or praying to any deity.

"That was some fuck up, William." The Lord Mayor snarled.

The Chief Constable glared at the politician. "It is true we underestimated our nemesis, but such a comment does not become you, Charles."

"Christ almighty, Bill," the Mayor retorted sharply. "You cannot play down such an incident. You have two men in a private hospital and one downstairs on a slab, his chest smashed and every organ punctured."

"Gentlemen, please," Samuel interrupted. "A different strategy will now be adopted. It was ridiculous anyway. He would have given up no information and trying to keep him in permanent captivity would have proved too dangerous."

The policeman and politician smiled through their teeth at the leader of their order. Samuel Carson was an American, born and raised in Chicago. His father a wealthy businessman having forged lucrative contracts in Saudi Arabia. This offered Samuel a privileged upbringing, including private schools both in the United States and the Middle East. However, there were many in the British wing of the Illuminati who distrusted Mr. Carson. He had only recently been appointed the Grandmaster for England following the death of the last leader. But through the thin veil of courtesy everyone knew of his fearsome temper, his ruthless ambition and history of terrible retribution for anyone that dared cross him. However, the American wing of the Illuminati under Samuel Carson's direction had an impressive legacy with forty-seven members of Congress fulfilling tasks for the organisation and two former Presidents; a contrary father and his drunkard son.

"This has been the most important objective of our order since its official creation in 1776, even though of course we existed many years before that date," the Grandmaster turned and shouted over the congregation, motioning all into silence. "Cain alone knows the location of Eden and the Tree of

Life. Within its roots lie a source of unimaginable magickal power which we can utilise to finally come out from the shadows and realise our true heritage as leaders of this world. No longer will we suffer global tyrants like China and Saudi Arabia. We can bring peace to Africa and establish the single world government to which we all aspire."

"Where is the suspect now?" The Lord Mayor enquired, turning to the Chief Constable.

"He has just left the hospital. I have three undercover detectives monitoring his every move. It is likely he will attempt to obtain a new identity since his current one has been blown."

"And do we know what forger he will use?" Samuel asked.

"Information we gathered from his laptop suggest an Irish master forger called Jack Mulcahy," the policeman stated. "I have two agents ready to intercept the Irishman."

"Hold on that order," Samuel said sharply. "I have a better idea than playing endless games of cat and mouse with Mr. Cain Kadmon."

The policeman stared at his Master in puzzlement. The side door to the hallway opened at that moment and in walked Alice Carson, the twenty-six year old daughter and only child of the Grandmaster. The congregation watched her entrance intensely, not just because of her blood connection to their fearsome leader but also for she was very beautiful. Quite tall at five foot ten inches and curly red hair which stretched almost to the small of her back. She had been trained in elocution and strict deportment exercises which must have proved difficult considering her thin frame in contrast to her large breasts. Female members of the

Illuminati were very rare as the order was inherently both racist and sexist.

"Father," Alice said softly in a sarcastic tone. She despised all these old men with their spiteful glares and ambitious thoughts. Despite her link to their Grandmaster she knew they only thought of her as weak because of her gender and lacking the ruthlessness required to fill her parent's shoes.

"I have a task for you," Samuel announced. "One which only you can accomplish and which will secure your place as my heir to the organisation."

"Master," the Chief Constable interrupted. "I must protest. The Illuminati is a male member only order. Besides, there are few amongst us that would follow Alice."

The Grandmaster turned and grabbed the policeman by the throat. "You forget your place," Samuel snarled. "Perhaps one of your lieutenants should be sitting in your office."

One of the detectives in the background came forth. "I will bow to Alice as our leader after your demise, Master."

"Well done," Samuel declared, releasing the Chief Constable, allowing him to stumble backwards, gasping for breath. "Maybe all the congregation will follow your example. What is your name?"

The policeman smiled. "Detective Chief Inspector Richard Bellings of New Scotland Yard," he announced proudly. "Furthermore Master, I have links to the criminal underworld that will secure weapons for our journey to Iraq. As everyone is aware, the Al Qaeda troubles the country has will likely pale in comparison to what we might discover in Eden."

"You speak true," the Grandmaster nodded. "The very earth became poisoned after Abel's blood was spilt by the Tree. Who knows what creatures roam Eden over the last six thousand years?"

"Perhaps even Lilith still resides there?" The Mayor said fearfully. "The she-demon is dangerous, magickal powers she obtained from the Apple might be formidable."

"We cannot surmise on her," Samuel said. "Adam's first wife might just be a myth. However, it would be prudent to plan for any eventuality. I want top of the range armaments, including flamethrowers."

"And what of Cain?" Bellings enquired.

"A scientist we have on our payroll has obtained titanium steel," Samuel retorted. "Even his strength would find it difficult to break those chains."

"And my task, father?" Alice asked.

"I need someone to get close to Cain, gain his trust and gather as much information as possible. Perhaps even the location of Eden."

Alice sneered. "Do I have to have sex with him?"

"No," Samuel replied. "Cain prefers the damsel in distress," the Grandmaster declared and everybody laughed. "He has spent all his years attempting to find redemption for the crime of killing his brother. However, you might have to harm or even kill some of our members to secure his loyalty. In short, do whatever it takes to discover his plans and new identities he will assume."

"I will do as you command, father." Alice said and left the hallway, all eyes fixed on her back in mistrust and envy.

CHAPTER THREE

Cain waited until nightfall before leaving the grounds of the hospital, knowing the cover of darkness would aid his escape from prying eyes. He knew detectives from New Scotland Yard were likely watching his every move, but a few tired policemen out past their bedtime were not much of a concern, and would be relatively easy to evade for someone of his experience. MI5 and CIA operatives would be more difficult. Cain knew those spies were far more persistent and had espionage tools to hear him fart a mile away. Satellite observation could also not be ruled out. However, even they would not be able to match his speed and strength as he prepared to duck through hotel entrances and restaurant exits in a matter of seconds. A few minutes later and he would be blocks away as they scrambled to keep up.

No, it was something else that gave him concern. It was not Scotland Yard detectives or smug spooks that caused his unease. It was the breathing of something more ancient and evil at his neck, for he knew it was they who arranged his 'mugging' the night before and the burglary at his apartment. The same flat he dared not approach lest they await his presence for another attempt. The sooner he obtained new identity papers the better and leave England for good.

Cain set to running, darting in and out of hotel and fast food restaurants, startling staff and customers. He laughed as he heard several men across the street curse and give chase, trying their best to appear inconspicuous. He vaguely heard their astonishment at their nemesis' speed and watched in dismay as their suspect disappeared into the night, fearing their morning report and their superior's rant.

Cain slowed and caught his breath at a back alley. He glanced back down the street to make sure he had not been followed before entering the door of Jack Mulcahy the forger. Cain smiled, he and the elderly Irishman had a long history. Jack was sixty-five years old, standing at six foot, grey and balding. Cain would always remark his old friend was in the wrong employment, despite his brutish temperament, providing false documents for such dubious clients such as illegal Chinese immigrants to Muslim extremists. Politics was never my business, he would often say, English money always folds into the pocket the same way no matter its origin. But he would draw the line at Ulster Freedom Fighters, saying anyone who could murder his fellow Irish people would always find a closed door.

People on the street who came to know and despise Jack would remark the only thing he inherited from his father was arrogance and a grossly inflated opinion of himself. Desperately craving respect, he bestowed none to others under his command, belittling and threatening his colleagues at every opportunity in boredom and resentment at a contrary boss who hated Jack, but let him have free rein over his employees. He and his employer enjoyed a twisted symbiotic relationship not unlike Doctor Frankenstein and his monster, both relishing the misery they inflicted on others. Jack in particular was both incredibly insecure and ignorant, and often expressed apathy at the estranged relationship with his brother and son;

an animosity he had encouraged. It was small wonder Cain was his only friend in the world.

Even Jack's own mother would bring insult upon herself by remarking to any that might listen, that her child was an egocentric son of a bitch. It was only when the proprietor retired did Jack finally acknowledge his demonic behaviour, as he was denied ownership of the company and his fellow workers ignored their lifelong cowardice and rose up against him. They realised a dole queue was preferable than serving a petty spiteful man who practised hypocrisy and laziness, but criticised others for even considering such apathy. Jack, offended the staff should dare reject his 'superior' wisdom, reacted in typical aggressive fashion, but was forced to resign and choose a different path. Not willing to serve another perceived tyrant and possessing a talent for machinery he soon followed a life of crime.

Cain quickly skipped up the narrow flight of stairs and approached the elderly man's office at the end of the hall. However, he stopped just at the door. Something was wrong. Jack was old, not deaf. The creaky floorboards that lined the hallway in the centuries old building always meant he would open the door long before any visitor gripped the handle.

Cain cautiously pulled down on the metal and peeked inside. He immediately saw Jack sitting in his favourite swivel office chair with his back to the door. Cain approached and tapped the Irishman on the shoulder, but to no response. Jack might have been a heavy sleeper, but this was something else. He turned the chair and sighed as Jack's head lay at an awkward angle, his throat cut so deep he had nearly been decapitated. His shirt and pants were soaked in blood and a dark pool had formed on the floor under the chair. Cain then noticed something odd. It appeared several of his fingers had been broken, the digits twisted and painfully deformed. Jack had been tortured, probably for the location of his counterfeit documents for established clients. Cain had to assume it was he the intruders were looking for and the name of his new identity.

He glanced around the room and noticed furniture had been thrown upside down, the fabric torn and stuffing left on the ground. Pictures were smashed and books torn to pieces, their spines cracked. However, Cain knew Jack had been in the business too long to leave his life's work in plain view. The Irish forger had earlier mentioned a concealed storage area beneath the office chair close to the desk. Cain gazed down and noticed a thin crack on the floor under the chair. He pushed his dead friend carefully aside and examined the dusty floor. Cain ran his fingers around the edge until he found a tiny ring, barely distinguishable. He gently pulled and up popped a latch revealing floorboards and insulation underneath. Hidden inside was a small package. Cain opened it and removed the contents, revealing various forged passports, drivers licences and birth certificates. A few marriage certificates were also present, Pakistani women eager to escape arranged nuptials by pretending to be already married.

Cain left the office, safely pocketing his new identity papers, leaving other clients' documents on the floor. They would have to take their chances with the police and custom officials. Just then he heard commotion coming from the bedroom. He approached his dead friend's resting place and kicked in the door, preparing to attack whoever was inside. But the room was empty. He shrugged his shoulders, it was probably rats in the attic considering the age of the building. However, he halted upon hearing muffled sounds coming from the wardrobe. Cain pulled on the two handles and a woman fell to the floor with a scream. She was shaking in fear and had been crying. The young female wore blue jeans and a red v-neck top, revealing substantial cleavage. She had long red hair stretching down nearly the full length of her back.

"Please, don't hurt me," she sobbed in an accent Cain thought sounded American. "Where is my uncle?"

Cain picked the woman up off the floor and stared at her in puzzlement. "How long have you been in there?"

"I'm not sure," she moaned, still shaking. "Perhaps two hours or more."

Cain gently wiped the tears from her face, noticing her makeup was smudged from crying. "Who are you? What are you doing here?"

"My name is Alice Mulcahy," she said softly, starting to regain her composure. "My mother was the sister of Jack. Where is he?"

"His niece?" Cain asked in confusion. "He never mentioned any family. How come you have the same surname if your mother is married?"

"My mother gave birth to me out of wedlock hence I retained her surname," Alice stated. "I came here to Britain from the United States to find Jack as he is my last remaining blood relative. Where is he?"

"I am sorry," Cain said, closing his eyes in remembrance of his old friend, and his tragic yet heroic death. "Your uncle is dead."

Alice stared at the man before her in disbelief and then sobbed. "I knew by his screams he was being murdered. The cries stopped before the men had left," she said as Cain gently wiped the tears from her cheeks. "No one could have tolerated such pain and suffering. I dared not move from the wardrobe. I am such a coward."

"You cannot blame yourself, for you would be dead also," Cain declared. "Do you know how many intruders were here? What accent did they have?"

"They were English," Alice replied firmly. "Of that I am certain. I believe judging by the voices there were at least three of them."

Cain sighed. "Three assassins to frighten an old man? They were expecting company."

"There's something else," Alice interjected. "I heard one murderer mention the word 'Illuminati.' Does that mean anything to you?"

Cain stared at her in hatred. She noticed he was however not surprised or shocked by her declaration.

"You're in way over your head," he said sharply. "Go back home to America. Don't leave this land in a body bag."

"I have nowhere else to go," Alice said, beginning to cry again. "I have no money and no relatives left. I came here on a college visa to study English at Oxford."

"Better you should work in some dingy bar in the United States than bleed out on the floor like your uncle."

Before she could respond a sudden noise was heard as the door downstairs was opened and frantic footsteps began to approach the apartment. Alice looked at him in abject terror.

"Quick, back into the wardrobe," Cain whispered. "Don't make a sound, no matter what you hear."

"What about you?" She said fearfully, grabbing his sleeve.

"I have a score to settle with these gentlemen." Cain snarled as he closed the doors of the wardrobe, shutting her inside.

He pushed the door of the bedroom nearly closed bar one inch so he could observe the intruders. Three men dressed in cheap suits entered the hallway and approached the office. One rather obese man who Cain presumed was the leader directed the other two to search the wooden floor of the office for any hidden compartments. He left out a growl upon noticing the fake documents that Cain had discarded strewn about the floor.

"It would appear our friend has been busy in our brief absence," the man snarled in obvious contempt. "Search the apartment, unless one of you would like to tell Samuel we returned empty-handed."

His two companions stared at him in fear, knowing all too well the price of failure. It was not a trait the Master accepted graciously. However, confronting their nemesis did not bode well either.

"He most likely has it on his person," one man said, the tremor in his voice noticeable. "You don't expect us to fight Cain alone, especially after what he did to Martin in the alley."

"We might not be able to kill him," their leader retorted sharply. "But we can certainly hurt him, or at the very least slow him down enough to seize the documents and make our escape."

"This paddy we killed was his friend," the intruder declared. "It is probably his intention that we not leave this apartment alive."

"Shut up and do your job!" Their leader shouted as he kicked Jack seated in his chair across the room, causing the dead forger to fall out and hit the floor with an audible thud. The man laughed. "You put too much faith in this Jew. The stories of his strength and penchant for violence are unfounded."

One of the men nodded in agreement before moving down the hallway and grabbing the handle of the door leading to the bedroom. He thought he heard a muffled sound just beyond the slightly ajar entrance and was about to cry out to his two companions when the wooden door suddenly came off its hinges and flew towards him, slamming the man against the wall.

The two intruders stared down the hallway in astonishment as the door had completely detached itself from its shattered frame and hit their friend in the face with a deafening crash. They watched as their comrade slumped to the ground, his features unrecognisable due to the blood pouring down his face and chest to the floor. Both men knew no-one could have survived such a blow. Their leader drew a semi-automatic handgun from his shoulder holster and pointed at the open bedroom entrance.

The other unarmed intruder cautiously approached the door, and while keeping some distance from the bedroom, stretched himself slant-ways and peered into the room. He turned to his armed leader in puzzlement, for he could see no sign of their mysterious assailant. He stepped towards the door, gazed at the ceiling and immediately realized where their attacker lay hidden. Cain had positioned himself above the broken door frame, left hand on the shattered wood and legs stretched, his feet on the top of the wardrobe. The assassin turned to cry out to his superior in fright, but Cain moved before he could respond and grabbed the man by his hair with his right hand, pulling him inside the bedroom.

The intruder let out a shrill scream of agony, as Cain still gripping a large tuft of hair threw the man against the far wall of the bedroom, knocking him unconscious. He then dropped to the floor as the last assassin ran down the hallway towards the open bedroom, shooting wildly at the entrance. The fat man turned and fired a round into the bedroom, catching his intended target in the left shoulder.

Cain let out no cry of pain, but instead stared fixedly at his attacker who dropped the now empty handgun in terror. The intruder turned to flee but Cain hit him in the back of the head with his right fist, sending the man flying down the hallway and crashing into the door of the office, pieces of his brain scattering all over the floor from his smashed skull.

Alice peeked out of the wardrobe. "Is it over?" She sobbed. "Are they gone?"

Cain gritted through his teeth. "Not yet," he sneered. "One yet remains before I send him to the Underworld."

Alice watched as Cain approached the fallen man and began to shake him vigorously. The assassin began to groan as his assailant picked him up onto his bottom and positioned him against the wall.

"Perhaps we should just leave and call the police," Alice declared. "Let them deal with this and bring this murderer to trial for the death of my uncle."

Cain sighed. "This bastard and the other two dead men *are* police," he said as he gripped the individual's hair, forcing him awake. "Isn't that right, my friend?"

"Go to hell, firstborn," the intruder snarled. "I answer only to the Grandmaster."

Cain hit the assassin in the face, breaking his nose. "And he will answer to me!" Cain shouted as the individual cried out in pain. "No longer will I constantly look over my shoulder as you live comfortably in the shadows."

"You have no idea who you're dealing with, Jew," the policeman sneered. "We have orchestrated every major political and social event for centuries, our members have infiltrated every walk of life. You can't buy a pint of milk or read a newspaper without the Illuminati having a hand in it. You may have eluded the books of history for six thousand years, but in this era of the Internet you will no longer find a hiding place."

"You did all of that on your own? I'm impressed!" Cain laughed. "You, my friend, are just a pawn; an Illuminati wannabe. But the door will always be shut to the henchmen, only the elite can become members. Or do you think the Master shares power?"

"You waste your time attempting to corrupt me, firstborn," the policeman smiled. "And I have no information to give," he declared as he quickly reached inside his pocket and revealing a two inch blade, swiftly cut across his throat.

Cain cursed and grabbed the man's neck, trying to halt the stem of blood, but to no avail. The assassin bled to death within a few minutes. Cain allowed his lifeless body to drop to the floor in disgust.

"What was all that about?" Alice asked in puzzlement. "I thought the Illuminati were just a myth. And why did he call you firstborn?"

"The real police will be here soon," Cain interrupted. "Any shots fired in London will bring them running within a matter of minutes. We need to get out of here. You are no longer safe on your own; you will have to remain by my side from now on, it appears our destinies have become interlinked."

"Hang on a second," Alice said. "Who are you? What person would cut their own neck rather than give information?"

"The kind of individual who fears something worse than me," Cain replied. "Questions about me can wait. We really need to leave."

Sirens could be heard in the near distance as they quickly made their way out of the apartment and into the street. They darted in and out of several alleys before coming to a stop.

"Please wait," Alice panted. "I can't keep up."

"Sorry," Cain replied. "I keep forgetting most people cannot maintain my pace."

"You're not even winded," she gasped. "You must be super-fit."

Cain smiled. "Come on, it's not much further," he said as they approached a run-down looking hotel down a side alley.

"This looks charming." Alice sneered.

"It will do for the moment until the heat dies down," Cain retorted.

They entered the establishment and approached the counter where sat a small old man in a dirty tartan shirt, stained with what appeared to be several days old chips and curry. Cain threw enough notes on the desk sufficient for many nights board.

The short man grudgingly got up from the chair and stared at his new guests. "Will you two love birds make it down for breakfast?" He laughed.

"Mind your own fucking business!" Alice snarled and the man drew back.

Cain turned and gazed at her in astonishment. She had discovered a new born fire in her belly compared to the scared girl hiding in the wardrobe. It would appear this woman was full of surprises.

The old man threw a key with a number tag on the counter before returning to his chair. Cain and Alice ventured up the stairs and opened the door to their room. A single double bed lay in the centre with two adjoining bedside tables and lamps. The purple carpet below their feet was dirty and stained with marks Alice could not discern. The small bathroom and toilet were in a similar condition.

"Jesus," she announced. "What a shit hole. Tell me our stay here will be brief."

Cain nodded, he was too tired to argue as he sat on the edge of the bed. He took off the fleece jacket and t-shirt he was wearing, grimacing in pain. Alice glanced at the strange large tattoo that filled the entire width of his chest. Blood continued to run down his left arm from the gun shot wound. Cain pointed to the door, motioning for her to leave.

"Oh no," she said flatly. "You won't get rid of me that easy. Besides I have a strong stomach."

"That's not what worries me," Cain replied. "Your nausea will soon be replaced by astonishment and insatiable curiosity."

She stared at him in puzzlement as he pinched the wound with the fingers of his right hand as if it were a blackhead or spot he was about to squeeze. Cain drew his fingers in tighter and gritted his teeth in pain. He let out a cry as the bullet began to appear at the opening. Alice gasped in amazement as he squeezed and the metal came out and fell on the floor. Cain picked up the bullet and sighed in satisfaction. She could only stare fixedly in shock as the wound then began to spontaneously heal itself until the opening completely disappeared. Within seconds it was as if he had never been shot in the shoulder.

"That's not possible," Alice said. "What kind of man are you?"

"That's a long story," Cain replied with a laugh.

"I can only imagine," she said, shaking her head in curiosity. "Are you some kind of genetic military experiment, or an extraterrestrial?"

"Neither," Cain declared. "I am completely human like you, my blood and bones are no different than yours. This was a curse and gift bestowed onto me a long time ago."

Alice frowned in puzzlement as he stared first at the dirty ceiling and then directly at her.

"My name is Cain Kadmon, son of Adam and Eve Kadmon, brother to Abel and Seth, the founder of Judaism and ultimately all of humanity."

She stared at him in bewilderment. "You're having a laugh!" She replied. "That is just a religious myth propagated by a corrupt Roman Catholic Church as a means to blind us to the truth of Darwinism. Next you'll be telling me about Creationism and the lies about the dinosaurs, despite their bones being on display in the Natural History Museum!"

Cain sighed. "There is room for both. Jehovah takes many forms, humanity is just one of his little experiments. First it was the dinosaurs, now it is our turn. When he tires of us it will be something else. It was the conceit of man to believe we were created in his image. This world is but one of many in the Universe," he retorted, as he pointed to his chest where a large black tattoo filled most of his torso. "See this," he said and she nodded. "This was given to me by God when I killed Abel my brother as a punishment and warning to others who dared defy the will of Jehovah."

"So you're a murderer?" Alice growled. "Then you are no better than those monsters that killed my uncle."

"It was an accident," Cain said and bowed his head in shame, six thousand years had not removed his guilt. "I killed my brother in a fit of jealousy over him being rewarded for an animal offering and God rejecting my fruit. I pushed him and he knocked the back of his head against the Tree of Life."

"You were in Eden?" Alice asked in astonishment. "What was it like?"

"Words cannot adequately describe Paradise," Cain replied, his voice trembling in sorrow and regret. "The most beautiful plants and flowers abounded everywhere and beasts roamed, lions mingling with antelope and not attacking. Every creature at peace with themselves and everything else. And then there was the Tree of Life, the largest plant situated in the centre of Eden, the very epicentre of all creation. The Tree dominated the Garden, all the animals gathered around it but dared not touch for it was forbidden."

"Were there any Apples on it?" Alice asked. "Did you taste of its fruit?"

"Only one Apple ever grew on the Tree," Cain replied flatly. "That was the purpose and essence of temptation. Lilith picked the Apple, gave it first to my mother to taste and she then gave it to Adam. They were then damned for all eternity and exiled from the Garden. Except for Lilith, she was to remain in Eden, bitter and alone with nobody for companionship for all time."

"Did you ever meet her, the she-demon?"

"No," Cain retorted. "These events took place hundreds of years before I was born. I was conceived in the wilderness of what is now northern Iraq, prohibited from ever witnessing Paradise."

"It must have been tough for your parents," Alice said. "Nobody else to depend on and no food to eat."

"You have to realise Adam and Eve were immortals, destined to live forever, the founders of humanity for the Middle East." Cain replied. "And my father had ultimate knowledge which he had acquired from the Apple, giving him the power to build an entire stone village from nothing and tillage the land, providing many crops."

Alice frowned in puzzlement. "You said your parents were the creators of mankind for the Middle East, I thought the bible said Adam was the founder of all humanity?"

"Incest is strictly forbidden under God's law," Cain retorted. "If it were just us, we would have been forced to marry our unborn sisters to propagate mankind. However, Adam was unique and Jehovah wanted it that way. Only my father had been created directly by God making him immortal, and my mother made from one of Adam's ribs, a scar he bore all of his life."

"This was a subject always ignored by the Catholic Church," Alice said. "They preferred blind ignorance and their followers not ask too many questions, so they could maintain control and power over the last two thousand years."

"Yahweh first created Nok the Elder, an African king and his tribe of five hundred from the ribs of chimpanzees, making them fully human and subject to normal lifespans."

"That would explain the close DNA link to the monkeys," Alice interjected.

"God then copied the same formula for every region of the globe; from China, to the Aborigines in Australia, the Native Americans, and the Celts in Gaul and England, and so forth. Every tribe would be slightly different so their cultures would be unique and when they finally mingled it would provide mixed blood for all of humanity." Cain declared. "But as I said He wanted Adam to be separate and his bloodline to suffer as little contamination as possible. We were to marry only royalty, so it was decided my younger brother Seth and I become betrothed to princesses, the daughters of Nok the Elder."

"No wonder God always viewed the Jews as special," Alice said and smiled. "Does that mean by the way that you are circumcised?"

"No," Cain replied with a grin. "That practise was established long after I was born. However, it was Seth who was the true founder of Judaism, having written the first early scriptures."

"Don't take this the wrong way," Alice interjected. "But you have the appearance of an

Arab, and not the modern Jew one would commonly see on the streets of Israel."

Cain sighed. "Yes, this is true. Thousands of years after my birth the Jewish people became part of Egypt. They were accepted grudgingly as part of the Egyptian Empire because of their fighting skills, providing the elite first line defence against what is now Syria. However, the true Egyptians kept them in a perpetual state of poverty so young Jewish women were forced to marry Egyptian men to provide security and a home for their children. Over many hundreds of years much of the Jewish people developed a paler skin tone. But despite this, part of the Jewish population remained pure. It was only after the suicide of Saul, the first king of Israel, and the subsequent rise to power of David that things dramatically changed. King David was a psychopath, he had all of Saul's family wiped out, down to even nephews and nieces. After their deaths, the bloodline dating back to my father was extinguished. I was furious at David's actions, I wanted him to pay for his evil deeds, but the Israelites had been locked in three centuries of constant civil war. They were at all times in a state of battle-readiness so I was unable to get close."

"That must have been heartbreaking for you," Alice interrupted. "Having the blood heritage of Adam destroyed."

"I should have seen it coming," Cain retorted. "I was present with Moses at the Exodus. The elderly prophet required my presence to inspire and convince doubters of the motives of God and of their rightful place in history, or so I naively believed at that time." Cain sighed. "However, after Moses died power passed to his chosen successor Joshua. I understood Joshua's reasons for destroying Jericho and committing genocide, to promote fear across Canaan and provoke the city's neighbours into fleeing without raising a sword against the Jewish invaders. But I could never reconcile myself with killing every inhabitant of Jericho, even the impaling of infants upon spears before their screaming parents. Those same cries of anguish still fill my restless nights. I left soon afterwards and never returned."

"Do you believe humanity has become more civilised, with Europe finally at peace and the advent of such worldwide communication tools as the Internet, bringing people closer?"

Cain shook his head in dismay. "I firmly believe the opposite. Man has become more sophisticated in his torture tools, even so called democratic governments swapping innocent civilians between themselves, believing it is morally acceptable to water-board a kidnapped foreigner; placing a wet cloth over their face and continuously pouring a jug of water over it until they nearly drown, simply because they might dare to have a different opinion to capitalism than you," he declared. "The same Roman mob mentality I witnessed in the Coliseum still exists today. I always find it strangely amusing when you switch on your television, watching some perverse singing reality show where amateur karaoke contestants embarrass themselves, their lifelong dreams being shattered to the laughter of vacuous idiots, who believe just because no-one is being killed the mockery is not damaging."

"You must have lived an incredible life," Alice said. "The world events you would have witnessed, the important people you would have met."

"I tried my best to keep out of history's way," Cain replied. "I was an outcast, feared and despised by many. But it is true, I did bare witness to spectacular cities and persons. I visited Alexandria before it was destroyed and saw the Hanging Gardens of Babylon. Unfortunately I also ran foul of many despicable characters including the Romans and the Nazis. Doctor Josef Mengele carried out grotesque experiments, attempting to utilise or copy my strength and regenerative powers. The Romans on the other hand tried to crucify me on the road outside Pompeii. They were unaware of my curse. Anyone who attempted to slay me would have vengeance cast upon them 'sevenfold.' There might have been earthquakes in the region and a volcanic eruption on the horizon, but that little mistake of theirs tipped the balance and blew the mountain." Cain laughed. "Constantine, the first Christian Roman Emperor managed to capture me within the boundaries of Constantinople. He wanted to seal me inside a metal coffin and incorporate my body into the foundations of the new city, but decided it was best to free me, fearing the curse and God's retribution."

"Did you ever meet religious figures like Jesus or his disciples?" Alice asked. "It would certainly be intriguing to discover if he was indeed the son of God, or if such a thing was possible."

"No, I was in China at the time learning unarmed combat. Even my superior strength would not guarantee success in a fight with overwhelming odds, it was considered wise to have an edge over a large armed mob." Cain said. "As regards the Messiah, who knows? But if you had seen the majesty of Eden you would believe anything was possible. However, it is worth mentioning that

Christ, if he indeed did exist, was a demigod; half human and half divine having a human mother. My father Adam, on the other hand had no human parents, making him higher on the divine evolutionary ladder than Jesus."

"Is that why the Illuminati have such an interest in you," she enquired. "Your link to the divine, to God?"

Cain clenched his fists in rage. "Samuel Carson and his cronies are not really interested in me or Jehovah, their only desire is the Tree of Life, they believe an incredible power source lies at its roots."

"And does it?" Alice asked.

"To step foot in Eden is strictly forbidden," he declared. "It was blasphemy enough when Abel and I entered the Garden to make our offerings, I was not about to start digging. However, the Tree is the centre of all creation so it is likely great magick stems from that ground."

"Talking of Eden," Alice said. "You say you were cursed? I thought Abel was immortal like you and impervious to injury?"

"Yes," Cain replied, staring out of the window into the dark street, his voice shaking with guilt and regret. "But it is close proximity to the Tree of Life that makes you mortal, that strips you of your powers. Abel hit his head on the Tree, it was that wound that killed him. If I shoved him under a subway train here he would have survived, his injuries would have healed, but at the Tree he was vulnerable. I did not know that when I pushed him, it was an accident." Cain sighed. "There was a famine which had lasted for many years. We were all starving, being immortal does not mean you do not feel hunger, and my wife was only human.

Âwân especially found the wilderness of northern Mesopotamia difficult, she was not used to such hardship, being of royal blood and having many servants at her beck and call in Africa. Nearly all the animals had died, but Abel insisted we use the last lamb as a sacrifice to God to end the drought. I said Jehovah would understand in the circumstances if we made an offering of fruit gathered from the few remaining trees. I decided that Yahweh might be most receptive to our pleas in Eden itself, despite it being forbidden to enter. It was for this reason I did not tell Seth or our parents about what I planned. Jehovah rejected my offering and accepted Abel's blood sacrifice, ending the famine and bidding us to leave Paradise immediately. I was angry, furious that Abel had been chosen over me, always believing father favoured my younger brother. Without thinking, I pushed him and his head struck the side of the Tree. At first I thought he was uninjured, having many times seen him fall great heights, his wounds within seconds heal completely. But this time was different. He lay motionless as blood flowed down the Tree and into the ground. I was terrified and tried to bury the body, fearing father would notice our overdue absence and come looking." Cain declared, leaning against the window. "God cursed me, prohibiting me from growing crops of any kind. I was to be a vagabond, surviving on scraps and the generosity of strangers or even resorting to stealing. I was to walk the Earth for all eternity, knowing only loneliness and the death of loved ones around me as I lived forever."

"That's pretty harsh," Alice said, placing her hand on his shoulder. "And what of your young wife, what became of her, did she come with you into exile?"

"Yes, Âwân travelled with me." Cain sighed. "She was with child."

"So you had a son or daughter?"

"No," Cain said and began to cry, the tears running down his face. "The infant was stillborn. The curse included all crops, not just the ones in the ground. From that moment I was sterile, I would never again impregnate a woman." He turned and struck the wall in frustration, causing plaster to fall. "Since I could not tillage the land, we attempted to survive on small animals I would catch, but she became sick from malnutrition and died giving birth, not even one year into our marriage. I have had many lovers throughout my long life, but never again would I marry."

"It is a fascinating tale," Alice remarked. "Did you ever consider contacting a publisher or literary agent to make your story known to the world?"

"I do not believe the Illuminati would welcome such publicity, their reaction would be hostile and draw unnecessary attention to myself." Cain replied. "Furthermore, I once had the opportunity to be a spectator at a writers' group in New York. Their views on publishers and literary agents was quite negative which appeared to be the norm amongst all amateur authors seeking publication. They likened publishers and agents as if one was thrown into a pit of crocodiles; the difference being the reptiles having a greater understanding and empathy with humankind. They remarked that literary agents in particular for the majority were rude, dismissive, hostile, arrogant and often simply bonkers. Their hard-earned opinions did not inspire me to contact such people in the publishing industry where greed and profit-margins are all important, and dignity for their potential authors is worthless."

"What was Adam like?" Alice interjected. "It must have been extraordinary knowing him. What happened to him?"

"I don't know what became of Seth and my parents," Cain replied. "They were immortal after all. It is possible after our tribe achieved a certain size they were called back to Heaven without ever knowing death."

"What was that era like with your clan, intact before the tragedy?" Alice asked. "Can you remember? I know it was a long time ago."

"Recall?" Cain echoed, smiling at the memory. "I remember everything, as if it were just yesterday…"

CHAPTER FOUR

Eden

Cain awoke early, the sounds of pots breaking his slumber. He peered out of the stone hut and into the centre of the village where his mother was preparing breakfast.

Eve glanced at her eldest son in amusement. Never the early riser, even on a day as important as this one. Her husband was already awake, long before the morning heat had begun. Adam was staring out into the rocky wilderness of northern Mesopotamia awaiting the arrival of his youngest son, returning from a journey that had taken over a year. Cain approached his father, always amazed how he knew days in advance when another immortal was nearby.

"How close are they?" Cain asked, drawing alongside his father.

Adam sighed, his long dark hair blowing in the wind. "The group should arrive around midday if Seth continues at the same pace."

"Is this really necessary, father?" Cain asked, bowing his head in disgust. "These people are not like us, they seek only your divine knowledge and to contaminate your bloodline."

Adam turned to his eldest son in frustration. "What would you have me do, Cain?" He shouted in anger. "Would you rather fornicate with your unborn sisters and produce monsters, immortal and possessing incredible strength. They would be shunned by all humanity and destined to live forever, their suffering knowing no end."

"At least they would be Jewish," Cain retorted sharply. "Not some half-African heathen with a human lifespan and limited understanding. Your untainted bloodline with every successive generation will become so diluted that within just a few centuries nothing of our divine heritage will remain."

"Jehovah created Nok and his tribe for this reason, Cain." Adam replied. "It is God's law and my will. You will do as I command."

Cain shook his head in dismay, knowing it was unwise to argue with his father. Not only was it disrespectful, but Adam was considerably stronger. Cain could not be killed but he could certainly feel pain, memories of past arguments with his father resulting in him being thrown large distances.

Cain returned to the centre of the village to help his mother prepare breakfast. His younger brother Abel was now awake, busily squeezing the udders of a goat, the milk squirting into a bucket.

"Important day, brother." Abel declared. "Seth said your princess bride Âwân is very beautiful."

Cain laughed. "I am sure he did not acknowledge that when her younger sister Aclima was promised in betrothal to him."

"Our brother is a scholar above everything else, even the temptations of the flesh," Abel said. "I hope his teenage wife appreciates that."

"I believe Aclima is in for a shock," Cain smiled. "Seth is obsessed with the teachings of father, he will have no time for temper tantrums."

Abel stared into the bucket in disgust, barely half an inch of milk lined the bottom. "How am I expected to strain milk from a starving goat?"

"Nok the Elder won't be pleased with this drought." Cain interjected.

Abel sneered. "The African king seeks father's knowledge. He will tolerate a little hardship. His demands after all are very high."

"He does offer his two daughters in marriage." Cain retorted. "Perhaps that allows some concessions. But I do not understand why I have to marry. Why can it not be you instead, or is it the goat you desire?"

Abel stood and threw the bucket of milk at his eldest brother in rage. It missed its target however, scattering the liquid across the rocks. "Father has decreed it be you, Cain. My destiny lies elsewhere." Abel snarled. "I am the farmer and shepherd, it is my responsibility to transform this wilderness into being habitable for your offspring. Your hands have never known hard work, despite your great strength being equal to mine."

Cain turned away from his brother in disgust, knowing it was pointless to argue. Besides he always believed father favoured Abel over him, knowing that Adam had instructed Abel inherit all the lands and make them fruitful as God had commanded.

Several hours had passed before Eve cried out with delight. Her youngest child appeared over a hill with a small party following close behind. Her husband ran and embraced his son, clutching Seth tightly. The young man gasped, Adam's superior strength crushing his chest.

"Father, please I can't breathe," Seth declared. "Furthermore, you embarrass me in front of our guests."

Adam turned to his visitors. "My friend, Nok, welcome." He announced, reaching out to shake the elderly black man's hand in friendship.

The African king smiled, his wrinkled face displaying the fatigue of the long journey, his grey straggly hair wet with sweat from the midday sun. "Forgive me, I am accustomed to great heat back home, but here it bears down unrelenting on an old man."

Adam put his arm around Nok's shoulder. "Come, rest yourself in my village, for tonight we have much to discuss."

The African party entered the stone houses, thanking their host in gratitude. Cain stared at them, their faces obscured by black veils, not knowing which of the visitors was his new bride.

"I'll bet Âwân has the face of a horse," Cain whispered to Abel.

His brother laughed. "If you're disappointed, there's always my goat. It never complains no matter how hard you grab it."

Cain turned and pushed Abel to the ground in rage. His brother quickly rose to his feet and prepared to hit his eldest sibling.

"Do you ever stop?" Seth interrupted. "I thought I was the baby of the family. You should display greater decorum in the presence of our guests."

Abel brushed the dust off himself and walked away, leaving his brother to his tantrum. However, he turned back and shouted. "Your temper will be the death of me, Cain."

Nightfall approached as the party sat themselves around the fire in the centre of the village. Seth passed around a bowl of berries and nuts, his head bowed in embarrassment at the meagre offerings to their foreign allies.

"I must apologise for the lack of food," Adam announced. "This famine has lasted many years and we are now down to our last lamb and goat."

Nok frowned in puzzlement. "I thought the knowledge you gained from the Apple would have bestowed the location of greater food supplies in this wilderness."

"Father, you shame yourself with such presumptuous interrogation," the eldest African princess said, smiling across the fire at Cain, her soon to be husband.

Cain grinned in satisfaction. "You are wise as you are beautiful, princess."

"If this treaty is to succeed," Nok said sharply. "Then more than berries will be required. You know my terms."

"Yes," Adam replied. "The first child born of your daughters' union with Seth and Cain when they come of age will travel to Africa to build your nation with my knowledge."

Nok nodded in agreement. "I am curious, did your wife also gain divine wisdom from eating the Apple before she gave it to you?"

"No," Adam retorted. "The temptation and its powers were for me alone. Neither Eve nor Lilith gained anything from the fruit. It was my first wife's treachery that caused our exile. I was naïve and stupid, believing no harm would come from consuming the Apple. But Lilith knew the consequences. She is ancient, as old as Eden itself. Her punishment is to remain in the mountains forever, forbidden to leave and witness the rest of Earth's history. It was only after eating the Apple that I discovered I was to be given the fruit eventually anyway to prepare me to establish the foundations of humanity."

"What were Lilith's motives for such an action, if she knew it would bring terrible retribution and God's wrath?" Nok enquired.

"She was jealous," Adam replied. "Jehovah had created Eve from my rib to be wife and the mother of Jewish mankind. Lilith is a succubus, sterile and barren, incapable of creating life. Her sole function in Eden was to be my companion and sate my desire for sex."

"She must be very beautiful," Nok said. "No offence intended to Eve."

"She is very dangerous." Eve declared flatly. "Her magickal powers exceed even her skills of deception."

"Can you show me where Eden lies?" The African king asked. "I would very much like to see Paradise."

"That knowledge is not part of our treaty, Nok." Adam responded. "Besides only an immortal may open the barred entrance, Paradise is forbidden to enter."

"How is it you, your wife and your sons are all the same age?" The younger princess enquired, glancing over at Seth.

The youngest son of Adam smiled back at his bride. "My parents were created at the adult age they are now. When we were born we grew to the same age but no further, we will retain this appearance for all time."

"Then you cannot be killed?" Nok asked in curiosity.

Adam laughed. "I have not encountered anything that has killed me so far. I cannot suffer disease or fatigue, but I can feel pain, hunger and thirst, so the effects of this drought cause me distress as they would you. The children of the union between your daughters and my sons will produce heirs both stronger, faster and healthier than their mothers, but their descendants will become weaker until a child is eventually born completely human."

"And your divine knowledge?" The king enquired. "What will become of that?"

"Your grandchildren will possess sufficient information to create a great African nation. I will teach them most of what I know. My sons here will forge an empire across Mesopotamia and the entire globe, trading with peoples as far as China and beyond. I will establish a magnificent city not far from here and call it Babylon, displaying wonders to amaze and a beacon for learning. When the population reaches two thousand, I will ask God to take my wife and I from this world."

"What do you mean?" Nok asked in puzzlement. "Will you finally ask for death?"

"No," Eve interrupted. "We will beseech Jehovah that we may ascend to Heaven, our bodies intact so we can return to the Source, the place where all creation in the Universe begun."

The African party stared at them in shock, Nok grabbing Adam by the wrist. "That is incredible. What is this Source and Universe you speak of?"

"This world you spend your short lifespan on is but one of many in the cosmos." Adam declared. "A common misconception is that God is everywhere at all times watching everything. But the truth is He is a caretaker, observing many species on hundreds of planets across the Universe.

It is only when something monumental occurs does it draw his attention to a particular world. He prefers we have free will, to discover our own destiny, whether that be for good or for evil. Only when a planet comes close to its own destruction does he intervene. Great beasts called dinosaurs once roamed this land with no concern for each other or the advancement of the world. Jehovah allowed an enormous rock from the skies smash to the ground and cause their annihilation. Time passed and he decided to create Eden, preparing for the colonisation of the planet by humans. Evolution has already caused one species of ape to begin to resemble man, but they will never achieve modern Homosapien. These Neanderthals have spread far across the globe, but I fear the divinely created population of distant lands will not allow their inferior existence. Humans will be allowed life on this world for ten thousand years, achieving many wonders, even visiting distant planets in this solar system. But it will not be enough to guarantee their survival, they are only tenants on this world. Time will pass again and God will grant dominion to another species, probably the bees and ants."

"Extraordinary," Nok said in amazement. "The Apple gave you all this knowledge?"

"That and much more." Adam replied. "But I would have preferred ignorance to still remain in Paradise, to hear Jehovah's voice every day. The conversations we would have were incredible. That is most what I miss from my former life in Eden. But I would never have known my sons. So it is a noble sacrifice."

"What was God's voice like in your head?" Nok asked.

"It is natural we all call it His voice, but the truth is it was neither male nor female, more like something in between, certainly not human however." Adam responded. "Jehovah is a spirit form, like the air we breathe. He is ancient and extraterrestrial, older and foreign to this world, existing in a time long before the birth of this Universe."

Adam stood to his feet and his sons did likewise. "Come my friends, the hour is late and tomorrow brings two weddings."

The African party rose and thanked their host's hospitality before retiring for the night.

Adam turned and embraced Cain and Seth. "Don't look so glum," he laughed. "Tomorrow is not the end of your freedom, but the beginning of a new and better life…or at least that's what your mother said when I married her!"

The twin weddings took place early the following morning before the sun reached its zenith and passed without event. Days turned to weeks and the African party including Nok took their leave. In the months that followed both princesses became pregnant much to the delight of Eve, eager to be a grandmother.

"My father-in-law wants his grandson to be named Enoch," Cain declared. "And I should build a great city in his honour bearing the same title."

Abel burst out laughing. "You couldn't build a shed! How about I construct it and you tell my nephew you were the architect."

Cain's face turned red with anger. "We can't all be father's favourite, yes daddy, no daddy…three bags full dad. I wonder how many times I could smash your head in before your immortality ran out?"

"All words and no action, brother." Abel retorted. "If you are so clever how about constructing a plan to end this famine? Let us travel to the source of the Euphrates and see if we can make it flow again."

Adam stood to his feet. "Make an offering to Jehovah, for it is in His almighty wisdom we find nourishment."

Both brothers nodded in agreement. Cain spent all day climbing up the few remaining trees, stripping what remained of the berries and nuts. Abel watched him in amusement, great beads of sweat pouring down his rival's back from effort.

"Are you just going to sit there?" Cain snarled.

Abel smiled in response, rose and picked up the one lamb that still lived.

Cain watched him in astonishment. "You plan to sacrifice our last lamb? And if the offering is ignored my wife will surely starve."

"My blood sacrifice will not be rejected." Abel declared. "We will travel deep into the Zagros Mountains, close to Eden where God is sure to listen to our pleas."

"If we entered the Garden itself then the offering is sure to succeed."

"You know that is forbidden, brother." Abel replied. "Close proximity will have to suffice."

Their parents and Seth watched them leave, unaware of the tragedy that was about to unfold. Two days journey passed before they approached the mountains and began the steep climb.

Many hours later Cain gave a shout. "I see the entrance."

Abel followed his gaze to a nearby cave, remembering years before when Adam brought his three sons to the location of Eden, so they would always know it existed, but none had dared entry.

"Let's take a closer look." Cain said and ran towards the cave.

Abel shouted after him to stop but his brother had already reached the rocky entrance and entered. Carrying the lamb under his arm, he ran after Cain and into the cave, but could see no sign of his eldest sibling. He found Cain a short distance into the mountain standing before a massive golden door inscribed with markings, some in Sumerian, most in a language Abel did not recognise. There appeared to be no handle on the mysterious barrier, but right in the centre was an impression for what seemed to be a hand with fingers outstretched. Abel remembered what Adam had said, that only an immortal could open the door. He grabbed Cain by the arm but his brother pushed him aside and placed his right hand on the portal, fitting his fingers into the appropriate impressions.

At first nothing appeared to happen, but suddenly the golden door swung open. The brothers expected darkness and a wave of dust to assault their faces, but what greeted them instead was bright sunlight. They shut their eyes tightly such was the brightness of the light. They glanced at each other in amazement, knowing they were deep in the mountain where sunlight could not penetrate. The brothers slowly opened their eyes and peered through the entrance and into the cavern. Cain and Abel stood speechless at what lay before them.

A giant cavern stretching five miles into the distance completely enclosed within the Zagros Mountains filled their vision. Above them light seemed to emanate from the ceiling with no apparent sign of entry to the outside world. A great forest with several clearings filled the enormous cavern including a stream of clear water crisscrossing throughout Eden. Cain pointed to his brother and they watched as a group of elephants, zebras and tigers mingled together without attacking or fearing each other. Many other creatures could be seen strolling through the woodland, all apparently content with each other's company.

The brothers left the entrance behind and ran into the forest, feeling the bushes stroking their legs and feet. The cavern was warm and incredibly inviting, fruit of abundant varieties flourished everywhere they looked.

"We should not be here." Abel announced, gasping in wonder at the Garden. "Father will kill us."

Cain ignored him and ran on ahead. Abel chased after but had to catch his breath, a sensation he had never felt before. He suddenly felt tired and his muscles ached. He stopped and watched his brother disappear into the trees. The realisation that something was monumentally different about him began to dawn. He punched a nearby tree and grimaced in pain. The wound on his knuckle after a few minutes began to heal without trace but took much longer than he had ever seen before. The closer he got to the centre of Eden the weaker he felt and a sickening feeling began to consume his mind. His fears were confirmed as he ran through several bushes and saw before him the most incredible object he had ever seen in his long life.

Cain was about two hundred metres ahead, staring up in astonishment at an enormous Tree, the plant dominating not only the large clearing but the entire Garden itself. Abel estimated the Tree must be at least three hundred feet high, its many branches stretching far and wide in every direction. But it was the dazzling orange light that glowed off its trunk and leaves that caught the eye.

Abel gasped in fatigue as he finally approached his brother. "We should depart immediately. It's not safe here."

Cain ignored his pleas. "Have you ever seen anything so magnificent?"

"We should make our offerings and leave, brother." Abel repeated. "There is great magick here, we are not welcome in this strange place."

Cain shook himself from his trance. "You are right, we came here to end the famine," he said as he threw the skin bag of berries and fruit to the ground.

Cain emptied the contents on the grass adjacent the Tree of Life and striking up flint quickly set fire to the fruit using the bag as kindling. The brothers watched the smoke fill the clearing and stared at each other.

"Is that it? Is the drought over?" Cain asked his brother. "Was my sacrifice sufficient?"

Abel shrugged his shoulders, not knowing what to say or even expect. The brothers stared at each other in shock as the branches of the Tree suddenly began to shake and a chill breeze blew down its trunk and across their faces.

A faint androgynous whisper could be heard in the cold air. "Your offering is not acceptable, firstborn." The voice declared softly in a tone the siblings could not determine was male or female, but rather something in-between, but definitely not human. The brothers surmised the voice was that of an angel, or perhaps a guardian spirit of Eden, but was not Jehovah himself. His almighty presence was not warranted.

Abel glanced at his elder brother before setting the lamb on the ground, and using a short blade he carried quickly cut the animal's throat. The beast cried out briefly, its lifeblood seeping across the grass and into the soil. The siblings stood and stared up at the Tree as another breeze, this one much warmer shook the branches and blew across their entire bodies.

"Your offering is acceptable, second-born," the mysterious yet beautiful voice announced and Abel smiled. "The famine will end in three days and not return," it declared and disappeared, the entire forest falling silent as if all the creatures of Eden were listening intensely.

"It is done," Abel said proudly. "Now we can leave and tell father my good news, I have ended this terrible drought and assured the future for our clan."

Cain stared at him in rage. "The honour should be mine! You were always father's favourite, now he will celebrate for a hundred years telling this story to every passing stranger, the tale probably reaching Nok. The African king will say what a great son Adam has in Abel, and how he wished his daughter had married you and not the lesser brother!"

"You are hysterical and insane," Abel retorted. "But you speak truth for once. You may be older, but certainly not wiser. Only your great tantrums will be remembered, never your mediocre deeds."

Cain screamed in anger and swung at his brother, but Abel was too quick and side-stepped. He punched his elder brother squarely in the face, splitting Cain's lip. It was the first time Cain had tasted his own blood and the knowledge made him go berserk. He ran at Abel and pushed him hard in the chest. Abel faltered on his feet and fell back, striking the back of his head against the trunk of the Tree, a sickening thud echoing throughout the clearing.

Cain watched transfixed as Abel's body slid down the side of the Tree and come to rest on the grass. He stared at the lifeless corpse in speechless shock for several minutes, expecting his younger brother to stir and shout further abuse; anger from Abel he would welcome to bring an end to the eerie silence. Cain finally knelt down and shook his brother, but to no reaction. He felt the back of Abel's skull and cried out in fear as his hand was covered in blood. Cain had never seen so much blood before, even the killing of many animals had not shed so much. He stood to his feet and was only vaguely aware the cavern had fallen into a strange darkness like the blackest moonless night. The Tree of Life began to shake violently as Cain started to pull clumps of grass and soil up from the ground. He dragged Abel's corpse into the shallow hole he had made, placing loose dirt and rocks over the body, barely concealing it.

A tremendous roar like thunder filled Eden and Cain fell to the grass in terror. A voice much louder than the one which greeted the offerings shook the Garden and all the animals of Eden cried out in dismay and fled to the edge of the forest.

"Cain," the voice shouted. "Where is Abel thy brother?"

Cain started to cry, the tears flowing freely down his cheeks. He had never heard God before. Adam had told him many times how it might sound, but no tale told a hundred times could have prepared him for this event. The voice was both male and female, possessing traits of both sexes but certainly not human. There was a strange sound trailing off the end of the sentence like fierce wind blowing through a narrow crevasse.

Several moments passed before Cain could find the words to answer. "I know not," he whispered, his lips trembling in fear. "I am not my brother's keeper."

Another violent roar ripped throughout Eden and the mountains above, sending Cain onto his back. "What have thou done, Cain?" Jehovah said. "The voice of thy brother cries out to me from the ground, his very blood poisons the earth and destroys the Paradise I built for thy father. I curse thee that from this day henceforth you shall receive from the earth no strength, no crop shall thee sow come to fruit. You will never enter the gates of Heaven and see my face. A vagabond and fugitive shall thou live, surviving on the scraps of your enemies. Loneliness and despair will follow you all the days of your long life. Henceforth you are stripped of your immortality. If your enemy discovers your true identity they will surely slay you and put you to death like you did your brother."

Cain rose to his feet and faced the Tree, wiping the tears from his face. "This punishment is too great even for such a crime as I have committed. I beseech thee, let me one day see your face when I have achieved worthy redemption. Protect me from my enemies, for if they know who I am and slay me, I will be unable to make myself worthy of your love. Remember I am firstborn, the original child born on this planet, the foremost infant conceived from Adam who you made Eden for."

Several minutes passed and Cain began to grab locks of his hair in frustration at the silence.

This time the voice came as a whisper and brought pain.

"Very well," God declared. "I will allow you to retain your immortality. A mark I shall place on thee so your enemies will recognise you and dare not slay, for if they attempt to put your immortality to the test, vengeance I shall visit upon them sevenfold. Go now from this poisoned Paradise and return only when you achieve worthy redemption."

A bolt of lightening flew out of the base of the Tree and struck Cain in the torso, sending him flying through the air and into the bushes. He slowly rose to his feet and clutched his chest in agony. Cain looked down and saw a large tattoo in the form of a black symbol crisscrossed his torso, the name Firstborn written in Sumerian lay carved into his flesh, but part of the tattoo was in a language he recognised from the golden door at the cave entrance, it was obviously an enchantment but he could not decipher its meaning.

Cain glanced around Eden and noticed the peace of the Garden had vanished. The grass began to die and turn a blackish brown and the trees started to wither. He watched as a tiger attacked a zebra, bringing the animal to the ground and ripping into its flesh. Similar events were taking place all over Eden, the content nature the beasts once had for each other had disappeared, they knew now only loathing and hunger for one another. Only the Tree of Life appeared unaffected, soon it would be the only plant alive in the Garden. Once the predators had consumed all the other animals they would turn on each other. Cain knew he was weak and vulnerable here this close to the Tree, his regenerative powers would not work. If a tiger or lion focussed their attention on him, he would have neither the strength to defend himself or the power of healing to cure his wounds. For the first time in memory Cain was in fear of his life.

He began to run for the exit out of Eden and back to Mesopotamia, when he abruptly halted. A lone individual approached from the entrance. His heart sank when he recognised the person coming towards him. It was Adam.

"Cain," his father shouted. "What have you done?"

His son did not answer, he was both too ashamed of his crime and afraid to speak lest his father kill him in revenge.

"A thousand miles away I would have felt the death of an immortal," Adam declared. "But I would have never dared believe it would be at the hands of another, let alone one son of mine murder another."

"I am so sorry, father." Cain said. "It was an accident, I never meant to kill him."

"Apologies cannot suffice, your crime is too great. I will take Abel's body from here and build a temple in his honour. You must go into the wilderness with your young wife Âwân and never return. Do not speak to your mother or Seth about this, their souls will not be tainted with your deception."

Cain nodded and started to cry again. He ran for the exit, leaving Eden behind. Cain turned once more to look at Adam, knowing he would never see his father again.

CHAPTER FIVE

The phone rang incessantly forcing the tired hand to finally reach out.

"Al, you awake?" The voice on the telephone enquired.

"Sean, is that you?" Albert Maher growled. "Jesus, it's after 2am. Don't you ever sleep? That couch you call your best friend must keep you up all night. Why don't you just leave that psycho bitch of a wife and I can get some shut-eye?"

"We stay together to spite one another," Neilson laughed. "There's been a development with your friend Sam Philips. Apparently he gave his MI5 tails the slip. It also appears his covert job with that technology firm was bogus."

Albert sighed. "Well, that was no surprise. The CIA probably set up that employment history."

"It gets better," Sean said. "He was getting his false identities from an Irish master forger by the name of Jack Mulcahy. The same Irishman was found dead earlier tonight with his throat cut. The apartment he worked from is in a right mess, blood everywhere but no other bodies. Someone did a clean up job before police arrived."

"Do you think Sam Philips or whatever his real name is was responsible?"

"This Jack Mulcahy was his friend so it is unlikely Mr. Philips killed him," Neilson declared. "But his fingerprints were found elsewhere around the flat. It appears your suspect has powerful enemies."

"It might be gang related, perhaps even the Russian mob, they always have operatives in London."

"I have a contact in the Home Office," Neilson said. "It appears some influential businessmen are in town meeting in secret. He doesn't know where, but he believes some government cabinet members may be involved in illegal activity."

Maher laughed. "MPs up to no good. When are they not?"

"My contact thinks they are freemasons or something akin to such an organisation. But get this…" Neilson paused, savouring the moment. "It seems Chief Inspector Richard Bellings might be involved."

"Dick is a suspect?" Maher asked in astonishment and Sean laughed, knowing all too well his partner's hatred of their superior.

"He was spotted leaving a meeting at some mansion outside of London, which brings me to why I am ringing you at 2am. My contact needs concrete evidence of police corruption in this matter for his investigation to go to the next level."

Maher groaned. "I know I am not going to like this where this conversation is going."

"Everyone knows Bellings has a locked drawer in his office but nobody dare enquire as to its contents. Night security will allow us in before the next shift begins at 6am."

"You want us to break into an office of New Scotland Yard?" Albert shouted down the phone. "Losing our jobs will be the least of our problems if we are caught."

Neilson smiled. "Where's your sense of adventure? Just think of it, being finally rid of that arrogant prick."

Maher said nothing for several moments. "Alright, I'll meet you at the entrance to New Scotland Yard in one hour."

Detective Inspector Albert Maher arrived at his workplace just before 3am to find his partner, Detective Sean Neilson already present, shuffling his feet on the pavement in boredom.

"Christ, you took your time," Neilson said. "Don't you know there are a hundred cameras watching me scratch my nuts in the breeze."

Albert drew up alongside his partner. "This is insane. If we find nothing in that desk we are screwed."

"There's bound to be something we can use," Sean declared. "Nobody keeps a locked drawer unless they have something to hide, even if it's kiddie porn."

"Come on, let's get going." Albert said and opened the door.

The two policemen were immediately greeted by a night watchman. After briefly showing their identifications, the detectives were allowed entry. They made their way upstairs, passed their familiar desks and down the hallway to their superior's office door. Neilson removed a screwdriver from his inside pocket and jammed it into the frame. After about a minute he managed to get the door open and they walked inside.

Even in the dark Maher could discern the picture of Robert the Bruce on the wall and grinned. He pulled the frame off the wall and hit it off the side of the swivel chair, driving a large hole into the middle, destroying the picture. Neilson watched him in amusement.

"In for a penny, in for a pound." Albert smiled. "If we find nothing we are fucked. May as well have some fun as I destroy my career."

Detective Neilson sat down on the black chair and quickly thrust the screwdriver into the centre locked drawer. With a grunt of exertion the wood cracked and the drawer flew open. Various document were enclosed. Neilson threw the contents onto the desk and began to shuffle through them.

One invoice caught his attention. "Jesus, look at this," Sean said and showed the paper to his partner. "A whole range of armaments bought from some company in America and transported this morning to Baghdad. What is Bellings up to, trying to start some new civil war in Iraq?"

Maher scanned through the list. "Thirty-one handguns, twenty-five AK-47s, three flamethrowers and even two high-powered sniper rifles. He didn't finance this himself. He must have rich sponsors."

"Another document says here thirty mercenaries have been hired from an American military security contractor in Iraq and are to receive the same arms upon delivery. A ship leaves in three days from London docks with a passenger manifest containing the names Samuel and Alice Carson, various other unknowns and Richard Bellings."

"We have enough here to fry his ass." Albert said in satisfaction. "Let's get out of here."

"My Home Office contact will probably want to catch them in the act at the pier preparing to board." Neilson said. "I'll make sure we are in attendance. I can't wait to see that smug bastard's face when we arrest him."

"We can't wait that long. When he sees the mess here he will know that transport is compromised." Maher declared. "Ring your contact now. We can arrest Bellings once he leaves his home and he is alone. We can detain him until after his co-conspirators are apprehended at the pier."

"Agreed." Neilson said and they left the building, the night watchmen none the wiser to the chaos left in the office under their care.

CHAPTER SIX

"That's some story." Alice Mulcahy said. "You've been on the run all this time?"

Cain nodded. "Enough about me. Tell me about your life."

Alice laughed. "My story isn't quite as exciting as yours. I was raised an only child by my mother in Chicago. She was a schoolteacher of English and Geography."

"And your father?"

"I didn't see him often. My parents divorced when I was very young. All I know is my father was obsessed with his work, a trait he inherited from my grandfather who traded in the Middle East. When my mother died I came here to find my uncle. The rest you know." Alice said and made for the door.

"Where are you going?"

"I am expected in college for a lecture at 10am. If I don't show up questions will be asked. I need to telephone a friend and spin her some lie so the university won't be suspicious."

"Very well. But it's not even half past eight in the morning. Students like your friend are not early risers. Stay a while, keep me company. I have not told anybody about my life before. Surely such honesty grants me an hour of your time. Besides those men are looking for you. You don't want to risk your health for a quick phone call and some window shopping."

"I suppose I could stay a while," she smiled and sat down on the edge of the bed.

Cain sat up beside her. "You know you are very beautiful."

Alice laughed. "And how many times have you told that line over six thousand years? What was Cleopatra or Helen of Troy like? Did you inflict that charm on them as well?"

"Never met them," he replied flatly. "As I said before I stayed out of history's way. Only someone special like yourself warranted my attention." Cain declared and suddenly kissed her on the lips.

Alice drew back and stared at him, surprised. She rose to her feet. "A man's heart is a kingdom, he guards the keys to its locked doors firmly. Someone of your strength and survivor instinct would never let someone like me in."

"Interesting parable," Cain remarked in a sarcastic tone. "Did you pick that up on your English university course?"

Alice slapped him across the face but he just laughed. Cain grabbed her hard, wrapping his arms around her. He caught the hair at the back of her head and held it fast. Cain kissed her again, but she did not respond. He began to relax, preparing to let her go when Alice kissed him passionately. She pushed him hard and he fell onto the bed. She climbed on top of him, straddling him, sticking her feet under his legs. Cain stared up at her as she removed the red v-neck jumper and threw it on the floor. He could not help but notice how large her breasts were in contrast to her slender frame.

She reached back and removed the white bra and placed it on the bed. Cain reached up and holding the back of her neck, pulled her down onto him. He kissed her again and turned her over onto her back. He got up onto his knees and unbuttoning her blue jeans, pulled them down, her panties coming with them. Throwing them to the floor, he quickly removed his clothes and lay down beside her. Cain wrapped his right arm around her and pulled her close. He kissed her much stronger now, sticking his tongue forcefully into her mouth. He grabbed her left breast hard, pulling on the nipple. Alice left out a faint groan and seized his testicles in her left hand. His black pubic hair was wiry to the touch as she held his erect penis in her hand. She briefly looked down to see he was quite large endowed.

"It's been some time for me," Alice said and smirked. "Best to take it easy at first."

Cain laughed. "It may have been months or years for you. But it has been centuries for me."

He lifted himself up and she placed one leg at either side of him. He rubbed the head of his penis against her clitoris, causing her to shudder with excitement. He gently eased his penis inside her and she let out a brief cry of pain. Cain began to thrust himself in and out of her slowly at first as her juices started to flow and the movement was less constrictive. He felt her shake violently as her orgasm ripped through her slender body and he shouted only moments later as he came hard inside her. Cain lay in that position for several minutes and kissed her again, feeling her hair between his fingers. She smiled up at him and placed his right hand on her cheek, savouring the touch. Cain eased himself out of her and she let out another short moan. He lay down beside her but she quickly rose from the bed. Cain looked at her in puzzlement.

"I should really make that phone call," Alice announced. "Don't worry. I will simply say I am ill and I am alone."

He nodded and stretched himself out on the bed as she dressed and left the hotel. Alice made her way onto the main street and soon found an enclosed public phone box. Placing the coins into the slot she dialled the familiar number.

A man's voice appeared on the other side of the line. "Alice, I was beginning to wonder when you might call, your friend left some mess at that Irishman's office."

Alice gritted her teeth. "Father, for a second there you sounded almost concerned."

"Where is he and what information have you gathered?" Samuel enquired, ignoring his daughter's sarcastic tone.

Alice told her parent the location of Cain and the story he had told her of Adam and how Abel was killed.

"Interesting," Samuel declared. "But only little extra knowledge other than what we already knew. Perhaps it is time to finally bring Mr. Kadmon in for more intensive interrogation and prepare for the journey to Iraq."

"I don't believe he knows anything more," Alice said fearfully. "Simply hurting him would be pointless."

There was an audible sigh on the line. "Alice, I do hope you are not going soft on me. You will have to be ruthless if you want to inherit the title of Grandmaster after me." Samuel said sternly. "You didn't make love to him did you?"

Alice paused for some moments before answering. "Of course not. I would never let emotions or physical desire get in the way of my job."

"Good girl," her father replied. "From what you described only an immortal's hand may open the barred entrance to Eden. I could always chop his hand off when we got there, but there might be an enchantment on the door that requires the act to be voluntary." Samuel said and Alice let out a sigh of relief which the Grandmaster did not hear. "Do not return to the hotel. I have a squad nearby with tasers ready to apprehend Cain. It would be too dangerous for you now."

"He might suspect something and leave."

"No, I believe not." Samuel grinned. "He will patiently await your return. Remember he has a thing for damsels in distress. Wait nearby, I will send a car."

Alice hung up and stood at the phone box for a minute, glancing at the alley across the street where the hotel was located. She began to pace up and down the pavement in nervousness, biting her nails. Finally she darted across the road to the entrance to the hotel, but did not enter. Above she heard commotion and breaking glass shattered from the room windows fell near her feet.

A man dressed all in black and wearing a balaclava appeared alongside her. He was armed with a pump action shotgun and a revolver was strapped to his waist. "Madam," the guard said sharply. "You should not be here." He motioned to two other similarly dressed men who arrived and they escorted Alice to a waiting van. As she was guided inside, she noticed six more men all armed dragging Cain from the hotel doorway. He was half naked and unconscious but otherwise appeared unharmed. They bundled him into another dark van which quickly drove off.

Alice watched the vehicle speed away down the street as the guard closed the van door, trapping her inside. She placed her face in her hands and began to sob. "What have I done?" She cried out faintly into the silence.

CHAPTER SEVEN

"There he goes," the policeman said. "Should we move now and arrest?"

"Not yet," Detective Sean Neilson replied sharply, placing his hand on the arm of the nearby officer. "Let him say goodnight to his darling wife. Let her not suspect his involvement in any criminal activity. We cannot be certain she is innocent of any charges."

The two New Scotland Yard and eight Home Office officials watched Detective Chief Inspector Richard Bellings kiss his spouse on the cheek at the doorstep to their three storey home in the affluent part of central London from the darkness of the small truck.

"Remember our agreement," Detective Inspector Albert Maher said to the men in suits from the Home Office. "We get him for two hours before we hand him over to you."

"Just make sure he can still talk with most of his teeth," one of the men replied with a stern look. "He's no good to us unconscious."

"Agreed," Maher retorted and turned to look at his partner. "Christ, I can't tell you how much I am going to enjoy this. I thought losing my virginity at fourteen to the babysitter was great, but this is going to make my decade."

The company of men let out a laugh as they opened the door to the truck and made their way across the road, keeping to the shadows.

Albert approached his superior, who was at first surprised but then shocked as the other nine armed men drew up alongside him.

Maher grinned at the Chief Inspector in satisfaction. "Detective Richard Bellings of New Scotland Yard you are under arrest for treason against the Crown."

His superior smiled back. "You don't know who you are dealing with. You are way out of your league."

"Well, Dick," Maher said. "That's what we intend to find out. Take this piece of shit away."

The Chief Inspector was unceremoniously thrown into the van as one of the Home Office men turned to the two detectives. "Remember, we need names. You had to call us instead of MI5 and your colleagues at New Scotland Yard because you don't know who to trust. I believe some very important people are involved with these fringe freemasons or whatever they call themselves."

Albert Maher nodded as he got into the driver's seat of the van and began to speed away from the scene. Sean Neilson sat in the back, keeping a close eye on his former superior. Barely thirty minutes later they arrived at a derelict building. They carried Richard Bellings inside and strapped him to a plain wooden chair.

"Comfortable?" Albert said and Bellings smirked back.

"You're all mouth and no trousers," the Chief Inspector laughed. "You haven't got the bottle to beat me up. Imagine what they will do to me if I confess or implicate them."

Maher punched his superior squarely in the face, shocking Neilson. "What do you think I am going to do? Your life choices are diminishing by the second. Ninety minutes from now those men in suits will return, expecting answers. The Prime Minister himself has been informed of this operation, believing it to be a matter of national security. He has authorised those Home Office men to take you to an army base where interrogation by military officers familiar with torturing Islamic fundamentalists will interview you. This conversation with me will be gentle in comparison."

"We found the invoices in your office." Detective Neilson announced. "You funding a private army in Iraq?"

"Adding breaking and entering to your list? You had no right to access my private affairs." Bellings snarled.

Albert punched the Chief Inspector in the stomach, causing the policeman to double over in pain. "Christ, Dick, wake up and smell the fucking coffee. We are talking treason against the Crown here and you're worrying about your hidden stash of porno!"

"I'm afraid we had to smash that prized framed picture of Bob the Bruce as well." Neilson added and Albert laughed.

"I've had enough of this shit," Maher snarled. "Get me the pliers and medical scalpel from the van."

Bellings stared at Albert in sheer terror. "Alright, I'll tell you who is involved."

Neilson grabbed the hair at the back of Bellings' scalp and pulled the Chief Inspector towards him. "Don't leave out the juicy stuff, or its fingernails followed by toes. I promise those men in suits will be forced to carry you out of here."

Bellings nodded in fright. "Local operations are orchestrated by the Chief Constable and the Lord Mayor," he said and the two detectives stared at him speechless.

"We were right to not involve New Scotland Yard or MI5." Neilson interjected and turned to their captive. "But they don't call the shots, do they? What exactly is this organisation, what are their goals?"

Richard Bellings looked at them, saying nothing.

Maher slapped him across the face. "Speak up, Dick. I didn't hear an answer."

Albert was about to strike him again when Bellings whispered. "They are the British wing of the Illuminati."

The detectives stared at him. "The what?" Maher enquired. "What exactly is the Illuminati?"

"They are an organisation founded centuries ago, their original function to hide prohibited manuscripts from the Spanish Inquisition," Bellings declared. "But their goals have changed, particularly over the last fifty years. They have become obsessed with the occult and politics, believing the two to be intrinsically linked. They have altered or interfered in world matters, most especially the World Bank. Their ultimate aim is a united global single authority with them at its head. Members have left encoded messages down through the ages on churches and mausoleums, they believe they are the spiritual successors to the Knights Templar."

"And you buy into this shit?" Albert sneered.

Bellings laughed. "Of course not. But a few nods, handshakes and many bribes later and you can find your career advanced no end."

"Perform blowjobs on demand and I get whatever I want?" Neilson grinned. "Where do I sign up?"

"So, say I believe this fantasy for a minute," Maher interrupted. "Who runs this British wing?"

Bellings sighed in apprehension. "An American businessman called Samuel Carson, a real nasty piece of work. As ruthless as he is ambitious, he has no scruples whatsoever in the methods to achieve his personal objectives."

"And what are those aims?"

"All I know is it involves your mysterious friend from the hospital," the Chief Inspector responded. "He has information they desperately want."

"Who else is involved?" Maher enquired.

"Several MPs, including one current Minister." Bellings replied and the two detectives shook their head, not surprised by the confession.

"What information do they require from Sam Philips?" Albert said and leaned forward, nearly pressing his face against the Chief Inspector, deliberately invading his personal space.

"That's not his real name." Bellings replied.

"What a surprise," Maher smiled. "Tell me something I don't know, like what the fuck knowledge he has that is so important it involves the hiring of thirty mercenaries in Iraq?"

Richard Bellings was about to answer when a gunshot was heard across the street and the Chief Detective's head exploded, splattering blood and brain matter to the floor and onto the policemen.

"What the fuck..." Sean Neilson shouted before they dropped to their knees and removed their handguns from their shoulder holsters.

"I think it came from the house across the road," Maher said as he made his way to the open window. "Had to be a sniper rifle."

Detective Neilson glanced over the top of the window and saw a man running from the opposite derelict building and approach a waiting black Mercedes. He was carrying a long barrelled rifle with infra-red night scope attached. There appeared to be two more masked men inside the waiting vehicle, including the driver. Maher stood up at the open door and prepared to fire his revolver at the sniper before he entered his getaway car, but at that moment the man in the back seat pointed an automatic machine-gun through the window and started firing.

Albert ducked behind the adjoining wall as bullets streamed into the outer walls of the house and through the open door into the room where they crouched.

"Jesus Christ," Neilson screamed above the horrendous noise. "Sounds like an AK-47 like we were taught back at the academy."

His partner nodded as the gunman stopped firing and the Mercedes sped off down the road, tyres screeching as they took the right corner at high speed. The two detectives glanced out of the building but the car was long gone. Albert began to telephone headquarters to organise an armed roadblock as Sean Neilson approached the slumped body of the Chief Inspector.

"That must have been some high-powered rifle, considering the mess it made of his skull," Neilson said, walking around the chair. "They wanted to make sure his silence was assured."

Albert Maher stared at the body. "Now I am pissed!" He growled. "Who are these people that they can murder a high-ranking policeman and run off into the night. They must have followed us which means they had Bellings under surveillance."

"I guess they didn't trust him," Neilson stated. "Or he had valuable knowledge they didn't want revealed, and it looks like your Sam Philips is at the centre of it all."

"I knew he was full of shit," Maher declared. "I should have clapped handcuffs on him and chained him to that hospital bed."

"Some party you had here and we didn't get our invitation," a man laughed as the eight Home Office officials entered the building. "When I said don't leave him unconscious I didn't mean blow his brains out."

"We didn't do this to him, have Ballistics check our weapons if you don't believe us." Maher snarled back.

"Calm yourself, detective, I was only joking," the man smiled. "I know you only wanted to question him, besides I didn't really think you were responsible for the holes in the wall outside."

"How did you get here this fast?" Neilson enquired. "Uniformed policemen haven't even arrived yet, and we only just put out the bulletin."

"You didn't really believe we were going to let you amateurs have free rein without us being nearby," another suited man announced. "We were in the nearby restaurant having a nightcap when we heard the commotion."

"Christ," Maher laughed. "Isn't that just like a civil servant, always taking every opportunity to have a quick drink or a sly shag on the side."

"Watch your mouth, cop," the man retorted. "Remember it is civil servants who organise your taxes."

"Let it go, Albert." Neilson said. "Let's get back to the task at hand."

"Agreed," the Home Office official added. "What information did you gather?"

"Not a whole lot," Maher said and paused as his mobile phone rang. He listened to the operator for about a minute before turning to the company. "They found the black Mercedes, it was abandoned one mile away and then torched. The three occupants were seen running through a nearby housing estate, they must have had another vehicle nearby. They are gone!" He said and threw the phone against the wall in rage, smashing it to pieces.

His partner knelt down and collecting the small parts, began to reassemble the mobile. "Let us focus on what we do know. You may call us amateurs but these guys obviously are not, this was a professional execution."

"Bellings said he was part of some cult," Maher stated as sirens could be heard outside on the street as several police cars pulled up.

One of the Home Office men left the building to speak to the officers on the road, ensuring the company inside the house were left undisturbed.

"The Ku-Klux-Klan or followers of David Koresh didn't organise this," one of the officials interjected. "This wasn't the work of some banner-carrying brainwashing right-wing neo-nazi hell-bent on resurrecting the ghost of Adolf Hitler. This was orchestrated by someone or some group with connections and a tremendous amount of money at their disposal."

"New Scotland Yard officers are organising a search warrant for Bellings' London home and the rural mansion this cult frequented is at this moment being raided." Neilson announced, answering his mobile phone. "It appears to be vacant, we will ascertain further information once the building has been dusted for fingerprints."

"Bellings said the Chief Constable and the Lord Mayor were involved," Maher declared. "Including several members of Parliament and a serving Minister."

One of the men laughed. "The Mayor? Should have guessed that blond haired snob had a hand in this. Word is he had a taste for the high life."

Another mobile phone rang and a Home Office official answered it, turning to the two detectives. "Your friends at the Central Intelligence Agency have arrived at their hotel and wish for you both to debrief them immediately."

Maher sighed. "There are more pressing matters here than entertaining those damn spooks. I will talk to them in the morning. It will take all night filling out the report on this mess."

"This order comes direct from the Home Secretary," the official retorted. "It appears the man you know as Sam Philips has disappeared, leaving the back alley hotel he was residing at in quite a mess. There is evidence of a struggle and the owner reported several armed masked men dragging Mr. Philips from the building."

"Bellings indicated my suspect was at the heart of all this, Philips has vital knowledge they desperately require." Albert replied. "Obviously after their failed attempt earlier they resorted to sterner measures. Considering what these men did to the former Chief Inspector, I have no doubt they will get their information shortly by means of torture."

"Reading your report on what the wino witnessed, I would say Mr. Philips is someone not to be underestimated," the official interjected. "Nevertheless, I agree that it is only a matter of time before they crack your suspect. We need to ascertain the current location of this Samuel Carson and his cronies."

"Perhaps the CIA have that knowledge," Neilson interrupted. "They have resources at their disposal not available to Scotland Yard, and this Sam Philips was their operative during the Vietnam war."

"Good luck getting information from those covert bastards," the official sneered. "Conversations with the spooks is usually one-sided."

The two detectives left the building, leaving the Home Office men to remove the Chief Inspector's body and examine the scene for the missing bullet. The policemen arrived at the four-star hotel shortly afterwards and were quickly escorted to the room where their impatient interrogators awaited.

Upon opening the door, four men dressed in expensive suits stood up, drinking coffee and stared at the detectives. Maher noticed they had no luggage other than a single laptop which was placed on the bedside table, flashing text appearing on the screen, indicating a continuous wireless connection, probably with either MI5, MI6 or CIA operatives within London.

"Nice hotel room," Albert announced. "My wages could not afford such luxury. We are certainly privileged to be in the company of such distinguished visitors paid for by our taxpayers for our American benefactors. My father used to talk about how the yanks did not share their nuclear weapons programme knowledge with their British allies after the second world war, effectively holding the United Kingdom to ransom."

The four men said nothing at first, simply staring at the policeman, their expressions like stone. "We did not come to this country to debate our ancestors' political and military decisions," one of the men declared, a forty-two year old balding operative dressed all in black complete with grey featureless tie. "We have been informed you spoke to Mr. Bellings before his untimely death. We need to know the contents of the conversation that transpired."

"Untimely death?" Neilson sneered. "He had his brains blown across our faces by a sniper rifle. What exactly is this cult that he was a member of, and who is Samuel Carson?"

The four spies glanced at each other in nervousness, an emotion Maher guessed was unfamiliar to them. "We are not at liberty to disclose that information, suffice to say the motives of Mr. Carson would have a bearing on your national security."

The two detectives turned around and made for the door. "You need to start trusting us and share knowledge, or this conversation is at an end." Albert said.

The Americans took a collective deep breath before calling the policemen back. "Alright," the same balding spy shouted. "But this is off the record and does not leave this room. What exactly did Bellings tell you?"

Maher approached the company and sat down on one of the beds. "He mentioned he was a member of some group called the Illuminati, a pseudo-religious organisation hell-bent on world domination. They considered themselves the 'spiritual successor' to the Knights Templar."

The operative nodded. "The Illuminati bear similar ancestral traits to the Templars, in that they both left encoded messages on old churches and tombs all over Europe, but their motives differ somewhat. The Knights Templar was a very powerful and wealthy religious order of holy soldiers founded in 1118AD governed with the protection of Christian pilgrims on their way to the Holy Land. They once had their own headquarters during the Crusades near the site of King Solomon's Temple at Jerusalem. The Pope grew jealous of their wealth and influence and in 1312AD trumped up various charges of heresy and had them all burned at the stake. Scholars believe their mythical treasure the pontiff lusted after was never found. The Illuminati's aims were always less honourable and certainly more self-centred. They are more similar to freemasons but nothing like our American fore-founders. They were officially founded in Bavaria in 1776AD by a Professor Adam Weishaupt. Originally their intentions were spiritual enlightenment, but over the centuries they have become focussed on neo-conservative aims including domination of the World Bank and the International Monetary Fund, believing whoever controls these organisations ultimately controls all the economies of the globe, irrespective of whatever government holds power, either democratic or dictator."

"What does this have to with Sam Philips?" Maher enquired.

"The man you know by that name first came to our country's attention after the second world war when he was liberated from captivity in a specially designed nazi laboratory in Auschwitz. He was being experimented on by the German butcher Josef Mengele, intent on creating the fabled master race."

The two detectives stared at the spies in astonishment. "What are you saying? That this man is over a hundred years old?"

"We believe he is probably much, much older than that," the American replied.

"So he's an alien from Mars?" Neilson laughed.

"No," the operative retorted. "We tested him extensively, he's as human as you or me. The greatest puzzlement was the strange tattoo on his chest."

"He told me it meant 'firstborn' and was written in Sumerian. The doctors could not discover the process by which it was created, believing it to extend into the ribs itself."

"What is really bizarre is that it appears to have been burned into the flesh, the method should have killed him," the American said. "But he seems to possess incredible regenerative abilities, the most grievous of injuries healing almost immediately. Apparently under extreme tests, one scientist even shot him point blank in the head. But he recovered within minutes and the wound could not be found. We brought in a scholar in the occult who said the markings on his chest were akin to some type of magickal enchantment."

"So we should put out a missing bulletin for Gandalf?" Maher laughed.

"Now I understand your government's interest in him and why he was used for special operations in Cambodia during the Vietnam War."

Neilson smiled. "And also why this Samuel Carson desires him so badly."

The company of spies looked at each other in apprehension. "This Chief Inspector of yours had made friends with some very dangerous and powerful people, it was only a matter of time before his usefulness became redundant. Samuel Carson has a reputation for tiring quickly of lackeys," the operative declared. "Mr. Carson is an American businessman who revolutionised the Illuminati, dragging them into the twentieth first century and making many of their members very rich. There are several senators who regard him as a genius and utterly ruthless. His interest in Sam Philips has to be sinister."

"Mr. Philips was last seen being carried unconscious from a hotel by masked men with machine-guns," Maher said. "We have to assume he is being held by the Illuminati."

"Mr. Philips is very resourceful, there is a good chance he will escape captivity," the spy replied. "We have a list of all his aliases, so if he does succeed in freeing himself we should be able to discover his location very quickly."

"We get first crack at him," Maher said sharply. "I have a lot of questions for Mr. Philips."

"Agreed," the American nodded. "He indicated many years ago he no longer wished to work with us, his usefulness has run its course and coercion would be impossible. But Samuel Carson is ours. We need that planned ship sailing to take place tomorrow night, let the Illuminati members believe their departure is guaranteed and give them enough rope to hang themselves. It is essential we catch Carson red-handed so his sponsors in

Congress will wash their hands of him and thus ensure his conviction for international terrorism."

CHAPTER EIGHT

Cain awoke slowly, a throbbing pain in his head. He opened his eyes and tried to peer into the darkness of the small room in which he had been roughly thrown. There appeared to be no furniture or windows in the dust covered chamber and a single metal door lay across from him. It had all the familiar trademarks of a medieval dungeon, complete with thick rusty chains wrapped around his chest and arms. He tried to move his hands from behind his back but discovered they were handcuffed. He attempted to break free, wriggling his body to and fro across the dirty floor but to no avail. While the chains appeared old and worn, it would still take some time to free himself, the metal not being of sufficient quality to maintain his bondage indefinitely.

His frantic movements however brought attention as the door quickly swung open and in walked three masked men carrying what looked like tasers. They were soon accompanied by a fifty-five year old gentleman dressed in an expensive three-piece suit and rather odd looking tie, bearing strange symbols sewn into the fabric. Cain groaned, the markings were familiar icons normally attributed to the Illuminati. He knew he was in the presence of the Grandmaster who had sought him for so long.

"Apologies for your uncomfortable accommodation, Mr. Kadmon," Samuel Carson announced. "I promise better surroundings when you arrive in Iraq."

"A dungeon?" Cain laughed. "Rather appropriate, considering how many of your members have seen similar views down through the centuries."

"Very amusing," the American replied. "But you should be more concerned with your own fate. Don't you want to know why the Illuminati have searched for you for so long?"

"I can already surmise that reason," Cain sneered. "I know you desire the location of Eden, that is why you are arranging transport to Iraq."

Samuel Carson walked towards his captive and bent over, his wrinkled face nearly touching Cain. "It would be so much easier for you if you simply disclosed the exact location of the Garden, I know it lies somewhere deep within the Zagros Mountains."

"You must also know the door which bars entry can only be opened by an immortal," Cain smiled. "The act must be voluntary and without coercion, the magickal enchantment on the portal will know the difference. It is pointless maintaining my captivity, not to mention these mediocre chains will not keep me in place for very long."

The Grandmaster stood up and went back to the company of the soldiers. "Those chains had to be arranged in a hurry, we have titanium steel arriving later today, you will find that metal even for your incredible strength impossible to break. And yes, we know about the enchantments on the door at Eden. We had after all the best of spies, one in plain sight and right under your nose."

Cain looked at him in puzzlement and then in shock as in walked Alice, apparently unharmed and stood alongside the leader of the Illuminati. She stared at her former lover on the floor, his anger evident as he wriggled in the chains.

"I am so sorry, Cain," Alice said softly. "I never meant any of this to happen. I was ordered to simply carry out a fact-finding mission, to gather as much information as possible about Eden."

Cain glared at her in rage. "How much did they pay you for screwing me and leaving me at the mercy of the henchmen at the hotel?"

Alice glanced nervously at the fifty-five year old man next to her as he stared back at her in disgust. "It's not like that," she said in a trembling voice as the Grandmaster grabbed her arm and pinched it hard, shoving her towards the open door, the impact of her entrance into the dungeon somewhat diminished by the declaration that his spy had slept with Cain. "He's my father, I had no choice."

"There's always a choice," Cain snarled. "Our destiny is defined forever by our daily options, to turn left or right, to get on the bus or get off. A moment's hesitation or inaction can have ramifications on the rest of our lives. By pushing Abel, my fate was sealed for all time. Don't throw your life away following this maniac, he cares nothing for you, his only concern is the power source at the Garden."

"Very noble sentiments, Mr. Kadmon," Samuel said as his daughter was led away. "But utterly pointless. It is my choices that matter, my orders that seal a person's fate. I only have to give the word and someone dies."

As if to emphasise this point, a messenger in the form of a young man dressed in plain clothes composing of a white shirt and dark jeans appeared. The individual approached the Grandmaster and seemed to be somewhat out of breath from running.

"Master," the messenger panted. "The soldiers reported they successfully eliminated Chief Inspector Richard Bellings, however he was at the time being interviewed by two senior New Scotland Yard detectives. The policemen are alive and were summoned to a meeting with operatives from the Central Intelligence Agency."

Samuel Carson shouted in rage and revealing a seven inch dagger from his inside jacket pocket stabbed the young man in the stomach, the messenger screaming in pain and fright before slumping to the ground.

"This is what I mean by my choices, Mr. Kadmon," Carson growled. "I alone hold power here, you would do well to remember that."

Cain laughed in reply. "It always amuses me how the master rewards his servants' loyalty with death like a bad comic book or movie, you must have an inexhaustible supply of henchmen."

"What I don't possess is eternal patience," the Grandmaster shouted. "Pick him up and take him to the roof."

The masked soldiers grabbed Cain and pulled him to his feet, the chains scratching along the floor.

"Throwing me off the building won't achieve anything," Cain said. "You know I am immortal and can recover from any injury."

Samuel Carson smiled. "Why would I wish to harm you, Mr. Kadmon? You are too valuable. No, I have a lesson for you to learn."

Cain glanced at him in confusion as they climbed several flights of stairs and approached the top of the eight storey structure. A fierce breeze greeted the company's faces as they opened the door and strolled onto the flat roof, making for the edge. Cain noticed he was near to the centre of London, a large shopping centre and adjoining car-park lay before them. He watched as dozens of people went to and from the building, busily carrying bags of groceries and clothes, mothers placing their infants into buggies and the back seats of cars, oblivious to the presence of the armed soldiers on the roof across from them.

Samuel Carson turned towards his captive and revealed from his jacket a small transmitter, a single red button and aerial attached to it. "Now you will understand, Mr. Kadmon, there is nothing I won't do and nobody I won't kill to achieve my aims. My men have placed a large explosive device within that shopping centre, it is doubtful anybody present within will survive."

"You are truly insane," Cain sneered. "And mistaken if you believe I will cooperate. I have been witness to terrible events throughout my life, these people mean nothing to me."

"You have stayed out of history's way, but it is time you once again took an active part in its making," the Grandmaster declared. "I firmly know you desire above all things redemption, to pay for the act of killing Abel. I know you will feel overwhelming guilt for the deaths and suffering of these innocent people, their blood will be on your hands. Cooperate with us, lead us to Eden and I will spare their lives, this I promise you. Fail to answer our questions and it will be your choice, not mine that seals these poor slobs their fate."

Cain stared at him, certain he was not bluffing or would shirk from killing all those people. Several minutes passed before he replied. "I cannot show you where Eden lies, the destiny of the entire world is at stake, the power source at the Tree is too dangerous to let it fall into your evil hands."

Samuel Carson looked at him with a blank expression and Cain started to believe he would not go ahead with his terrible intent. But then he placed his finger on the red button and pushed it.

"No, don't do it," Cain shouted as a horrendous loud noise could be heard in the distance, the sounds of metal and glass mixed with screams echoing from the shopping centre and across the car-park.

Cain dropped to his knees at the edge of the roof as a great orange and reddish balloon of fire rose up from where the building once lay, cars and people blown across the road, smashing into the walls of the very house they resided in. Even from where Cain knelt, he could make out the broken bodies of women and children, their deformed corpses lay everywhere alongside severed limbs missing their owners.

Samuel Carson bent down next to him. "Now I believe you will cooperate, Mr. Kadmon," the Grandmaster laughed as Cain began to cry, a tear running down his cheek, a sensation he had not felt in centuries.

"You will burn in Hell for this, you bastard." Cain snarled in reply.

"Of that I have no doubt," Carson smiled. "But we will dine with the Devil together."

CHAPTER NINE

Cain was escorted back to his holding cell and thrown with force into the corner, the soldiers laughing before leaving him to his solitary confinement. He gazed down at the floor for some hours before the door slowly opened, the intruder trying its best to remain discrete, minimising the creaks as the metal door scratched along the stone ground.

Cain looked in surprise as Alice crept in and placed a finger to her lips, motioning for his silence. She was dressed in warm clothes comprising of a heavy fleece jacket and blue jeans. She carried similar garments in her hands and what appeared to be a small but expensive camcorder with attached viewer.

"Well, if it isn't the niece of my dead friend Jack Mulcahy," Cain whispered, "or should I say Judas with his betrayer's kiss."

"For someone so ancient, you certainly see things in black and white," Alice retorted sharply. "I told you I had no choice. It is easy for you, being so strong and invulnerable. Being a drifter and wanderer all your long life, never having to stop and consider other people and how trapped they are in circumstances beyond their control."

"What's the camcorder for? So you can tape my misery for your father to amuse himself later, that smug murdering bastard?"

"Yes, I heard about the shopping centre, it's all over the news." Alice said. "Now you know what my father is capable of, but still not truly the nature of his character."

"I would have thought killing hundreds of innocent people would be testament enough to a person's black personality." Cain retorted.

Alice turned on the camera and detached the viewer so the captive could see. "Let me show you something that will give you a true insight into the Grandmaster's evil nature. Witness what he would do to someone of his own bloodline."

Cain gazed at her in puzzlement as the film on the camcorder began to play, showing what appeared to be the inside of a mosque, the familiar attire of Arab Sheiks passing before his eyes. He guessed the events were taking place somewhere in the Middle East, quite likely Saudi Arabia or Jordan considering the dozens of middle-aged and elderly Sheiks lining the mosque, large quantities of thick-chained gold hanging from their necks, their wives dressed in full hijab, the black veil obscuring their faces.

The obviously wealthy guests appeared to be attending some type of social function, probably a wedding. As the movie continued to play, events moved to the front and Cain immediately recognised Samuel Carson. The leader of the Illuminati was pushing who was likely the bride to be alongside the solitary elderly Sheik before the altar. The cameraman continued to pan the view until the bride, dressed in the same strict Muslim dress as the other female guests came into sight. At first she was indistinct from the other women, but she removed the veil and Cain instantly saw with shock the face of Alice. Her cheeks were pale and her eyes were puffy from crying. Samuel Carson stepped forward and the film on the camcorder abruptly stopped.

Cain stared at her in curiosity. "I don't understand, what was it I was witnessing?"

"My wedding," Alice said and began to weep, tears streaming down her face. "My father had arranged nuptials to an old rich Arab, but at the last minute he halted the proceedings. It was an elaborate lesson for me to learn, to bear witness to both his absolute control over my life and his ruthlessness. Sometimes he plays this just to remind me in case I might forget who is always in charge and that my destiny is never my own."

"I am sorry," Cain replied. "He really is an evil piece of shit, I had no idea that you were being coerced. I now understand the betrayal was never yours, that you had no choice."

"My father's bullying influence always exists, pervades my every breath," Alice said softly. "Even when he is miles away I still feel his presence, his gaze upon my back, his cold voice whispering in my ear, poisoning my thoughts. But now at last I must find the courage to do the right thing, to prove to myself that he can no longer control my every action."

Cain watched in curiosity as she revealed a key and reaching behind his back shoved it into the lock of the handcuffs. The metal rings slid off his hands and she helped him remove the rusty chains wrapped around his torso. Cain stood to his feet, the ache in his arms and legs beginning to dissipate as he stretched himself.

"Father has ordered stronger bonds," Alice announced. "They are due to arrive soon."

"Yes, I heard," Cain replied flatly. "But now he will never get the opportunity to try them out. We need to leave immediately and let the authorities deal with the Illuminati. This time they have gone too far, killing hundreds of people, even their supporters within the British Parliament will not tolerate this and begin to distance themselves."

They made their way upstairs and halted around the corner from the front door. Three men armed with machineguns paced at the exit, talking about last Saturday's football game and the girls they met after the match.

"You're immortal, you could rush them and kill them before they get a chance to respond." Alice whispered.

"And if one manages to shoot me in the head or heart it will take me several minutes to recover," Cain retorted sharply. "By then I will be back in the cell with no chance of freedom. It would be more advisable to find a window."

They approached various windows but all were barred. Although Cain knew he could easily break the metal bars it would cause too much noise and alert the guards at the front door. They went upstairs to the next floor and noticed an open window free of any obstructions. However, two soldiers suddenly appeared from a nearby room. One was armed with a sawn-off shotgun and the other guard had at his side-holster a large revolver. Cain sighed in frustration as they continued to walk in the direction of where they stood, hidden just around the corner.

Cain waved his hand at Alice, motioning for her to stay back out of harm's way. He waited until they were nearly at the corner before jumping out. The two mercenaries stared at their freed captive at first in surprise, not believing their eyes, wondering how he could have escaped. But training and duty soon took over. The guard began to raise the shotgun but Cain snatched the weapon from the astonished man and turning it quickly around, punched the soldier hard in the face with the short barrel, the mercenary falling to the floor unconscious. Cain knew he could have just as easily shot the man with the weapon, but silence was their greatest ally. The other guard removed the revolver from its hip holster but Cain head-butted him, sending the soldier to the ground, blood running down his nose and onto the carpet. Before he could react or call out for help, Cain bent forward and punched the mercenary in the forehead, smashing the man's skull with his incredible strength. There was an awful squishy sound as he hit the soldier and Alice shuddered at the noise.

"I am so pleased we sorted out our differences," Alice said, not daring to look at the dead man. "I would hate to be your enemy."

"Contrary to popular belief, I do not enjoy killing people, even if they deserve it," Cain sighed. "It's just I am so used to it, an unfortunate consequence of a long life dominated by violence."

Cain jumped out of the window and landed on the ground outside on his feet. He spread his legs and opened his arms, motioning for Alice who waited at the second storey window to leap down, ready to catch her.

"Don't drop me," she said fearfully.

"Do not worry," Cain replied. "My strength is much greater than any mere mortal man."

"Christ, I hope so," she cried out and jumped, landing into his outstretched arms safely.

He let her to the ground unharmed as they could see over the adjacent wall several ambulances and fire-engines in the near distance, ferrying the dead from the collapsed shopping centre. Hundreds of onlookers and volunteers lined the road leading to the car-park. Using that route as their escape path would be impossible, at the very least they would be stopped as possible witnesses.

"What has the monster done?" Alice asked. "To think I was part of his madness."

"It's not your fault," Cain retorted. "Your father has proved he is the master of his own fate, he will now have to answer for his terrible crimes."

They went back the other way and climbing over several walls and through the back gardens of many startled residents, they soon found themselves on a main road. Cain and Alice ducked under an overpass so she could catch her breath before spotting a nearby taxi, just about to depart after depositing its latest fare. They got in and directed the driver to the outskirts of London, finally stopping outside a bed and breakfast some distance off the motorway. Cain gave false identities to the receptionist before they made their way to the room, exhausted.

"I am going for a shower," Alice said as Cain collapsed on the bed and soon fell asleep.

Alice returned to the bedroom some minutes later, wrapped in a nightgown she found in the bathroom. She sat down to watch the television for about an hour, but did not switch on the daily news, too horrified to witness further the onslaught of her father's butchery.

She fell off the bed in fright as there was suddenly a knock on the door. Cain also awoke and instantly rose to his feet and approached the door.

"Open the door, Mr. Philips," a voice at the other side declared. "This is Detective Inspector Albert Maher. Let me in immediately or I will have twenty policemen dressed in riot gear and shotguns here in five minutes."

Cain slowly opened the door. "Did you bring pizza?" He laughed. "I have such a hunger escaping from trigger-happy lunatics."

"We know all about your *friends*, Mr. Philips." Detective Sean Neilson said. "Albert and I have been appointed Special Operations Managers, meaning we control a large task force composing of over one thousand policemen in London City with the sole intent of bringing the Illuminati to justice. MI5 and MI6 have their own dedicated task forces with everyone having a shoot to kill procedure if necessary in effect, orders coming directly from the Prime Minister."

"We didn't have anything to do with the shopping centre." Alice said, her voice trembling.

"We know that, Ms. Carson." Albert replied. "Yes, we know exactly who you are and that your father Samuel Carson is responsible for this carnage. What you may not be aware is that he has released a private broadcast to the police notifying that another ten similar bombs are hidden under shopping centres somewhere in the country. Naturally all the buildings have been closed and cleared of all civilians, but even if the report is a hoax the damage to the fragile retail trade in Britain will be substantial. We raided the rural mansion where the Illuminati held their last meeting, only to find the house cleared of all evidence even down to no furniture, bearing the trademark precision of a police operation. A house to house sweep was carried out in the area surrounding the destroyed shopping centre. We found evidence in a dungeon on the premises suggesting you were held captive, however the rest of the building was completely cleared except for bloodstains upstairs on the carpet."

"How did you find us?" Cain asked.

"The Central Intelligence Agency gave us all your former aliases, you used one of them booking into this hotel." Neilson said. "Nice job by the way on the fake employment history with the Information Technology firm, the CIA told us they had a hand in its creation."

"What do you want from us?" Alice enquired, holding onto the bathrobe she still wore.

"We have a problem," Maher declared. "All commercial airlines, train stations and ports are being strictly monitored by armed police and army personnel. The Queen herself couldn't get on a plane without being strip searched. The scheduled ship departure from the docks is still going ahead tomorrow night, despite Samuel Carson knowing he and his cronies will be either arrested or shot on sight. It is our belief he will allow or coerce these accomplices to continue to the boat, knowing they will be apprehended, in effect offering them up as lambs to the slaughter. We firmly believe only the former Detective Chief Inspector Richard Bellings knew intimately all the operations within the Illuminati outside of Samuel himself, that is why they eliminated him. The ship departure has to be a diversion, we need to know the Grandmaster's real destination and plans. Furthermore, he said in his bulletin he would not detonate the bombs at the shopping centres if he had his 'property' returned to him at a designated drop point at dawn tomorrow."

Cain sighed heavily and Alice turned around and made for the bathroom, embarrassed for the policemen to see her crying. "You have no idea what this psychopath will do to his daughter after her betrayal," Cain said sharply. "I am used to pain and torture, all manner of peoples have been trying to kill me for a long time. But it is her safety and well-being that concerns me."

"I know what we ask of you both," Maher said. "And I would not dare to ask of you being bait, if only we were not in this situation."

Cain walked over to the window and stared out into the darkness of the night, as Alice came out of the bathroom and approached him. "You mentioned before about choices," she said softly. "Perhaps it is time to make the right choice, the only option left open to us. Maybe we can finally bring my father's evil to an end, it is worth that to risk my life."

Cain grabbed hold of her hand before turning to the two detectives. "Have your men station themselves outside the room. We will not try to escape, and in the morning we will fully cooperate and go to this rendezvous. I just hope you know what you are doing, I will hold you responsible for what happens to her."

Albert Maher nodded and they left the hotel, giving orders for several armed officers to guard the outside of the room.

Alice lay down on the bed and Cain stretched himself next to her, as she cuddled into his open arms. "I won't be able to sleep a wink knowing what awaits us in the morning," she said, the terror in her voice evident. "Speak to me more about your life, tell me about what happened to your wife after Adam banished you, and the incredible people and events you witnessed."

Cain smiled. "That's a long story…"

CHAPTER TEN

Death of a Princess

Cain appeared out of the Zagros Mountains alone, the absence of his brother Abel evident.

Eve and Seth ran out and approached him. "What have you done, Cain?" Seth asked, his face contorted with rage. "Father said he felt the death of an immortal, and here you return to us alone, your head hanging in shame."

"I have committed a terrible crime and Jehovah has punished me," Cain replied, pulling aside his robe, revealing the black tattoo freshly burnt into his chest. "I am to be banished, prohibited from ever entering Paradise and to be a vagabond upon the Earth."

"God should have killed you, brother," Seth retorted sharply. "You have been shown unreasonable mercy, but who am I to question the will of the Lord. However, you are to leave immediately and take Âwân, never to see the faces of your parents again. For my part, perhaps in several thousand years I may bestow forgiveness."

Eve began to cry but nevertheless kissed her eldest child on the forehead. "Go now Cain, and never return."

Cain went into the village and grabbing Âwân's hand, left his family behind and went into the wilderness of bare rock and hot sand. He pulled the princess by the wrist for several hours before she could take no more.

"Please husband, I must rest," Âwân stated. "I do not possess your energy and I am heavy with child."

"I see some trees," Cain said. "I can build a shelter there and then I will look for food."

"I need a roof over my head, husband," the young princess panted. "I am not used to such hardship, I am royalty. In the land of my father I would have five servants always at my beck and call, offering fruit and cooked meat."

Cain sighed in frustration. "We are far from the country of Nok the Elder."

"We must return to your parents, my beloved," Âwân sobbed. "I cannot bear a child into the wilderness. Even the drought has not yet ended."

Cain sat down on the ground and she collapsed next to him. "Don't worry, I will take care of you," he said and picked her up in his arms and carried her to the shade of the trees.

Cain set to building a makeshift shelter of branches and leaves, ensuring his young bride was as comfortable as possible given their barren surroundings. Grabbing a long branch, he ran his hand down the shaft removing all foliage, creating a basic spear.

Several hours spent hunting for small animals proved fruitless but Cain did discover something on his travels. "I found a deep cave in a nearby hill," he said. "It will provide better protection from the elements than mere twigs."

"I must eat, husband." Âwân moaned. "Otherwise our child will not survive. I should have never left the land of my father. You have brought shame on both our houses."

Cain turned to her in anger. "We are far from the country of the African kingdom, we must make do with what the Lord has given."

"It is because your God has bestowed so generously that we are in this predicament," Âwân snarled. "You are the firstborn, the original immortal conceived from the perfect superhuman Adam, and this is how Jehovah has rewarded us, with pain, suffering and early death for me and my baby."

"You should not speak such blasphemy," Cain said fearfully.

"I will say what I please, what further punishment could your God inflict upon me," Âwân said firmly. "I curse your Lord Jehovah and all He stands for, and I also hex you my husband, for it is your crime of murder that has sealed my doom. Long after I am dead and the eternity of time stretches endlessly before you, may you never know happiness and peace of mind always elude you." Âwân growled. "Never again will we converse, I will go to my grave in silence."

Cain stared at her in astonishment, speechless. Several minutes of stillness passed between them before Cain finally reached over and picked her up, carrying her into the wilderness. They soon arrived at the cave and he made her as comfortable as possible despite the hard rock against her back.

Weeks turned into months and Cain returned one day from another hunt of rats and other similar desert rodents to find his wife in labour. His mother Eve had explained to her son what to expect, but nothing could have prepared Cain for this event and the tragedy that was about to unfold.

After months of silence from his young wife's mouth, it might have been a blessing to hear Âwân's voice, unfortunately it was only screams, first of pain and then anguish. After five hours of grunting and shouts Âwân finally delivered her son, Enoch. Cain gazed down at the bloody infant, its umbilical cord still attached. He cut the tube and held the child in his arms, smiling as the baby stared at his father before closing his eyes, the arms hanging loose. Cain looked at the infant, not comprehending at first what was happening, before placing the newborn child on the ground and started to breathe into its tiny mouth. Âwân began to cry, her frail starving body barely having the strength to sit up.

Cain continued the process for nearly twenty minutes, before realising it was pointless. His son was dead. He knew immediately the curse God had placed upon him, prohibiting any crops he attempted to sow would not flourish was responsible. Jehovah's commandment extended even into the womb of his wife. Âwân glared at her husband in rage and Cain knew in his heart that she realised the same reason for the death of her child. She reached out and with the last of her energy slapped Cain across the face.

Cain put a hand to his cheek to soothe the stinging pain as he watched Âwân slump to the rocky floor. He picked her head up and looked into her lifeless open eyes. Her pale face was wet with tears and despite the hardship of the recent months, Cain could still see how very young and beautiful the African princess was.

He laid her down on the ground before starting to claw at the rocks and soil, his great strength throwing up huge amounts of dirt and debris into the air. Soon he had dug a hole four feet deep by three feet wide, and into it he gently placed his dead wife and child. He placed the soil and stones quickly back over the bodies, promising no animals would feast on his loved ones.

Cain left the cave behind and screamed at the sky, his shouts echoing throughout the region, all nearby life in Mesopotamia bearing witness to his grief, before he ran into the wilderness.

CHAPTER ELEVEN

An Exodus of Blood

Cain wandered the barren country of Mesopotamia for many centuries, surviving on insects and rodents, dying hundreds of times from starvation, only to be revived moments later to relive the horror all over again.

It was now the Bronze Age in the year 2895BC, the era of King Menes, a direct divine descendant of Seth Kadmon. It was at the gates of Memphis, the world's first imperial city that Cain suddenly found himself, and collapsed from exhaustion. He would have rather avoided any contact with relatives of his former immortal family, but the priests of the temple discovered Cain and brought him in.

He stayed in the magnificent city of grandiose buildings, decorated in beautiful drawings for only a few days until his strength returned. Thanking the priests for their kindness, he listened briefly to their tales of their warrior king, his passion for arts and culture, and his obsession for the conquering of the Sinai. He also heard with interest the beginnings of the Persian Empire, their influence stretching across the Tigris and Euphrates Rivers, Cain's former homeland and a source of concern for King Menes and his princes. Cain knew civilisation had now reached a certain point in its evolution where conflict on a large scale was becoming inevitable with many nations competing for dominance. He realised this was his father's legacy, ten thousand years of war, slavery, suffering and mindless death. He wondered if Adam was still alive and would he be proud of what he had created.

Cain left the city behind and made his camp for several centuries more on the banks of the Red Sea, fishing and providing shepherd duties for nearby farmers, even occasionally acting as bodyguard for travelling merchants. Only a few times did he venture north to the great city Alexandria to buy supplies. Eventually the isolation forced him to head south, in search of human companionship.

It was now around the year 1500BC and Cain was about to become a participant in one of history's defining moments, events that would leave an imprint upon his memory for all time, and which would force him to question his Jewish heritage.

He passed through an endless sea of sand, bearing witness to incredible triangular-shaped mountains of manmade stone. Cain stopped a man holding a spear, dressed in a white tunic and square towel on his head, fixed in place with a bronze ring. He was directing twenty bare-chested young men, ten at either side pulling a thick rope onto which was attached a huge rectangular block of carved stone. The labourers were clearly tired and hot, the sweat dripping from their naked sun-scorched backs. One began to stumble from exhaustion and the guard responded by kicking the unfortunate individual in the face. The man briefly screamed in pain before rising to his feet and resuming his duties.

"Was that really necessary?" Cain growled at the soldier. "Why not let him rest for a few minutes and give him some water?"

"What business have you questioning a servant of the Pharaoh?" The guard retorted, his arrogance quite evident. "Would you rather join him, stranger, or have you left your company of slaves without permission, the punishment for which is death."

"Better men than you have tried to kill me," Cain smiled. "And your eventual demise would only come after seven terrible afflictions of the body and mind have ravaged you."

The soldier responded by raising his spear towards Cain, but instead of running the lance through him, the guard reached and pulled open Cain's robe. The soldier peered at Cain's penis before letting him go and dropping the spear away from Cain's chest.

"You are not circumcised," the man declared. "Be on your way, stranger, make your commerce at Luxor[1] and leave before you are mistaken for a Jew."

"How can you be so certain I am not Jewish?" Cain retorted.

"These Jews if nothing else are sticklers for tradition," the guard laughed. "The rabbis insist upon the cutting of the foreskin, I believe the slaves fear them even more than they despise us."

Cain sneered at the man before going further south towards civilisation. The huge gates of Luxor greeted him, a pleasant view after days of sand. He was only barely through the portal and witnessing the many buildings when he caught sight of what appeared to be a scuffle down an adjacent side-alley.

Three men dressed in the now familiar white tunics and head towels were hassling a middle-aged man. The soldiers brandished curved-shaped short-

---

[1] Now known as *Thebes*.

swords and were pushing the unarmed individual against the wall.

"Where's your brother, Aaron?" One guard snarled.

"You know he is protected by Pharaoh's command," the man replied sharply. "Or do you dare to question the will of the Morning Star?"

The soldier slapped the man across the face. "Do not lecture me about the motives of our living god, he is fickle and his moods change by the minute. Your brother could lose favour at a moment's notice and order his arrest. We simply want to chat about how he has turned the Nile River to blood red and these other plagues he has promised."

Cain approached the guards. "Three armed men to persecute this poor traveller?"

The soldiers turned and snarled. "This is none of your business, stranger. Be on your way or suffer the same fate."

One of the guards pushed Cain hard in the chest, causing him to stumble back. Cain responded by hitting the soldier in the face, breaking his jaw and left cheekbone. The man screamed and clutched at his face, a stream of blood pouring from his mouth. The other two soldiers looked first at each other before fleeing, leaving their unfortunate comrade to sink to his knees in agony, holding his shattered jaw up with shaking hands.

"Thank you stranger," Aaron said. "But we should leave before reinforcements arrive. Follow me."

The slave ran past several buildings and out of the city. He led Cain four hundred metres away down a hill into a large manmade valley where lay what appeared to be thousands of slums; houses roughly and quickly constructed from mud and straw, much more primitive than the fine structures inside Luxor. The buildings were closely built together to maximise space and Cain estimated there were probably in excess of five thousand people residing in such a narrow space.

"Welcome to the Land of Goshen, my home to over six thousand Jews or slave-soldiers as Ramesses II refers to us," Aaron announced. "We are on occasion the frontline troops against Assyria and Egypt's other enemies, so Pharaoh does not have to risk any of his own men. But our usual life is dominated by endless labour and starvation. It has been our sole task for generations to construct the temples and the pyramids, the burial tombs of kings long dead. We are essentially worked to death, this being the unavoidable destiny for our sons and daughters."

"If your people are the elite force with such military experience, why not simply rise up and take your birthright from these tyrants?" Cain enquired.

"Weapons are kept far from here," Aaron replied. "The soldiers always keep us in small groups of twenty, always rotating so a friend you might work with one day, you probably won't see again for a month. Besides, the Pharaoh that came before this one, came up with a better idea to exercise population control."

"What do you mean?"

"Pharaoh Seti grew afraid that our numbers became too great," Aaron said, his voice shaking with rage. "He ordered his guards to collect all newborns and carrying them off, threw them into the Nile to drown."

Cain stared at him in shock, not believing that genocide had now become part of human nature, but remembering that Adam had told him mankind would be capable of terrible acts in the future, even far worse than this. Off in the distance they could see a young man waving.

"We are being called," Aaron said. "Come, my friend, speak to my brother, the Prince of Egypt."

Cain looked at him in puzzlement, wondering what royalty would be finding sanctuary in such banal conditions. He followed his new comrade inside the small building where lay a six foot rectangular wooden table and two plain benches. There were two men inside, the young man who hailed them carrying a knife and another older Jew who was bearded and appeared to be in his mid-thirties. Aaron ran and embraced the older robed individual and they spoke briefly, whispering so Cain could not hear.

The man turned to Cain and smiled. "Welcome to my brother's home, stranger, and thank you for saving Aaron from persecution."

The younger armed individual interrupted. "Master, I must protest. We know not who this intruder is, for all we know he could be a spy sent by Pharaoh to discover the secrets of the plagues," the guard said and pulled on Cain's robe, glancing inside. "Just as I believed, this man is no Jew."

The young soldier slashed Cain across the chest with the short blade and tried to stab him in the face, but Cain grabbed his hand and twisting his wrist, forced him to drop the weapon. Aaron and his brother ran forward to examine the injury to see if the stranger might die, only to stand back in astonishment as the wound began to heal almost immediately until it had completely disappeared.

"Incredible," Aaron said. "Your injury has healed within moments and not even a scar can be seen."

"I recognise those markings," Aaron's brother declared, pointing to the black tattoo on Cain's chest. "I spent most of my childhood being tutored in the scriptures of ancient times. Pharaoh Seti might have been a pagan, but he believed in the knowledge of other cultures and religions, saying it was wise to know the ways of your enemies. I am Moses, otherwise known as the Prince of Egypt."

"I do not understand, my brother," Aaron said. "Who is this man, how do you know what he is?"

Moses grabbed the hands of his eldest brother. "This is Cain Kadmon, son of Adam and Eve from the dawn of time."

Aaron and the young guard stared at the guest in shock. "We should kill him or send him to the Pharaoh, if the rest of our people find him they will surely demand the same, or ask for our lives in return." Aaron said.

"Firstly, I am the prophesied leader sent to deliver our people to the promised land, they will not harm me," Moses interjected. "Secondly, Cain could prove very useful both in the persuasion of Ramesses and the journey into the desert, and thirdly which is most important, anyone who tries to kill Cain will suffer sevenfold before death, isn't that correct?"

Cain nodded in agreement. "Why do they call you the Prince of Egypt, and what are these plagues the Pharaoh fears so much?"

"Many years ago, my parents worked as servants within the palace where my mother became friends with Pharaoh Seti's wife." Moses said.

"Considering how your people are viewed by the Egyptians, I would not have thought any member of the royal house would converse with a mere slave, no offence intended." Cain replied.

"None taken," Moses said. "But the Pharaoh's wife was Assyrian[2], she did not suffer from the same prejudice as the majority of Egyptians. She was also lonely and despaired at her husband's actions when he ordered the massacre of the infants. When my parents died under the heel of the soldiers' boots in the Valley of the Kings when the slaves organised a minor rebellion, the Pharaoh's wife insisted that I come under the care of the palace. Aaron and my sister were much older and able to fend for themselves, but I was only a few months old. I was raised as an Egyptian and because I was the same age as the infant Ramesses II, we became close friends. Servants and visitors to the palace often commented we were more like brothers than friends, separated only by blood and heritage. Henceforth, I became known as a Prince of Egypt, if only to poke fun at my true slave history. However, when I reached my twenty-second year, things changed."

"What happened?" Cain enquired. "Did Ramesses II finally tire of his adopted slave brother?"

"Watch your tongue," Aaron retorted sharply. "You are in no position to comment on the relationship between brothers, considering what you did to your sibling."

"Aaron, let me continue," Moses said, placing a hand on the shoulder of the older man. "I was appointed a Captain of the Guard by Ramesses

---

[2] Now known as *Syria.*

II, chosen to oversee the construction of the newest temple, destined to be the burial tomb of his father. One day, I witnessed an old man being whipped mercilessly by a soldier. The elderly slave was unable to partake in the dragging of a stone tablet up the hill towards the base of the temple. When I tried to intervene, the guard fell over and struck his head against the stone, killing him. I panicked and ran, knowing even though I had a good relationship with the Pharaoh's son, and considered by many an Egyptian, I was still an outsider and would be executed for murder and potentially inciting a riot. I fled into the desert where I remained for more than ten years. There I shepherded sheep for a farmer and eventually married his daughter."

"Up to your waist in sheep shit and nagged endlessly by some bandit's brat, no wonder you returned to civilisation and the luxury of the palace," Cain laughed.

"On the contrary," Moses replied. "Life was good and simple, until one day I heard the call of Yahweh, beckoning to me in the wilderness from a bush that was ablaze but did not burn."

Cain stared at him in astonishment. "Interesting. That's definitely something new. What did the burning twig say, besides crackle?"

"It told me to return to Egypt, to free my people from slavery and would give me the knowledge to convince the superstitious Pharaoh to release the Jews by the way of ten plagues, each one more worse than the preceding one."

"So essentially Jehovah told you God helps those who help themselves, in essence provide your own miracles and let the Lord take all the credit. The Almighty was always large on punishments and short on mercy. In fact, if it were not for these regular and brutal reminders of His divine presence, one might doubt He even existed," Cain remarked. "And what are these ten plagues that will afflict Egypt so terribly to persuade the Pharaoh to relinquish his hold on a free workforce, and therefore abandon all construction on the temples, not to mention the elite front line of defence against its border's many enemies?"

"The first plague has already begun, the Lord God has turned the waters of the Nile to blood red, making it undrinkable to both man and beast. Thousands of dead fish float everywhere, from the steps of the palace to the resting barracks of the Great Pyramid guards at Giza," Aaron laughed.

"And the real truth behind the changing of the liquid?" Cain asked. "And won't that also affect your people and animals?"

"The volcano Thera[3] has exploded, and this mixed with recent heavy rainfall will wash the red silt from the eruption downstream into the Nile, transforming the colour of the waters to blood and making it poisonous. Pharaoh is very superstitious but incredibly stubborn, and the court sorcerers were able to duplicate the event in a bowl of clear liquid and red dust. However, the plagues yet to come will shock even his cold heart as we bring promises of a tsunami of frogs, flies and locusts to decimate his crops and blight his heathen populace with boils." Moses declared. "We have commissioned Libyan merchants to provide us with the raw materials in the form of frog eggs and maggots among other things, vowing to reward them with a mountain of stolen Egyptian gold when we enter the desert. Only the first few plagues will

---

[3] The volcano *Santorini.*

affect the Jews, the remainder and the more serious will exclusively trouble our captors."

"Does it not bother you the hardship you bring to the Egyptian people, who also have to suffer under the yolk of a tyrant from which there is no escape?" Cain asked. "And where you not raised as a prince and close friend of the Pharaoh you now persecute, using God as a shield to hide under, a deity the Egyptians cannot possibly understand or fight against while their children starve?"

"You sincerely believe I wish the people of Ramesses II harm, the same tribe that took me in and gave me sanctuary?" Moses replied sharply. "These heathens are by majority innocent of any crime against the Jews, but there is simply no other way to convince Pharaoh, his will is resolute and he will not listen to reason. But nine chances will my royal brother get before I unleash the most terrible of all the plagues and take from him the greatest of his possessions."

"And won't you require divine intervention to bring to life any of these catastrophic events?" Cain enquired. "That flaming bush was short on knowledge, it would appear only your efforts and cunning will deliver the Jews to freedom?"

"If I told Ramesses that I alone was responsible, he would immediately forget our combined childhood and simply have me put to death," Moses replied. "However, by informing my superstitious brother that a deity is organising this retribution, he is far less likely to question it's origin and grudgingly accept the inevitable outcome. The second plague will also come from the Nile in the form of an epidemic of frogs, driven out of the river by the poisonous waters, coupled with the eggs we are growing in secret in hundreds of slave homes throughout the Land of Goshen. The third and fourth affliction will be waves of flies, now having grown abundant by the lack of frogs in the Nile, the insects' population greatly increased by maggots we have feasting on the shit scraps the Egyptians call food they throw over the wall at us. These same flies will transmit diseases to the animals in the fields throughout Egypt, giving us the fifth and sixth plagues as our enemies eat the poisoned flesh, giving rise to painful boils before the remainder of the cattle and sheep die. The seventh catastrophe will be in the form of 'fiery hail' which our allied neighbouring Libyan astrologers claim will arrive shortly due to a giant cloud of ash and brimstone coming from the volcanic eruption, dramatically altering the weather producing freak lightening storms, enough to strike terror into the hearts of even the bravest Egyptians. The eighth plague will be that of locusts, normally a minor irritant at this time of year, but with most crops either destroyed by the hail or the waves of insects, the remaining harvest will be targeted exclusively by the starving locusts, bringing further misery to our captors. The ninth event will be that of a solar eclipse, the primary sun god Ra being obscured by the moon for several hours, a cosmic occasion again prophesied by our Libyan allies, eager to take advantage of any weakness of Egypt in preparation of an invasion. Even Ramesses witnessing all of his kingdom falling into sudden darkness in the middle of the day will be shocked and willing to listen to reason. If not, I will be forced to deliver the tenth and most terrible of all the plagues, that being death of the firstborn. The first child of any Egyptian family is given priority above all other infants, and therefore will be given the largest portion of contaminated food when they emerge after the brief period of darkness. What remains of all the animals and crops lying in deep storage after the ravages of the fiery hail and locusts will be distributed first to the eldest child of every household, whereas the Jews consume their food immediately after preparation. I can forestall this horrible event if Pharaoh is ready to release my people and inform him of the poisoned food."

"You appear to have done your research," Cain interjected. "Of course the prophesied Angel of Death that comes with the tenth plague is certain to guarantee the deaths of the firstborn, if the consuming of contaminated food does not succeed."

"The benefits of a royal education, courtesy of Seti who was obsessed with the learning of foreign and domestic cultures." Moses smiled. "Sit with us and wait out these plagues in the safety of Aaron's home. We will have much need of you in the years to come in the wilderness."

The dagger-wielding guard at the door interrupted. "You said before any person that might dare to try and kill you will suffer seven brutal afflictions before dying," the man said fearfully. "I do not feel ill, neither have I broken out with boils, sores or any other disease."

Cain looked at him in puzzlement. "That is odd," he responded. "Perhaps your intention was never to kill me, simply to wound, or maybe Jehovah saw into your heart and witnessed no true malice in your soul. You should just be grateful and offer your thanks to Yahweh that he spared your life this day."

Moses and Aaron nodded in agreement before leaving the slum, preparing to organise the other nine plagues and inflict suffering across the land of Egypt.

In the months that passed, Cain was a silent witness to the catastrophes that ravaged the Egyptian Empire. Safe in the Land of Goshen he watched in horrified fascination as tsunamis of flies and locusts filled the sky, the screams of people heard for miles. In the months that followed the same cries turned to anguish as Egyptians gathered around the palace, pleading with the court sorcerers to free them of the unhealable boils that afflicted their flesh. Ramesses struggled to provide his populace with easy answers as the midday sun disappeared for several hours, obscured by the moon they regularly prayed to. It was only when *Makat b'choro*, the final and deadliest plague, that of death of the firstborn came to pass did Pharaoh finally relinquish.

Aaron and Moses entered the blood-soaked door and approached Cain. "At long last, it is done." The Prince of Egypt declared. "When my royal brother saw the corpse of his own son did he finally realise the power of Yahweh."

"I thought he was too stubborn and proud to ever let your people go?" Cain asked.

"The reign of the temple builder Ramesses is far different from that of the Great Pyramid architect Khufu who lived more than a thousand years ago," Aaron said. "This Pharaoh is more accountable for his actions, particularly after his disastrous twelve year war with the Hittites. Khufu could command total obedience without question, but Ramesses must always be wary of revolution, his so called divine authority is not guaranteed. Even he could not ignore the cries of his populace, in particular his starving army who continued their duties with increasing protest."

"It is fortunate we covered all the doors of our people with the blood of the sacrificed lamb, including this one." Moses said slyly. "We surely prevented all the deaths of our own firstborn. I wonder what might have become of you, Cain first son of Adam, had this house not been blessed. Would the same God that cursed you with eternal life have been compelled to remove that hex and finally kill you, allowing the Angel of Death to enter this building and make you a corpse?"

"Interesting theory, but ultimately pointless." Cain replied sharply. "Perhaps Jehovah would then suffer the same seven terrible agonies he promised anyone who dared to murder me, would he have to follow his own rules to the letter?" Cain laughed.

The two men stared at him in puzzlement before returning to the matter at hand. "We have managed to gather a large quantity of gold over the centuries, from trading with Egyptian and Assyrian merchants, enough to purchase food and water for the long journey into the desert and Canaan. It is imperative we leave immediately lest my royal brother changes his mind and returns us to bondage." Moses said.

"What is it you desire of me?" Cain enquired.

"Only to walk by my side into the wilderness, your link to the divine, to Yahweh will secure the trust of the more nervous Jews who will hesitate. Even a life of unending hardship and suffering is more preferable to the unknown, to a journey of likely starvation and without the security of a roof over your head, in essence a case of better the Devil you know."

Cain sighed. "It is my intention to keep out of history's way, to avoid the great events of humankind, it is not my place to interfere in such momentous occasions."

"And yet you desire above all things redemption?" Aaron shouted in anger. "How do you propose to amend for the murder of Abel and one day return to Eden to seek God's forgiveness, if all you do is sit in a hole in the desert tending to sheep and eating rats?"

Cain gazed at him in temper and the two brothers feared their death was upon them, but he relaxed and smiled. "I understand your viewpoint, if I don't entirely agree with it. Very well, I will go with you and help you lead the Jews to this land of milk and honey."

Moses let out a laugh and embraced him, before escorting him out of the slum and into the street where already thousands of Jews from all over the Land of Goshen had begun to gather in excitement. Cain saw people from every age and walk of life, from the very young infants being carried in the arms of their parents to the elderly being assisted by their adult children. He knew this was going to be an epic task, to transport such a vulnerable populace and the many hundreds of sheep and goats into the desert.

Moses climbed up onto the edge of a well to give himself height. "My people, at last we are free from bondage and the tyranny of the Pharaoh. No longer will we build temples to foreign gods adorned with tributes while the Jews starved," the prophet declared. "Be not afraid, for we have Yahweh always at our side, and now delivered to us out of the wilderness, Jehovah's first conceived child."

Cain glanced nervously at the amassed crowd staring at him, all eyes transfixed at his presence. "It is just as the Prince of Egypt said," Cain shouted quickly. "Let us leave now and find your destiny in the land of Canaan."

The people turned and began to pick up their meagre belongings as Moses smiled at Cain in satisfaction. Many hours later they left Luxor behind and entered the desert, heading first south to confuse Pharaoh and his generals, before heading north towards the direction of the Red Sea. They came to the vast tributary east of Akhetaten where the waters were at their narrowest. Moses declared they should rest and break bread. The exhausted people had only begun to relax their weary bodies when a scout appeared and told the prophet that Ramesses and his army of chariots were only a few miles away in hot pursuit. The crowd began to cry and yell in terror, knowing the vengeful Pharaoh was only an hour away from their current position.

Moses gathered them together. "Be silent," the Prince shouted. "My father-in-law told me of a secret path through the marsh, my royal brother and his soldiers know not of this road through the wetlands of the Red Sea."

Cain helped the people with their animals and small children as the six thousand populace entered the shallow waters of the sea, quickly up to their knees in mud and tall grass. They had only entered a short distance into the marshland when Ramesses appeared at their abandoned camp. The Pharaoh yelled obscenities which the Jews ignored. He finally halted his yelling and ordered his army into the Red Sea. The guards glanced at their king in apprehension, but knowing only too well of his anger and the ruthless manner in which he treated Hittite prisoners, they rapidly entered the marsh. The chariots however were not suited to such wet ground and soon became entangled in long weeds. The soldiers left the horses behind and attempted to pursue their former slaves on foot, but it quickly became apparent that Moses had outwitted them as they sank into the mud to their waists and could not move.

The Prince of Egypt began to laugh as he faintly heard his royal brother curse in frustration, knowing the Jewish people were finally free of Pharaoh and would never see him or the Egyptians again.

Weeks turned into months as the Jewish populace became used to harsh life in the wilderness. Moses travelled alone up Mount Sinai, accompanied part of the journey by a young Jew called Joshua. Cain was fascinated by the stone tablets that the prophet returned several days later with, this being the first time he had seen an object directly created by Jehovah since he left Eden many centuries before.

Moses sent twelve spies including his prodigy Joshua and another young man called Caleb into Canaan. They came back with negative reports, save Joshua and Caleb who told of small city states like Jericho that could be overcome with greater manpower than the Jews currently possessed. Moses informed the crowd of six thousand that they would have to remain in the desert for forty years so a generation of fighting men might be born and trained to achieve victory in Canaan. The populace reacted in dismay but dared not question the Prince of Egypt, even when he nominated Joshua as his successor.

In the months that followed, Cain began to view Moses' prodigy with deep suspicion as the ten spies who had failed the prophet were killed in mysterious and violent manners. He knew Moses had likely not ordered their assassination as the ten men were already prohibited from entering the promised land and were of no threat to Joshua. The young prodigy had taken it upon himself to execute the spies as they had no voice to object, and Joshua needed an outlet for his growing taste for bloodshed. Cain spoke of his fears to Moses but the Prince was deaf to any opinions, saying Yaweh had declared Joshua the rightful heir to lead the Jews.

Forty years passed and Moses died peacefully, never seeing the promised land that he had sacrificed so much for. Joshua quickly stepped into the role as leader, appointing thirty elite men his personal lieutenants, their duties being the organising of an army and Cain suspected watchers of his every move, lest he might challenge Moses' prodigy.

The population of now twelve thousand travelled deep into Canaan. After a victory over the Amalekites in Rephidim, they set their sights on the rich trading city Jericho. Joshua declared that the city was to be an example to the region, ordering that no person or animal be allowed to survive the assault. Cain understood the reason for this command, knowing that such a massacre would frighten the other city states into submission, but still expressed an objection that such barbarity would mark the emerging Jewish nation for centuries and make them no better than their former Egyptian masters. Joshua reacted with rage at this protest spoken from a man who would murder his own flesh and blood, and that this was the will of the Lord. Cain responded that such an order came from Joshua alone and he used God as a mask to hide his increasing sociopathic mindset.

The Jewish army was commanded to march around the walls of Jericho for three days without cessation. The population inside viewed the behaviour in puzzlement and laughed that decades spent in the desert without proper shelter had warped Joshua's brain. However, the Jewish leader ordered several men to climb the wall in secret and entered the room of a prostitute, who harboured the men and even hide them as her chambers were searched for spies. She was to be rewarded to leave the city alive as her neighbours who purchased her flesh would perish. The dozen Jewish soldiers opened the gates in the early hours of the night and the army entered unhindered.

The following two hours were spent dragging women and children into the street as their husbands were murdered in their sleep. Cain protested as the guards set to killing the screaming infants in front of their mothers, impaling them on their swords and spears before executing the women before finally moving onto the animals. Cain saw Joshua only once throughout the entire assault, his face contorted with bloodlust as he drove his sword repeatedly into young children, his body covered with blood and splatters of what Cain suspected was brain matter. The Jewish leader then disappeared into the crowd, eager for more victims. Cain left the city in disgust and waited outside the city walls. This was not the destiny that Moses had persuaded him to adopt back in Egypt, and he knew the prophet would not have approved of such violence, no matter its strategic value.

Cain stayed with the elderly men of the Jewish populace in the main camp from then on, not wishing to engage in any conversation with Joshua or his murderous soldiers. He did not partake in the battle against the next city state Ai to the west beyond the Jordan River. Joshua and his men however were defeated with thirty-six Israelite deaths. The Jewish leader attributed the disastrous assault to Achan, one of his lieutenants who had taken a golden idol in the form of a foreign deity from Jericho. He ordered Achan, his family and even his personal animals to be stoned to death to restore Jehovah's favour. One of the victims was a young baby whom the wife of Achan cradled in fear.

After witnessing the massacre of children at Jericho, this butchery was too much for Cain, he could not bear to see another infant so mercilessly murdered. "This is too much," Cain shouted. "This mindless bloodshed must end, send Achan and his family into exile instead. It is not necessary to execute them, they are Jews after all. This was not the promised land that Moses had envisaged."

"Too many times have you questioned my authority and the will of the Lord," Joshua retorted in anger. "God has abandoned you, killer of your brother. I lead my people in Yahweh's name."

"You hide under Jehovah's aura, knowing that the Jewish populace are too frightened to object, and could not bear another forty years in the wilderness. Murder this innocent family and you do not deserve the promised land," Cain replied sharply. "History will mark the Jewish nation as genocidal monsters. Thousands of years from now, another murderous people might view the Jews as fair game; a blood-thirsty race worthy of extermination and bring them to the brink of extinction, and other nations might very well stand back in contented safety, feeling deep down that the Jews brought it upon themselves, and the world would be a better place without them."

"This is blasphemy," Joshua shouted in rage and pointed to five of his lieutenants. "Take this foreign devil and throw him into the dry well, let him drink of the sand and harsh rocks below for all eternity until Gabriel's trumpet sets him free at Judgement Day. Farewell, Cain son of Adam Kadmon, for I will never set my gaze upon you again."

Cain did not fight back as the five soldiers carried him on their shoulders and threw him head first into the deep hole. He fell nearly a hundred feet before striking the dry floor. The guards then proceeded to heave rocks and sand into the hole for several minutes until Joshua was satisfied that Cain would not emerge. The Jewish leader began to laugh, knowing that this threat had been removed and ordered his army to break camp to begin a fresh assault against the city Ai, vowing victory this time.

However, the smile disappeared from his face as the five lieutenants doubled over in pain, clutching their stomachs. They declared the agony was terrible, but after some moments it passed. Joshua believed that was the end of the mysterious illness until the same men began to vomit continuously for several more minutes, again the affliction ceasing almost as quickly as it had commenced. Next the guards began to cry out as their bowels shifted, their cloths destroyed with their faeces and urine, their entire systems emptying all food. The men stared at their leader in confusion before screaming in pain as the nails on their fingers and toes suddenly bent backwards, blood beginning to stream down the digits and into the sand. Their flesh then broke out into blisters and boils, the putrefying smell of the infection making Joshua turn away in disgust. The lieutenants believed it could not get any worse until their teeth suddenly fell out, blood running from their open mouths. Finally blood began to come from their eyes and ears as the eardrums burst. The men yelled in terror and agony as the eyeballs exploded, sending fragments of flesh and pupils onto the clothes of Joshua. The Jewish leader could only stare in fascination as the five soldiers fell over, their corpses coming to rest on the sand.

Joshua gazed at the men for several more moments before regaining his composure and ordering his army away from what he declared as an accursed region, never to return. It was two days before Cain managed to drag himself out of the dry well, his body covered in mud and small stones. He glanced at what remained of the dead lieutenants, their cadavers already in the process of being consumed by desert rodents and insects, their features indistinguishable. However, Cain knew the sevenfold curse that was imprinted on his chest and soul had claimed the lives of these men. He did not feel any pity for such murderers, especially when he saw only a short distance away the corpses of Achan and his family, resting with their sheep and goats, their broken bodies distorted by heavy stones which had been hurled at them.

Cain spent three hours burying the innocent Jewish family, but left the five soldiers where they lay, food for the maggots that now covered their cadavers. He gazed out into the barren wilderness, not knowing or caring where Joshua and the Jewish people had gone. His destiny and theirs were now separate, that bargain he had agreed with Moses in Egypt had come to an end. He would now find his own fate elsewhere far from this place, and the redemption he so desperately craved.

CHAPTER TWELVE

A Roman Catastrophe

Cain found himself many years later in 79AD, an unfortunate slave of the Roman Empire. Found wandering in the streets of Napoli,[4] he was rounded up with the homeless and newly arrived Christians and formally declared Noxii.[5] After a brief and routine trial before the city magistrate, he was escorted to the nearby coastal town Pompeii.

His robust physique meant he was immediately sold to the local Ludus Magnus[6] situated on the outskirts of the twenty thousand population settlement. He was to be trained in the fighting style of the gladiators, his weaker companion prisoners were to be sent straight to the Coliseum to be condemned to a swift death, brief entertainment for the jeering crowd as they were torn apart by wild tigers.

---

[4] The Italian City *Naples*.

[5] *Obnoxious* to the State, those considered the lowest caste in society: usually criminals, Jews and Christians whom were subject to Rome's harshest punishments. This was normally death in the Coliseum after a bloody and humiliating charade, e.g. a bizarre re-enactment such as the fall of Carthage where the participants were forced to wear comical costumes and defend themselves unarmed against wild animals or gladiators. Those unlucky enough to survive this torture were dragged off with metal hooks driven into their flesh and swiftly decapitated, their headless bodies dumped unceremoniously into the river.

[6] *Gladiatorial training school*, usually situated near to the local Coliseum.

Cain watched as these unfortunate men and women were branded on the forehead, marking them as fugitives, enemies of the State. Cain glanced at the tunic-wearing soldiers, brandishing their spears in disgust. The Roman Empire had been in existence now for over one hundred years and Cain feared would dominate most of Europe for centuries more. The Romans had a history of extreme violence mixed with dangerous narcissism, believing they were some sort of master race destined to rule the known world and weren't afraid to enslave any country to build their empire. Outsiders from Gaul to Palestine were never permitted citizenship, the more fortunate and wealthy were allowed limited trade, the less lucky found themselves in the galley ships as slaves, worse still a few stronger men and some women were consigned to a brief life in the arena, providing bloody entertainment for the mindless mob, whom Rome hoped would be too distracted by the excitement of the Coliseum to realise their own true poverty and miserable existence.

The Romans were not the first cruel despots to attempt total annihilation of the globe, history having born witness to other races like the Hittites, the Greeks and the Persians who possessed similar aims, but Rome was the only nation strong and militarily disciplined enough to carry it through. The only races that would escape their gaze were beyond their supply lines such as China and peoples in far off countries yet to be discovered.

A well-built middle-aged man dressed in a fine robe flanked by four soldiers approached Cain and his fellow prisoners. "Welcome to my Ludus Magnus of Pompeii. It will be your glorious destiny to clash swords in the Coliseum," their new owner shouted. "Those of you who do not fight well, can at least die well. Your life up to this moment is over, consider them as wasted years growing crops and feeding your brats. Rejoice for the fate that truly awaited you is now before you. My name is Darius, but you will always refer to me as master."

Cain started laughing and the other gladiators drew back, fearful they might be associated with him and suffer their owner's wrath. Darius drew alongside his smiling slave as one of the soldiers moved to strike Cain, but the Roman lord stopped him.

"Something amuses you, slave?" Darius said. "Perhaps a few days in solitary confinement would silence your laughter?" The master stared at Cain's chest. "That is an interesting tattoo you have, were you affiliated to another Ludus, did you once serve another master?"

Cain did not answer and this time the Roman lord allowed the soldier to hit the slave in the face with his rectangular large shield, sending Cain to the dusty ground. He picked himself up and gazed straight into the eyes of the legionary, as if daring him to repeat the assault. "The master who carved this mark has left this land long ago, if he had not, the Roman Empire would not have been allowed to exist."

Darius looked at his slave in amusement. "Was He a great ruler of men? The last stubborn leader of barbarians who displayed such defiance was executed alongside all of his men in Gaul at the hands of the glorious Emperor Julius Caesar. A magnificent munus[7] in celebration was held by the

---

[7] Gladiatorial games held to commemorate the death of a noteworthy ancestor, i.e. a famour senator.

returning Emperor to rival even the great games he had put on for his father who died twenty years before. On that occasion he had paid for an incredible three hundred and twenty gladiators all dressed in the finest silver armour.[8] Despite his own huge debts he had wished to place five hundred men in the Coliseum in Rome, but the frightened Senate refused his request, fearing putting so many gladiators in one area at the same time might give rise to another Spartacus type revolt."

"There is no doubt Julius Caesar was very intelligent, having the wisdom on the field of battle to secure victory against overwhelming numbers in Gaul," Cain responded and the Romans nodded in agreement. "But perhaps he was most wise in the sponsoring of huge gladiatorial games to appease the ignorant mob so they were never aware he fleeced them for his war chest, and simultaneously sated their bloodlust which has always been so characteristic of the parasitic Roman Empire."

Darius stared at Cain in astonishment that a common slave could speak so eloquently and without fear show such open contempt for Rome. "Take him to solitary," the master said to the soldiers. "Let us hope his sword arm can display the same finery as his tongue."

Cain passed by the cells of his comrades-in-arms which encircled the training arena of the Ludus, containing a bare mat of dried straw and an old rag for sleeping on. He noticed further into the

---

[8] Such a lavish combat would have cost about 40,000 denarii (approximately $800,000). It is worth noting that during the entire lifetime of the gladiatorial games (63BC – 476AD), approximately one million men and women were killed and whole species of domestic and wild animals were made extinct.

building lay the larger chambers which housed the animals. Three tigers, a lion and two panthers growled at Cain and the legionaries as he approached. Their quarters appeared much cleaner and had large soft cloths to sleep on in comparison to the gladiators' cells. It was obvious the creatures were prized and more valuable than the men, having been secured at great expense from foreign traders travelling from Africa. The humans were expendable as most gladiators rarely lived beyond their second combat in the Coliseum. But the animals almost always returned safely home and well fed on a diet of criminals and Christians.

The guards arrived at an iron door and threw Cain into the small room. There were no straw or rags for comfort present, only the cold stone floor. Once the legionaries had left, Cain gazed at the walls in silence, pondering his next move. He knew the talents he possessed such as his incredible strength and self-healing attributes would attract unwanted attention, and he would be swiftly transported to Rome for a larger audience in the grand Coliseum. It would be far wiser to avoid trouble until it became inevitable and seize an opportunity for freedom when it presented itself. Then on that occasion it would not matter how many soldiers and bloodthirsty citizens got in his way.

Hours passed before the legionaries returned and dragged Cain from the cell. They brought him into the training arena in the centre of the Ludus where his fellow apprentice gladiators where in attendance, bare-chested and brandishing wooden swords and staffs. Lethal weapons were prohibited by law in the Ludus, there would be time and opportunity enough for real steel in the Coliseum which awaited them in only a few days.

Cain noticed most of them were nervous and even frightened of combat and he guessed many of them were simple farmers and labourers, the concept of hurting and especially killing another human being never entered their minds. Cain knew even with months of training these men would never be ready and would be easy deaths for the most amateur of gladiators in the arena. However, Cain had promised himself to stay out of history's way, it was not up to him to be a leader for these unfortunates. Better charismatic individuals than he had tried and failed such as Spartacus, who after a revolt met his end against overwhelming odds from Rome and was then crucified on the road, a warning to others that might dare to challenge the Empire.

The few days and nights passed quickly and Darius approached the men. He ordered the legionaries to dress the gladiators in bronze armour and short-swords before escorting them to the nearby Coliseum situated on the outskirts of the Pompeii town centre. The arena was tiny by Rome's standards, but still accommodated several thousand spectators.

Cain drew up alongside Darius as the ground beneath their feet began to shake, the tremors appearing quite shallow and close to the surface. "Is it the excitement of the people in the Coliseum that causes the earth to move?"

Darius laughed in reply. "I wish that were true and they awaited my gladiators with such enthusiasm. But the truth is the ground has been shaking every few days and with increasing strength. Perhaps it is a sign from the gods that they want spectacular games today and are bored with the usual amateurs who die too quickly."

"Have you ever considered the enormous mountain that overlooks this town and Herculaneum might be ready to explode?" Cain asked.

Darius looked at his slave in amusement. "There is no record of an active volcano in this region. If there was the slightest possibility of danger our glorious Emperor would have ordered the evacuation of the towns under the shadow of Vesuvius. Pompeii has been a popular tourist destination for decades and is an important trading port, giving sea access to Greece and Africa."

"The Roman Empire cannot foresee every outcome, particularly something as unpredictable as nature." Cain responded sharply.

Darius laughed. "There is nothing to fear from such tremors. Earthquakes in this region are very common. Only seventeen years ago did a great shake rip through Pompeii,[9] killing hundreds of people and destroyed most of the houses. Much of the populace left and never returned, but several thousand came back, seeking fortune in this rich tourist destination. We have rebuilt this great city, with the help of Rome and the gods. Even the noted scholar Pliny said tremors are frequent and not to be feared."

"You underestimate the power of nature," Cain retorted. "You blindly believe because the Roman Empire has conquered a quarter of the world, you are beyond all dangers. It amuses me that Rome considers all peoples other than

---

[9] An earthquake measuring 7.5 on the Richter Scale occurred in the area on 5th February 62AD, causing the destruction of many of the buildings in the city. Ironically it was the feast day of the guardians of Pompeii.

themselves mindless savages and barbarians, and yet it is they who are by majority peaceful and culturally enlightened. The rest of the globe is disgusted at the butchery in the Coliseum which you mask as banal entertainment, where thousands of men are torn apart and animals are brought to the brink of extinction."

"You speak like an experienced Senator," Darius said in amazement. "Every gladiator who passed through these doors only cursed and grunted, even the few volunteers I have witnessed were usually too drunk to mouth anything intelligible. You must have had a formal education from someone with great knowledge."

Cain bowed his head in regret. "The only teacher I ever had was my father. But he is now long departed this world."

Darius grinned. "You should consider yourself fortunate to have known him, most of these bastards never knew their parents. The local brothel provided them with mothers and the Ludus was their only father."

"Family is all important," Cain sighed. "When your blood relatives are dead, then you truly know you are alone in this life."

"Then be glad your miserable existence is about to come to an end," Darius sneered. "Remember the only rule of the Coliseum; if you cannot fight well, at least have the dignity and honour to die well."

Darius led his slaves into the amphitheatre where Cain saw hundreds of jeering spectators surrounding the central arena, safely protected by rampaging beasts and enraged gladiators by twelve-foot walls. Already taking place before their arrival were four pairs of fighters locked in mortal combat.

Cain saw a secutor[10] and parmularii[11] were drawing the greatest attraction of the baying crowd, eager for blood and severed limbs. Each wore a large helmet, seemingly too big for any normal head, as if to add to the pomposity. Despite the ferocity of their attacks, it would be unlikely either gladiator could suffer any injury to the skull, outside of being hit with a heavy object like a hammer. Cain noticed both men were quite overweight as seemed to be the norm for all participants in the arena, as if to perhaps protect the vital organs from slashing wounds. However, Darius had pointed out earlier it was usually loss of blood that caused a fighter's death. Mortal injuries between pairs of gladiators in the Coliseum were rare, and were frequently delivered by the masked attendant at the far wall who executed the wounded man by means of a sledgehammer to the unprotected skull.

The secutor suddenly struck his opponent on the right thigh and as the parmularii fell to one knee, the other gladiator slashed his short-sword across the fighter's bare back. The man screamed in pain and collapsed on his side. The secutor raised his weapon in triumph as the wounded slave began to crawl away. The Editor of the games, seated in prominent position on a balcony overlooking the amphitheatre, signalled to the masked attendant and the strange cloaked figure dragged a long hammer across the sand towards the fallen gladiator. The parmularii removed his helmet and raised two fingers in submission to the Editor, but the obese man on the balcony ignored his pleas as the

---

[10] A gladiator equipped with a large shield.

[11] A different type of fighter, usually armed with a small shield.

attendant swung the sledgehammer and struck the gladiator on the side of the head, killing him.

Cain gazed on in disgust as the crowd began to shout hysterically in excitement, an execution in the Coliseum in Pompeii was very rare; tales they would enthusiastically tell their jealous friends. "How can you applaud such savagery?"

Darius smiled. "When the games first began centuries ago when Rome was a republic, the arena would have been littered with dead fighters. It was the era of Sine Missio[12], when every gladiator who entered the arena was certain to kill or be killed, he was forced to eliminate his opponent or not leave the Coliseum alive. Now it is far more civilised."

Cain gasped. "I would hate to see your concept of anarchy."

"We had a taste of chaos when Spartacus led his revolt of gladiators against the Empire," Darius replied. "It took several legions to quell that uprising."

The remaining participants left the arena and the crowd began to cheer at the sight of Darius and his new influx of combatants. The assembly of new gladiators gathered together before the balcony of the Editor and declared the solemn oath of all participants of the arena. "We vow to endure to be burned, to be bound, to be beaten and to be killed by the sword."[13]

The obese well-dressed man stood to his feet, overlooking the amphitheatre grounds. "Go now and may your deaths be legendary."

The fighters were paired off and each handed a small shield and short-sword. None were

---

[12] *Without release* from pre-determined death in the arena.
[13] The gladiator's oath as written by the noted scribe and philosopher Petronius.

given a helmet, the crowd wishing to see decapitation in all its bloody glory. The jeering mob did not have to wait long for a kill as one gladiator was swiftly executed by his partner as he thrust his weapon into the other man's exposed chest, the blade protruding from the fighter's back.

Cain found himself facing a tall well-built bald man in probably his late twenties who stared fixedly at him, displaying a maniacal grin. The gladiator began to wave the short blade in front of Cain's face.

"It would be better for you to simply surrender and drop the sword," Cain declared. "You are not my enemy and therefore I will not hurt you. But if you continue in your attack, your death will be horrendous, however not by my hands."

"I don't understand what gibberish you spout, barbarian," the fighter snarled. "But there is no surrendering in the Coliseum. Only one of us may leave alive this day and I promise that man will be me."

The gladiator swung again at his opponent, but Cain sidestepped and hit the fighter in the face with his right fist. The man dropped to the sandy ground dead as the crowd gasped in shock.

Darius approached, astonished at Cain's actions. "How did you do that? I have never in all my years seen a gladiator killed by a single blow delivered only by the naked hand."

The Editor of the games called Darius to the base of the balcony and leaned down to speak to the Ludus proprietor. Cain could not hear the whispered conversation but it quickly became apparent to him the secret contents of the speech.

Darius returned to his new star gladiator. "The master of the Coliseum wishes to see you repeat the attack, this time against multiple opponents. On the one hand, this is most unfortunate and unusual as a gladiator who normally wins his bout does not have to enter into combat again for several days. But you should instead consider this as a glorious opportunity to prove yourself worthy of becoming the new champion of Pompeii."

"I killed that fighter in self-defence," Cain retorted sharply. "I do not murder people for profit or sport. I once took an innocent man's life in rage, I will not allow myself to be in that situation again, even under the threat of death or torture."

Darius laughed. "These gladiators will give you no choice. They will cut you into tiny pieces and enjoy every minute of it. That last fighter you executed was a simple farmer driven wild by terror. These men are highly trained professional gladiators who have each seen dozens of bouts and killed every opponent they faced. High and mighty principles are worthless without the head on your shoulders to express them."

"If I kill these fighters, can I earn my freedom?"

Darius sneered. "You will earn your life until the next bout, more comfortable sleeping quarters, plenty of denarii and a girl or boy for your pleasure once a month."

"I require none of those," Cain said. "But my freedom will be given to me this day by one means or another."

Darius looked at him in puzzlement before turning and signalling to the Editor to release the professional gladiators into the amphitheatre. Cain watched as five heavily armoured thraex[14] entered the arena. Three carried the Roman standard short-sword and large rectangular shield, one was a secutor bearing a smaller shield and blade, and the last gladiator appeared to be a bestiarius,[15] dragging behind him on a long chain an adult lion which he kept at bay using a metre long trident.

Cain watched as the men separated themselves about the Coliseum, in particular keeping their distance from the lion which did its best to circle around its master in hope of seizing a weakness in the gladiators' defences. The Editor had decided that Cain possess no weapons of any kind, considering if his strength was so great he might have an unfair advantage against his opponents, despite their overwhelming numbers and armament.

Two of the thraex launched themselves at Cain, swinging their swords towards his unprotected head and upper torso. Cain jumped out of the way and hit one of the fighters on the back, sending him face down into the sand. Before the Thracian could recover, Cain struck his fallen opponent on the back of the neck with the side of his hand, severing the gladiator's upper spine. The crowd let out a loud cheer in excitement as the second man swung for the top of Cain's skull, meaning to plant the blade deep into his bent head. However, Cain rolled forward and in between the fighter's outstretched legs. As he dived, he punched upwards and struck the man in the crotch. The gladiator dropped to his knees in agony and Cain easily removed his large

---

[14] *Thracian.*

[15] A specific type of gladiator trained in using wild animals for use in the arena.

rectangular shield. Lifting the metal object high into the air, he brought it down onto the fighter's skull, splitting the head open. The man cried out as Cain removed it and threw the shield away, sending a shower of blood and grey brain matter onto the sand.

The assembled mob began to scream even louder in enthusiasm as the three remaining gladiators advanced, the two thraex facing Cain as the bestiarius went to his back from a safe distance, letting the lion loose on the full rein of the chains so the animal would be just within striking Cain's legs. Cain turned around and running forward, hit the beast on the top of its head with his fist, stunning the lion. The animal began to stagger in confusion, as Cain grabbed the chain and pulled the gladiator towards him. The bestiarius panicked and attempted to drag the metal back which was tethered to his wrist. Cain gave an enormous heave and brought the fighter all the distance between them. He then struck the gladiator in the chest with colossal force, shattering the bestiarius' ribcage and breaking the spine. The two Thracians gasped in astonishment as Cain then proceeded to lift the lion from the ground and threw the dazed animal at one of the fighters.

The beast appeared to recover its composure and sank its fangs into the gladiator's thigh. The man screamed in pain and fright as Cain ran at his partner. Cain dived as the fighter swung the blade and head-butted him in the torso, sending him to the sand with a grunt. Cain relieved the gladiator of his short-sword and drove the weapon into the man's open mouth, pinning him to the ground. The thraex began to gargle his last minutes of life, as Cain watched the lion remove its teeth from the last remaining gladiator's leg and sink its fangs into the

Thracian's face. The man cried out in agony as the beast pulled off much of his facial features including his nose and a large part of his jaw. The bloodthirsty crowd went hysterical, screaming in delight.

The Editor called for lanista[16] Darius to appear and personally congratulate his champion gladiator. A dozen armed legionaries came into the arena, escorting the Ludus owner lest the feasting lion still feeding on the fallen Thracian consider him its next meal.

Darius moved to embrace Cain in appreciation of his magnificent victory, but Cain pushed the lanista to the ground.

"What is the meaning of this outrage?" The Editor shouted. "How dare you strike your master?"

In response, Cain grabbed a spear from one of the guards and threw the long weapon at the Editor seated in the balcony overlooking the central amphitheatre. The tip of the blade hit the well-dressed fat man in the left arm. Although it was merely a flesh wound, the Editor went berserk with rage.

"As I told this miserable excuse for a human being at my feet," Cain said, pointing to the humiliated Darius. "I don't murder for money or pleasure. However, you and your army of savages I will gladly kill for free."

The Editor moved and stood at the edge of the balcony so the entire audience could see him. "Such an incredible spectacle as we have witnessed by your hands would normally excuse an act like striking your master, and the punishment would be sufficient by way of a hundred strokes of a whip.

---

[16] Proprietor of a Ludus.

But daring to try and eliminate the Editor of the games in front of all of Pompeii is punishable by death," the obese man snarled. "Guards, take him to the road outside town and crucify him like a common criminal. I will compensate you Darius, for your loss sufficient to bestow twenty gladiators in replacement of this warrior."

The legionaries removed Cain from the arena as the mob booed at his insolence. Darius watched his prize gladiator depart from the Coliseum with a mixture of relief and regret. Two miles beyond the outskirts of Pompeii they set to the execution of Cain. Placing his naked body on the makeshift wooden cross, they hammered six inch nails into his outstretched wrists and feet. Cain grunted at the pain and discomfort as the soldiers hoisted the cross into a freshly dug deep hole and slipped the wood into place.

Cain watched the legionaries down below as they opened flasks of wine and began drinking to their labour and out of sight of their superiors. However, their party did not last long as terrific cramps ripped through their stomachs. Cain immediately recognised the familiar first signs of the sevenfold curse. But his attention was drawn abruptly to the distant mountain Vesuvius, overlooking the towns of Pompeii and Herculaem.

A great shudder went through the earth, rocking the cross and sending the soldiers to their backs. The legionaries rose and gasped in shock as they saw the top of the mountain which overlooked their beloved town five miles away suddenly explode in a cloud of black smoke and ash. An enormous haze of pumice and stone flew hundreds of feet into the atmosphere, obscuring the sky in darkness. Already the guards could hear many of the populace of Pompeii begin to scream in terror. Several more legionaries arrived as the first legion of men started to vomit violently, entering the second stage of the sevenfold curse. The captain of the new group of soldiers relieved the first legion, believing their collective illness was attributed to witnessing the terrifying spectacle of the volcanic eruption. Cain watched them leave in amusement, knowing his crucifers did not have long to live. They would be dead long before Vesuvius showed its full fury.

"No matter what happens, do not take your eyes from the prisoner," the captain declared. "I will contact Pliny the Elder in Misenum. As Admiral of the fleet stationed in the bay of Napoli, he will have the authority to organise an evacuation of the population. The council and much of the people are content to reside indoors and wait out the storm, but I believe this is going to get much worse. The great earthquake seventeen years ago will be minor by comparison."

"Your superior speaks truth," Cain sneered. "I warned the lanista Darius the dangers of ignoring the wrath of nature. However, perhaps your gods will keep you safe."

The officer ignored the crucified prisoner and swiftly departed, arguing with the condemned was a waste of his valuable time. The legion watched the eruption from what they believed was a safe distance, Vesuvius a comfortable eight kilometres away. Several hundred refugees fleeing the volcano emerged on the roadside, carrying what little belongings they could lift on their shoulders. Cain noticed one of them was the Editor of the games, still nursing his injured arm, accompanied by three legionaries.

"I'll wager those nails hurt," the obese man laughed, as his horse drew up alongside the cross. "You could have been the champion of Campania,[17] but instead you will live out your last moments in disgrace and agony, and all for lofty principles a gladiator cannot afford."

"I will still be alive tomorrow, which is more than can be said for many of your bloodthirsty citizens." Cain retorted sharply. "Best you ride fast on that donkey before I remove myself from this cross and finish the job I started on that arm."

The Editor glared at the slave before hitting the reins on his beast and departed down the road. A tremendous shake abruptly ripped through the region and the refugees quickened their pace. However, the soldiers could now see no further people on the path leading to Pompeii, it appeared the remainder of the populace had decided to hide inside their homes and wait for the volcano to subside.

Hours passed and nightfall approached, Vesuvius continuing to spew tons of ash and cinder into the sky, an enormous dark cloud of pumice beginning to rain down on Pompeii. The legionaries watched in horror as the atmosphere above the raging mountain was lit up by a huge fountain of orange fire, fiery rock smashing into roofs of houses and onto empty streets. When dawn finally came after a sleepless night, the guards could scarcely believe it was a new day as the sky was dark as far as the eye could see in every direction, an un-penetrable haze obscuring the town.

---

[17] The Italian region comprising of many small towns including Pompeii, Herculaneum and Misenum.

Cain laughed as two of the legionaries dropped their spears and fled down the road, finally succumbing to their terror. The remaining members of the legion watched in interest as a crowd of citizens appeared on the path from Pompeii, a well dressed noble towing a dozen well-built bare-chested men behind him. They began to run as Vesuvius roared suddenly, a tremendous explosion driving hundreds of tons of molten debris into the atmosphere and over the region. Cain knew the primary eruption had now begun, all the previous volcanic activity been only a minor precursor to the main event. Any Romans that had stayed in the town and the soldiers before him were doomed, they would never outrun the fury of the mountain.

Darius dragged his gladiators to the base of the cross and stopped for a minute to gaze up at his prized fighter. "Well, if it isn't the great hero with the big mouth," the lanista snarled. "Are you enjoying the view from up there? Is the destruction of my beloved town preferable as you breathe your last moments, compared to the privileges of wine and women you would have experienced in the Ludus, the envy of all of Campania?"

"Behold, the supreme arrogance of the Roman Empire, offended the slave should dare to revolt and reject their gifts of suffering and servitude," Cain shouted down to his former owner. "Worry not 'master', about the loss to your purse and reputation as a perpetrator of butchery, for soon you will receive your just reward."

At that precise moment, another gigantic explosion came from the mountain and an even larger eruption of fiery pumice and ash filled the sky. The congregation of legionaries and gladiators watched in speechless awe as an enormous pyroclastic cloud descended from Vesuvius, and rushed into the streets and devastated houses of Pompeii and Herculaneum. The searing hot haze blew down wooden doors and instantly filled the lungs of terrified citizens cowering under tables and beds, their blood boiling within seconds and causing their brains to implode.

Cain grinned as the speeding black mist reached his captors and former arena comrades in moments, their brief screams cut short as their bodies became frozen in time, stone statues of fright and pain forever transfixed. Cain fell from the shattered cross, shaking in agony as the flesh which had been burnt from his bones with the heat began to refuse and heal itself. It was several minutes before he could stand to his feet, his body whole again. The fire cloud had destroyed his clothes and he struggled to see the path ahead, the ground hidden under a foot of ash, his surroundings obscured by a strange heavy black snow.

Every step brought sharp pain as the pumice was hot under his naked feet, however he could make out the corpses of Darius and the company of gladiators a short distance away. Cain stopped to stare at the peculiar statue of his cruel master, both knees bent as if he was praying, the mouth open in a silent cry as if he were pleading with his deaf gods for another day to live out his greedy unscrupulous life.

Cain noticed in the dark snow a large purse. Opening the cloth bag he saw several hundred denarii inside, the contents being the winnings at the Coliseum.

Cain removed one coin and gently placed the metal into the gaping mouth of the lanista of the Ludus of Pompeii. "Consider us now even Darius, here is your payment for my disobedience. The rest I will keep for my travels out of Campania, and donate the remainder to some charitable cause to offset the blood and lives that stain these coins."

Cain turned and entered the hazy wilderness, his fate now restored to his own hands and no longer at the whim of slave merchants, until his next encounter with the Roman Empire hundreds of years later and a despot masquerading as a saint.

CHAPTER THIRTEEN

Roman Christian Hypocrisy

Cain tried his best to keep to his word, performing charitable deeds whenever possible, in the hope that by spending the centuries helping the most vulnerable members of society, he might at last find redemption for his past misdeeds, in particular the murder of his brother.

Cain spent all his daylight hours handing out free bread to the homeless and sick, donations from the Christian church situated not far from the centre of the city Constantinople, only recently renamed from Byzantium in what was now the year 330AD. While Cain did not believe in Jesus Christ or any of his doctrines, he was prepared to overlook any hypocrisy this might highlight as the Church was the only organisation within the city possessing the financial means to hand out donations.

He at first had been concerned that he was still within the domain of the Roman Empire, despite this was the western capital and completely separate from Rome. A powerful, militarily successful and egotistical Emperor called Constantine held sway, having carved out his own private section of the now dying empire by winning a crucial victory at Milvian Bridge, outside Rome in 312AD against Maxentius, the son of his dead father-in-law who had conspired against Constantine and the Emperor had strangled. The founder of Constantinople declared he had witnessed a vision from God on the eve of the battle in the sun showing an image of a cross and the words 'in hoc signo vinces.'[18] After ordering his soldiers to paint the holy icon on their shields, the battle was a success and Constantine immediately converted to Christianity becoming the first Roman Christian Emperor.

His victory at Milvian Bridge allowed him to crown himself Augustus of the western part of the Roman Empire, depriving the Senate in Rome of all military and economic authority as Constantinople flourished. However, Cain firmly believed this vision in the sun was simply a clever ruse to denounce paganism and allow Constantine to sack wealthy temples of what he now regarded as foreign and false deities. While Cain as a believer in Jehovah, having the privilege of personally conversing with the Almighty, did not shed any tears for the passing of a dead religion, he found distasteful the greed and extreme violence by which the Emperor executed its demise. Like former Caesars before him he took advantage of spirituality to support his vital and expensive war chest.

One of the last remaining temples dedicated to Roman mythology was located across the square from the Christian church. As Cain continued to hand out bread to beggars, he noticed a gathering of approximately twenty legionaries approach the doors of the building. Entering inside, they began to throw robe-wearing pagans onto the street. Several soldiers appeared carrying a bag each of golden idols and trinkets, treasure to be smelted and carved into Constantinople denarii, the local currency and wages for a rapidly increasing in size army.

The Christian priest grabbed hold of Cain's sleeve, knowing only too well of his hatred for the

---

[18] *In this sign you shall conquer.*

Romans and concerned he might try to intervene in State matters. Cain turned and patted the old man on the shoulder, smiling and putting the priest at ease. However, as events began to descend into a riot, Cain became increasingly alarmed at the manner in which the guards handled unarmed and normally peaceful pagan worshippers.

The residents of the temple began to snatch at the bags containing their prized icons, resulting in the heavily armed legionaries knocking them to the ground. When one member attempted to strike a nearby soldier, the guard responded by hitting the pagan across the face with the handle of his sword. Another robed individual tried to grab the weapon and the legionary instinctively ran the man through the chest with the blade, killing him. The other pagans then grabbed at the guards, trying to bring them to the ground and relieve them of their weapons. The legionaries were forced to defend themselves and responded by drawing their standard short-swords and set to attacking the men.

Cain reached the temple within a few minutes and immediately struck one of the soldiers on the left temple, shattering his skull. The other guards were too preoccupied with the rioting pagans to notice Cain's arrival. However, when Cain relieved one of the soldiers of his spear and impaled the legionary, pinning him to the door of the temple they became aware of his presence.

The guards growled at their comrade's condition, still transfixed to the pagan temple door. Cain laughed as they advanced, but was unaware of the legionary behind him who suddenly struck him across the back with the short blade. Cain cried out as the weapon cut deep into his flesh, the blood flowing freely down his legs to form a pool on the ground. He turned to kill the guard who had injured him, as another soldier managed to hit Cain on the wrist with his sword, severing his right hand. Cain watched the hand fly from his arm and into the street. He stared intently at the gaping wound, this being the first time he had suffered such a grievous injury. The stump continued to squirt blood into his face and clothes and the guards gazed on in amusement, perplexed their assailant was more interested in how such a wound could have taken place, rather than the horror and pain he must be feeling.

The legionaries' confusion turned quickly to shock and awe as the missing hand began to take on a life of its own, moving across the ground in the direction of its owner. Cain knelt down and stretched out the stump as the limb flew through the air and reattached itself to its master. The soldiers watched in fascination as bone and sinew reformed on the arm. Within minutes Cain could move his fingers and grabbed the dead legionary's blade.

The guards took a step back as more reinforcements arrived. The remaining pagans fled into the crowd but the soldiers did not pursue, their interest was now solely on their mysterious attacker. Cain knew he could not defend himself against an entire army despite his superior strength, regenerative abilities and training he had acquired over the centuries, particularly in China and Japan under samurai masters. Cain was swiftly surrounded by more than two dozen legionaries, all brandishing their spears towards him. However, he took a few steps forward towards the guard who had severed his hand. He dropped the sword at the man's feet in apparent submission and the soldier grinned in satisfaction. But as he leaned down to pick up the weapon, Cain suddenly kicked him in the groin with his right foot. The legionary collapsed to the ground, clutching his privates in agony as the guards led him away to the city prison.

Approaching the city centre, he caught sight of the Great Palace overlooking the Marmara Sea and nearby the enormous Hippodrome, dominating a large area of the wealthy settlement. Constantine had constructed his living quarters surrounded by luxury, to the north within a few minutes walk was the huge Baths of Zeuxippos and further northeast the Acropolis. Cain was amused to hear one of the soldiers comment that no less than seventeen churches and monasteries lay dotted around the adjacent coast, and close by the colossal Hagia Sophia Church in case the Emperor should wake in the middle of the night, fearful his sinful soul might be in jeopardy.

His accommodation in the prison was however far less hospitable, the cell walls decorated in crude writings of Latin, former occupants listing their favourite whores in the city and comparing scores of provided services versus breast size. Cain noticed a rat in the corner chewing on a piece of rotting meat in the centre of a pool of dried blood. Presumably the last owner of the chamber had not survived the daily beatings of the warden and his imbecilic cronies.

"Don't get too comfortable," the legionary declared. "It appears word of your extraordinary self-healing talents have reached the ears of the Emperor himself. He wishes that you have an audience with him shortly to explain your mysterious origins and reason for being in his city. Normally you would be crucified within the hour or fed to the Coliseum lions as punishment for daring to kill one of my men, but it seems you are becoming somewhat of a celebrity," the centurion laughed. "But I would not entertain myself with thoughts of freedom if I were you, failure to please our contrary and deeply paranoid ruler usually results in a death far worse than we could deliver. One has to only examine what he has done to members of his own blood family on a whim, to be fearful of his dramatic mood swings."

True to his word, Cain lay in the filthy cell for little more than an hour, the incessant gnawing of the rodent on his dubious meal becoming increasingly more annoying. He was led out of the prison and stripped naked before being paraded before an excited throng of people in the street, rumour of his fighting prowess and supernatural abilities reaching the furthest points of the city. The populace only recently being forced to relinquish their pagan religion in favour of a foreign Christian one were glad for some distraction. Cain noticed they were not embarrassed by his nudeness and did not avert their curious eyes, the Roman heritage of orgies and wild sex still fresh in their memories.

The Great Palace lay only a short distance away and the legionaries quickly escorted their prisoner inside, nervous the growing mob might seize an opportunity to grab onto the stranger and encourage his escape. Cain was amazed at the opulence inside the enormous building, tapestries lined every wall featuring depictions of the Battle of Milvian Bridge and the Emperor's vision in the sun, prompting his conversion to Christianity. As he entered further into the palace he saw pictures of Christ's crucifixion, in stages from scourging to resurrection. Despite many conversations with priests of both religions in Constantinople and the common gossiper on the street, Cain could not determine whether Constantine's spiritual awakening was genuine or part of some greater plot against Rome. Certainly the dying empire was suspicious of Constantine's true motives and supported an uprising against him, in the form of his brother-in-law Maxentius whom after being defeated at Milvian Bridge in 312AD drowned in its deep waters.

Finally after what seemed like endless corridors of marbled floors and gold jewel-encrusted doors he entered the great throne room of Flavius Valerius Aurelius Constantinus, sole Emperor and founder of the richest city in the known world Constantinople.[19] Standing before him was a robust fifty-five year old man dressed in fine attire consisting of silken pants and jerkin under a thick purple robe. He had the familiar facial features consistent with most Romans, well defined chiselled cheekbones and large nose. Cain found interesting he had enormous eyes, quite uncommon for his race under finely trimmed bowl-shaped hairline. He was handsome and was an imposing figure, transmitting a statesmanlike aura of power and respect.

The Emperor turned to the centurion. "Nakedness might be appropriate in the cells of vulgar criminals," Constantine boomed. "But it is unbecoming in the throne chamber of the Caesar, particularly for a honoured guest such as Cain Kadmon."

The nude prisoner stared at the ruler in puzzlement, his identity until this moment was unknown to the Empire.

---

[19] Now known as the capital of Turkey *Istanbul*.

Constantine saw his reaction and laughed as a legionary appeared with clothes for their captive. "I have an extensive library here in the palace and several staff, their sole duties being research into ancient Christian mythology," the Emperor said. "That tattoo upon your chest is quite unique, no other person in history has had both the privilege and curse to bare that mark."

"So you are not surprised or shocked to witness a living testament to the existence of Jehovah?" Cain enquired.

Constantine smiled. "Not in the slightest, for I myself have seen the majesty and wisdom of the Lord. It was God who appeared in my dreams on the eve of my victorious battle at Milvian Bridge and bestowed the vision of the cross in the sun, the glorious star which up until then I worshipped as a pagan deity."

Cain sneered. "The story of your sunstroke is well known in the taverns of the city, it is amazing you still retain sight after delusions brought on by heat and too much time staring at the sun."

"The defeat of Maxentius was no illusion, his army outnumbered mine by two to one." Constantine retorted, his robe dragging across the marbled floor as he approached the now dressed prisoner. "My generals and military advisers warned a pre-emptive attack against my brother-in-law was doomed to failure. I however ignored their pagan sacrifices of ill omen, and taking a quarter of my army numbering some forty thousand, I crossed the Cottian Alps and swiftly took the heavily guarded town Segusium.[20] I then ordered the army to

---

[20] *Susa* in modern Italy.

advance to the strategic city Augusta Taurinorum,[21] where we encountered a large cavalry force on the outskirts of the settlement, but they were no match for the iron-tipped clubs of my horseback legionaries. Augusta Taurinorum was so impressed by the victory they refused entry to the fleeing cavalry and instead welcomed me with open arms. Milan and the rest of the northern cities sent emissaries carrying messages of congratulations and offers of unconditional treaties. Maxentius sent his praetorian prefect Ruricius Pompeianus with a large army to intercept us at Verona. Even though the town was heavily fortified and impenetrable on three sides because of the river Adige, I laid siege and successfully routed his forces. The general however escaped and returned with an even larger army, but I sent only a small group to intercept him for I still wished to continue the siege. In the short frantic battle, Ruricius was killed and the force annihilated. The city Verona immediately then surrendered along with the remainder of the Roman settlements. Maxentius, still in control of most of Rome's city soldiers and possessing a large quantity of African grain prepared himself for a long siege. He had ordered the destruction of all bridges across the Tiber river, thus causing a claustrophobic sense of panic and frustration to the citizens within. I continued through the country at a slow pace, taking my time on the road to Rome, allowing this dissent to fester. At the chariot races in the Coliseum, the crowd shouted abuse at Maxentius and proclaimed my victories. In response of fearing a citywide revolt, he built a temporary bridge and advanced north to meet me in open battle. He gathered his

---

[21] *Turin*, Italy.

forces together in lines with their backs to the Tiber. I had ordered my men to paint the sign of the Christian cross on their shields and with this new supernatural power I vanquished Maxentius. My infantry and cavalry smashed into his and pushing his men back, they either drowned in the river or died by the sword. Maxentius attempted to flee by small boat but such was the panic of his fleeing army, they pulled the craft down with their weight and he perished with his generals in the waters. The war was over and I was proclaimed sole ruler of Rome."

"Your military expertise is impressive, you showed truly remarkable insight and ingenuity on the battlefield," Cain said and the Emperor smiled. "But is it any wonder your brother-in-law tried to kill you for what you did to his father Maximian?"

"Maxentius hated his parent," Constantine snarled. "Such was the level of loathing between them, Maximian fled Rome and came here to Constantinople. It was only when my father-in-law conspired against me did I have him strangled."

"You made it look like suicide, as if it were his choice after his daughter, your second wife the Empress Fausta discovered her father's plans," Cain interjected. "You put a eunuch[22] in your bed. When Maximian murdered the slave, you had the perfect proof of his treason."

"I destroyed all statues and markings of him throughout the city, I wanted his memory expunged from national history." Constantine sneered.

Cain laughed. "The only reason your wife allowed the execution of her own father was to

---

[22] Slave who has been castrated, the testicles removed so as to ensure no possibility of adultery with the Empress, therefore providing the perfect personal bodyguard and manservant.

further the ambitions of her children over yours from your first marriage. She concocted a story of false adultery between her and your eldest son the heir apparent Caesar Crispus. You had your own son eliminated on rumour from a woman with a proven history of treachery."

"And she paid for it with her own life, drowned in the bath a year later on the orders of my mother Helena who adored Crispus. Besides it was good timing to execute certain members of my family who probably would have been troublesome later in my reign."

Cain sneered. "You killed your nephew Licinianus who was only eleven years old after ordering the death of his father your own brother."

"Fausta got her wish however," the Emperor said. "Our sons Constantine II, Constantius and Constans were made Caesars and potential heirs to the throne."

"Interesting choice of names," Cain remarked in a sarcastic tone. "It was not sufficient to name this city after yourself, you gave titles to your children bearing your signature also. Your ego is quite fantastic, even by Roman Emperors' standards."

Constantine moved forward and punched Cain in the face, sending the prisoner to the floor. The centurion drew his sword in defence of his ruler but the Emperor motioned for him to relax his blade.

"I have the blessing of God," Constantine declared. "I gave the Christian Church freedom from persecution in the Edict of Milan and erected dozens of their temples throughout Constantinople. I destroyed almost all pagan buildings and banned their false religion from being spoken in the street.

Pope Sylvester himself has recognised me as being instrumental in the birth of Christianity throughout Europe and safeguarded its future for all time. Next to Jesus Christ himself, I am the closest thing they have to a Saviour. I believe this grants me some leeway in naming my own children!"

Cain smirked. "Hold a person's head in the sand long enough and they will regard the first person to offer them water their Messiah. Not to mention the pagan temples had gotten fat with wealth from donations and support from Rome for centuries; an easy and convenient target to feed your depleted war-chest. The battles against Maxentius and in Gaul would have been expensive, and the Christians would be only too happy to be conscripted into the army to replenish your manpower losses."

"Those wars were necessary," Constantine retorted. "After my coronation in Britannia,[23] the Franks[24] invaded the lower Rhine valley twenty-four years ago seeking to accomplish a foothold in Gaul. I captured their kings Ascaric and Merogaisus, and fed them and all their surrendered soldiers to the lions and tigers in Augusta Treverorum[25] in the victory celebrations which lasted several days."

"You call such battles necessary," Cain remarked. "Or was it simply an exercise in brutality and to entertain the baying mob? You still maintain the sacrifices and gladiatorial games in the Coliseums throughout the Empire, but penalise any

---

[23] *Britain.*

[24] Large barbarian tribe in Gaul (France).

[25] *Trier.*

magistrate that might send an innocent Christian to his death in the form of a minor fine. You have enforced serfdom on your peasant farmers so as to ensure a son or daughter has to continue the family tradition of farming without profit, removing any possibility of escape to a better life in another profession."

"These decisions were required to build a wealthier and peaceful Constantinople for unborn generations, a little hardship now will provide great rewards for their descendants."

"Kill them now with unrelenting labour and no wages so future sons would have to only work twenty hours a day instead," Cain sneered. "Constantine, you are a hypocrite and slave-master; a true child of the Roman Empire like Nero and Julius Caesar before you. You claim to effort tirelessly for the good of the populace of Constantinople, but you are simply an ambitious opportunist and dictator instead. The Christian Church may regard you for centuries to come as a Saviour, but true history will see you only as a devious and manipulative despot who murders his own family for amusement and enslaves his people on a whim."

The Emperor motioned to the centurion. "I have conversed enough with this heretic," Constantine said. "I cannot put you to death, but I can certainly ensure you spend an eternity in starving darkness. The western wall of the palace is currently been repaired, place the prisoner inside and replace the stones. There he shall remain until this house disintegrates or the Archangel Gabriel blows his trumpet at Judgement Day and releases you from captivity. You could have been an enormous force for good, a living witness to the majesty of Christ and encouraged thousands of Christian pilgrims to visit the city to hear your sermons. Perhaps you might have even become one of the new cardinals that Pope Sylvester is swearing in to administer countries all over the world, but instead in your arrogance and wilful resentment of God you have chosen oblivion."

Cain smiled. "It's probably just as well I don't become a Christian priest, not only do I despise their ridiculous clothing, I fail to fulfil one of their prime enrolment requirements in that I don't have a sexual attraction to altar boys."

Constantine sneered at his prisoner. "Despite what you may have heard from the drunken gossipers on the street, that practice is rare and outlawed on punishment of death. Popes and bishops may overlook or shift paedophile priests around dioceses, but I do not accept such evil behaviour."

"That must be comforting to both their adult male and female parishioners," Cain grinned. "The safety of their children is guaranteed under your auspicious rule, and they can rest assured their grubby favours will be granted in return for receiving the local priest's 'holy' seed, and that the semen is not wasted on an innocent unfortunate infant."

"Get this man out of my sight," the Emperor snarled to the legionary. "I want him buried alive before nightfall."

Cain burst out laughing as the centurion dragged him away. "I may not die this evening, but your miserable reign will end soon thanks to the sevenfold curse, for anyone attempting to kill me will suffer seven terrible afflictions of the body before inevitable death."

Constantine stopped the soldier in his actions. "The scribes did mention an ancient hex that marks you as untouchable and free from persecution. Perhaps it would be better to escort you to the borders of Constantinople instead, but if you ever return I will put the curse to the test and imprison you in the walls of my castle for all eternity."

Cain smiled at Constantine as he was led away. "Perhaps after our historic encounter you will witness more apparitions tonight in your dreams or in the midday sun, bestowing onto you divine wisdom as to what fate you should have given me. But the reality is after now my second visit with the despicable Roman Empire, I will be glad to leave this place and never set eyes on either a legionary or Emperor again." Cain said and sighed. "However, I fear worse monsters and horrors await me still in the unending centuries to come."

CHAPTER FOURTEEN

Massacre at Passchendaele

"You must have a fondness for mud and dirty water," Simon laughed. "I know we are friends, but it is not necessary to get yourself blown up. Better you enjoy some Canadian wine and women instead. After three years of worldwide combat in what is now 1917, the war to end all wars should be coming to a conclusion. The Germans cannot sustain these losses."

Cain leaned across the table where he and his comrade sat in a secluded café down a quiet side-street in Ontario, rattling the coffee cups in their china saucers. "If you had seen as many conflicts as I have witnessed, you would not say such things. In my extensive experience, these wars inevitably continue until a nation reaches exhaustion through attrition. The Kaiser does not know the meaning of surrender."

"Neither do the British, despite their incredible casualties in the Battle of the Somme,"[26] Simon declared. "However, they claim their commander, General Douglas Haig is a genius who believes the war will reach a conclusion soon. With that in mind, the Canadian Prime Minister Robert

---

[26] The Somme Offensive took place in France between 1st July and 18th November 1916. It was one of the bloodiest battles of World War One with a total in excess of 1½ million deaths. The British alone lost 60,000 troops in the first day of combat, marking it as the single greatest defeat in the history of the country. Interestingly, the Battle of the Somme was also famous for the introduction of the tank.

Borden has promised half a million soldiers for England. The war effort has spread throughout the nation, Church ministers preaching combating the Germans is our Christian duty, army officials proudly displaying their highland dresses and even womenfolk wearing badges bearing the symbol 'knit or fight.' The government has even authorised for the young, the old, mentally and even physically handicapped may be admitted. This will be a glorious war with much honour to be won."

"There is nothing honourable in getting your head blown off or drowning in a waterlogged shell crater," Cain retorted sharply. "It is only because of Canada's history with the British Empire that compels them to enter this pointless conflict over some Archduke in Serbia getting himself assassinated. Ironically it is because of the great losses being incurred that the army has extended its recruitment to include Indian, Japanese and even black men of Canadian descent. Thankfully this also includes me as I have been a resident in this country for over twenty years, which means I can watch your back and return you alive as I have promised your father."

Simon smiled. "I have been meaning to ask you about your strange history with my parents and how you appear to have not aged a day since I was a child."

"I became friends with your father when he was a student at Ontario University," Cain stated. "He was being mugged by three older men, one of whom was threatening him with a knife."

"Yes, father said you broke the robber's arm and they ran off. He believed you saved his life, which is why he gave you a job at grandfather's farm which is now his," Simon declared. "This is why my parent keeps you as a labourer and caretaker, despite your bizarre ability to kill every crop you touch. After several trees in the orchard inexplicably died, he moved your employment to that of maintenance; performing upkeep of the straw warehouse and farm animals."

Cain grinned. "He was correct to do that, I am afraid plants and I do not mix well. As regards my youthful appearance, we Iraqis age very slowly."

"I would love to possess that talent," Simon said. "Especially in the conflict to come."

"There is still time to change your mind," Cain whispered. "Return to your apprehensive parents and put my own mind at ease. Don't force me to tell your father in a month's time his child perished in Belgium fighting a foreign king's war."

Simon smiled. "How can I die with someone like you to watch my back and save my ass like you did my parent?"

"Even with my remarkable skills, I cannot guarantee your safety." Cain retorted. "The reports I hear from the trenches bear stories of horrific conditions amidst a sea of mud; dead unburied soldiers lie everywhere to be devoured by rodents the size of Jack Russells, their wounded comrades screaming into the darkest nights, frequently lit up by incessant bombing. It has all the hallmarks of a hell on Earth. There is no glory or honour to be found there, just a premature death and a tragic waste of a promising life. This is not the destiny God has planned for you, rather this war is the Devil's work."

"Some fates are unavoidable," Simon replied. "If I do not volunteer, it is only a matter of time before they conscript me. At least this way, I have some chance of being promoted quickly. They are in dire need of front-line lieutenants to lead their platoons.”

"It is the officers who are usually shot first, that is why they are in such short supply," Cain stated. "This German nation has been throwing its weight around for decades, the Serbian assassination was a convenient excuse for the Kaiser's expansion plans into Europe. Even if the Germanic Empire loses this conflict, they will return in another twenty years to try again. It is only when they are utterly defeated on their home soil will they finally acknowledge surrender. Millions more soldiers and innocent civilians throughout the globe must perish before this matter will be completely resolved."

"Jesus Christ," Simon announced. "How did you get so cynical?"

"A lifetime's experience with humanity gave me this unique viewpoint," Cain replied flatly. "Mankind has been involved in countless wars throughout the ages. What amazes me is they never learn the lesson history teaches us; a failure to realise their mistakes and are therefore doomed to repeat them, and most importantly is that history like the weather patterns are circular. The Hittite society rises and is defeated, the Romans are born and destroyed after bullying their neighbours, and now we have the British and Germanic Empires fighting over a patch of mud. In a hundred years it will be two different superpowers going to war over some worthless piece of land or misunderstanding."

"However, this is a valuable field of mud," Simon interjected. "Ypres is the last remaining city in Belgium held by the English. If it falls to the Germans, the whole of Belgium will have been conquered and the British supply lines will be under threat. This battle at Passchendaele could decide the outcome of the war."

"Isn't that what General Haig said about the Somme?" Cain asked. "A whole generation of men annihilated and for what? The English claimed just two miles in the whole Somme campaign and yet it cost them four hundred and twenty thousand men; that is the equivalent of about one man per every half centimetre. The only success of the battle was the attrition was equally grievous to the Germans, they could no longer maintain the losses and had to withdraw. This of course meant they also retreated to Belgium where they nearly took over the entire country."

Simon laughed. "Perhaps you should be recommended for officer's training as well, possessing such passion in the subject matter."

"Authority and I do not mix well," Cain replied. "Even my parents had difficulty telling me what to do, but at least I had common sense enough to not deliberately put myself in harm's way. Therefore I am going to have my work cut out protecting your neck, your father will never forgive me if anything happens to you. Time for silence now, here they come."

The two friends watched three soldiers approach, shouting to them and the nearby other recruits to gather their belongings and depart for the army base and their one week training event. The next seven days were filled with endless marching, an arduous assault course which focussed more on the novices' ability to carry heavy rucksacks and hold their heads submerged under muddy water rather than any proper military experience. They were also taught in the weapons of both Allies and the Germans, including the Maxim heavy calibre mounted machinegun,[27] the British officers' six round capacity pistol, the German Luger and the standard small-bore, bolt action rife[28] which was capable of firing off between eight to twelve rounds per minute under normal conditions. They were also trained in the main sniper rifles; the German Mauser,[29] the French Lebel[30] and the English Lee-Enfield.[31]

---

[27] A primitive mounted water or oil-cooled machinegun invented by Hiram Maxim at the beginning of the Twentieth Century. Operated by a crew of up to six soldiers at any one time, was very prone to overheating and required a constant supply of water; troops were known to even urinate on the weapon to cool the device. However, it could fire between 400-600 small calibre rounds per minute. Maxim first offered the use of the machinegun to the British, but they refused citing its many faults. The inventor subsequently sold it to the Germans who modified the device and produced 100,000 machineguns. This German Maschinengewehr 08 weapon proved to be devastating against the British.

[28] Research into advancing the technology of the rifle prior to the war was intense and carried out by many nations. However, when world conflict erupted in 1914, this research ceased and the focus was on manufacturing large quantities instead of the current model. This by modern standards would be highly unusual, as it is normally in times of war that technology of weapons increases and groundbreaking advances are not uncommon, producing a more efficient model.

[29] The 7.92mm Mauser Gewehr 98 which was invented by Peter Mauser in 1898 had a distinct advantage over other sniper rifles of the time in that the clip and magazine could be detached together saving valuable time on the battlefield, and that it had a fitted scope attached. However, it was unable to achieve rapid fire due to its limited five round cartridge and bolt mechanism.

Cain discovered to his shock that there appeared to be more of an emphasis on a soldier firing off as many bullets as possible before he was shot himself, rather than on preserving the life of the individual. It seemed this world conflict was promoted purely as a war of attrition where bravery and military strategy were of little importance. Cain was not surprised however by this assumption that life was cheap and expendable, this was a viewpoint he had witnessed many times over the centuries by dozens of nations; in essence the ends justified the means.

The week passed quickly and Cain found that the average age of the recruits was between sixteen to nineteen years old, somewhat younger than Simon's twenty-three years. Because of this, Cain's friend was automatically promoted to the rank of lieutenant and was assigned to taking charge of a platoon of thirty men. Simon was delighted with this decision by his superiors, but Cain did not share his pleasure believing this would place his comrade in additional danger. The thousands of soldiers were transported to Ontario docks where a

---

[30] The Lebel 8mm rifle or Fusil model was invented in 1886, but suffered from serious flaws compared to its German and British counterparts in that all eight rounds had to be loaded one after another continuously into a tube-like cartridge below the barrel. If one bullet hit the primer of another, an explosion could occur and kill or seriously maim the soldier. Interestingly the rifle fired smokeless cartridges.

[31] The British Lee-Enfield 0.303 inch rifle or otherwise known Short Magazine Lee-Enfield Mark III was invented in 1907 by James Lee, and a trained soldier could usually fire twelve rounds a minute. The design was far superior to both the German Mauser and the French Lebel and it therefore became standard issue for American and Canadian troops. The rifle continued to be in use in World War 2.

steamboat awaited to deliver them to the French coastline and then walk to Belgium.

Several weeks passed before they arrived in Ypres on the 18th October 1917, the settlement surrounded on all sides by the German infantry and artillery. Cain noticed there was an atmosphere of silent fear throughout the town, people hurrying past them to perform essential tasks such as purchasing food from the market stalls that still operated and returning to the relative safety of their homes.

A senior British officer greeted them and informed the Canadian platoons they were to relieve the Anzac Corps of their position in the valley separating Gravenstafel ridge and the hills of Passchendaele. The battle of Poelcappelle had taken place just nine days earlier, with ten divisions of the French and English having engaged the German brigades in fierce combat. Although the conflict had been technically a success for the Allies, they gained only a minor section of land and lost thirteen thousand troops. The Australian and New Zealand[32] armies had also fought in the battle and suffered very large casualties.

The four Canadian divisions were informed they would be partaking in four separate assaults, each attack taking place in three day intervals. They would be supported by the British Fifth platoon and the French First Army currently in Houthulst Forest. Cain and his brigade marched out of Ypres and took

---

[32] New Zealand suffered their greatest defeat in the history of their nation at the first battle of Passchendaele, having lost 2,700 men of which 45 were officers. A further 800 men who were seriously injured had to be abandoned on the field as they were unable to retrieve them due to heavy shelling by the Germans.

their ordered position in Gravenstafel. The first conflict began on the 26th October where the largest Canadian division was assigned to the high ground at Bellevue Spur, the remainder of the troops would take position at the central railway. Cain and his soldiers successfully captured the crucial Wolf Copse before linking up with the British Fifth Army. The rest of the Canadian platoons had less success having to retreat due to fierce German attacks and misunderstandings with the Australian division over troop deployments.

Cain was shocked by the ferocity of the fighting, having difficulty at times to stay close to Simon and protect him. Many times he saw soldiers fall off the narrow duckboard that ran through the marshland and disappear into waterlogged craters; deep holes twenty feet or more now submerged and hidden by heavy rainfall through the month of August. No single tree or even blade of grass could Cain make out through the sea of mud, his shoes and pants thick with the brown substance, any injury suffered by the young men would lead to infection and a long lingering death where antibiotics had yet to be invented. Tanks including the British Mark I found the terrain extremely difficult to traverse and Cain witnessed the soldiers having to carry machineguns and tripods into the wilderness, dropping parts of the device in their rush to cross the mud and avoid the shelling.

The general impression Cain discovered was the haphazard way the battles were orchestrated where inexperienced troops barely out of childhood were led by officers lacking even the basics of training. Strategy was obviously something the Allies were unaware of which Cain could understand, simply because this was the first world war; the first unique never before seen opportunity for generals to learn and discover valuable experience in trench warfare which would be highly regarded in later years. Unfortunately for the troops under their command, this meant millions of lives would be tragically and needlessly lost while they gathered this knowledge.

They were allowed to rest until the 30th October, though Cain and Simon found this difficult out in the open with no shelter and the incessant gunfire and bombing going on all around them. The Canadian platoons were ordered along with their English and French counterparts to capture a vital patch of ground in preparation for the final assault on Passchendaele. They were to lead an assault on the heavily fortified Crest Farm, the village Meetcheele and the region of Goudberg. The Crest Farm was easily captured but the other two objectives could not be met due to extreme resistance from the Germans. In the days that followed the British Second Army took control of the English Fifth platoon and the remaining Canadian brigades, unifying the groups into a single force.

The final stage of the Passchendaele assault began on 6th November and within three hours of fierce combat they had captured the vital town. The Canadian army was ordered to take the high grounds outside the settlement and this they achieved with small resistance four days later, bringing an end to the long drawn out battle of Passchendaele.[33] Of the full company of twenty

---

[33] The Germans retook most of the land gained by the Allies through the entire Passchendaele campaign in three days in April of the following year. The Allies however easily fought

thousand Canadian troops, less then five thousand remained.[34]

As they departed from the barren wilderness of mud and lakes of black water in the direction of Ypres and much needed recuperation, Cain and Simon breathed a deep sigh of relief.

"I was wrong," Simon declared to his lifelong friend. "There was no glory to be found in this hell on Earth. However, some measure of honour can be found in fighting alongside these fine men and most especially you, my fabled protector. You can report back to my parents of your success in preventing my premature death."

Cain smiled. "That is a task I will be glad to undertake…"

Cain's conversation was abruptly cut short as a single shot fired across the wasteland from a hidden German sniper struck Simon in the chest. Several Canadian soldiers ran to the location of the enemy soldier and upon discovering his makeshift bunker-hole, swiftly killed him by use of bayonets. Cain knelt down by his friend as Simon's blood began to pool around his uniform and the muddy ground.

---

them off in September and October 1918, forever driving them out of Belgium.

[34] British and German casualties are in much dispute with many authors and historians arguing over the exact number of deaths suffered by most sides. However, it is generally estimated the English suffered losses of at least 200,000 and the Germans in excess of 275,000 and could be as high as 350,000 during the battles of Ypres and Passchendaele. Canada suffered losses of over 60,000 during the entire first world war. Interestingly, Adolf Hitler was a soldier during the conflict with the Sixth Bavarian Reserve Division. He became injured during a British gas attack in October 1918.

"I will carry you to Ypres and take care of you," Cain said, beginning to pick his comrade up. "I will not allow you to die in this place."

Simon screamed in pain and twisted himself so Cain had to put him back on the ground. "It is too late for that, my old friend," the young officer whispered. "You have done your duty, my father can be proud of you for that and hopefully feel some measure of satisfaction in how I lived my brief life and saved many soldiers in this platoon under my command."

"I will never forget you," Cain said softly to the dying Canadian. "My friends throughout my long travels have been few, but you have been amongst the greatest of those."

Simon smiled as his eyes went blank, his face expressionless as the life left him. Cain got up and dropping his rifle into the mud, ran off into the wasteland. One of the soldiers prepared to fire on him for deserting, but another Canadian stopped him, signalling that Cain had done much for their safety and deserved better. They decided they would report him as killed in action so the military police would not look for him. The platoon lifted up their dead commander and carried the lieutenant into Ypres for a hero's funeral.

After securing accommodation on a train, Cain left Belgium behind and keeping hidden in forests and mountain areas, secretly entered Germany. He decided to find shelter with the Jewish community, and perform charitable acts in return for food and boarding, hoping that after witnessing the battles of Passchendaele, he might avoid another world war.

CHAPTER FIFTEEN

The Nazi Butcher

"Move for inspection Jew," the soldier growled, prodding his prisoner in the chest with the machinegun. "The Chief Medical Officer of the main infirmary of Auschwitz-Birkenau is waiting."

Cain was lined up with hundreds of people of different ages ranging from the elderly being assisted by their adult children to small infants held in the arms of terrified mothers. German stormtroopers walked past the crowd, pushing a random person back, sometimes with the butt of their rifle. Much of the assembly carried what meagre belongings they could find in a hurry after being forcibly deported from all over France and Poland. Cain noticed some were dressed in finer attire than their neighbours, presumably wealthy businessmen. The guards however did not appear to treat them any better for the golden trinkets they attempted to show to the dismissive infantry.

Standing apart from the crowd at the far side on a makeshift platform was a thirty-three year old dark-haired man dressed in the familiar clothes of a doctor. Cain watched this peculiar official point at various people within the gathering, motioning for some to move to the left while others where told to go right, all the while he seemed to have a sly grin as if he were sharing a private joke with himself.

"Behold the White Angel,"[35] a woman whispered to Cain as she moved alongside. "So called with his arms outstretched dressed in his white overcoat, separating the doomed from the slaves; those consigned immediately to the gas chamber and the remainder to service the guards and maintain the camp. But a few most unfortunates will be selected by the doctor for special treatment in his private medical ward, there to be experimented on in grotesque surgeries for the advancement of the Third Reich."

"The Master Race?" Laughed another man nearby, listening to the woman. "This nazi butcher and his cronies will never inherit the earth. They liken themselves to the dead Roman Empire, believing they will reign over the world for a thousand years. But I hear the Russian army whom they despise and say are subhuman are tearing apart Europe in revenge for the Battle of Stalingrad, driving the German infantry back to the Rhine, and the Americans are smashing their armoured divisions in France. Apparently a colossal beach landing took place three months ago in June 1944 at Normandy and has the Führer on the run. Even the Angel of Death's experiments and belief he can bestow immortality on their beloved psychotic leader cannot hold back the Allies."

"You think the Russians care about us, or that the English government don't know about the concentration camps?" The woman retorted sharply. "The Jews have been ignored and persecuted since the time of Adam. The Allies have their hands full with the war, we are low down on the priority list.

---

[35] Known to the inmates of the concentration camp in German as *"Der Weisse Engel."*

We will all have long been exterminated before they gather the interest to liberate us, just be thankful your children are not twins, Doctor Josef Mengele has an obsession with dissecting and torturing similar-appearance infants."

Cain stared at them horrified. "How can the common German people accept this barbarity? Surely there must be a majority objectionable to such needless savagery?"

The two laughed in response. "You are truly naïve, my friend," the man sneered. "The German population know only too well of our fate, they watched with their arms folded as Jewish families were dragged onto the street before being deposited on waiting trucks, the propaganda of Hitler ringing in their ears of their inferior greedy neighbours who stole their jobs and polluted the minds of their children. When the first two million of our race were executed by machinegun before being dumped in a mass grave, crowds of German townspeople would gather and take photographs to show their friends. Himmler himself had to get personally involved to erect barriers and position guards to keep the morbid gawkers away."

"Silence," the woman interjected. "It's our turn soon. Watch the White Angel as he observes the assembly of youngsters."

Cain stared as Mengele lined a gathering of some three hundred children against the wall of the nearby building where he had drawn a white chalk mark on the wood. One by one he measured the youngsters against the line and any that could not reach the five-foot mark he ordered to be taken immediately to the gas chamber.

Cain was shocked by the arbitrary manner in which the prisoners were dealt with. Not since the early Roman Empire had he witnessed such cruel methods of selecting the weak from the strong, how human life was valueless and without merit. He contemplated intervening and try and save the lives of the children, but the sheer number of armed guards would quickly overpower him. Nevertheless, he could not simply stand by and watch such unnecessary suffering.

Cain stepped forward to the gasps of his neighbours, the woman whispering to him to get back in line or risk the soldiers' wrath. A stormtrooper immediately saw him and moved to intercept the prisoner.

"Back in line Jew," the guard shouted. "Or would you rather skip the selection process and go straight to the showers?"

Cain did not move, but simply stared at the German in defiance. The stormtrooper responded by raising his rifle to hit the captive in the face with the butt of his weapon. Cain however sidestepped out of the way at the last moment and the instrument failed to reach its target. He instead hit the soldier in the chest with his fist, breaking several ribs. The man screamed in pain and fell to his knees as another guard ran forward and taking aim, shot off a single round from his rifle. The bullet struck Cain in the forehead and he collapsed to the ground, blood streaming into the dirt from the gaping hole.

The soldier approached and standing over his victim, leaned over to drag the lifeless body away by the arm. However he quickly let go of the limb as the prisoner's eyes opened and the injury to his skull healed within minutes, the hole disappearing and the torn flesh repaired.

Cain rose to his feet and smiled. "Now bear witness to your true God, and not the egotistical lunatic with the ridiculous moustache who resides in Berlin."

Doctor Mengele walked towards them in fascination as the soldier began clutching at his stomach in agony. The White Angel gazed on in an almost trance like state and grinned as the stormtrooper went through the sevenfold curse before finally dying, his face contorted in pain.

"That was astonishing," Josef Mengele said. "I have never seen anything like that, even when I was under the tutelage of the great Doctor Otmar Freiherr von Verschuer who pioneered enormous advances in human genetics in Frankfurt,[36] in the pursuit of the German superman we have promised the Führer. If it were possible to mass-produce that effect on a large population or specific race, we could eliminate the need for cyanide capsules and even the concentration camps altogether."

"You are a true humanitarian," Cain responded sarcastically. "You could remove all this unnecessary suffering and tragic waste of life. No longer would you have to parade human beings like cattle to slaughter or starving slavery."

The Angel of Death laughed. "I was talking about the waste of resources and manpower that has to be set aside to organise and carry out the orderly disposal of these sub-humans. Hundreds of soldiers whose sole responsibility is to hunt hidden Jews in the cities and towns, transportation to the camps and even burial detail for their stinking corpses, not to mention the sorting of clothes after they are stripped and removal of gold teeth. These ungrateful

---

[36] Mengele was assistant to the infamous researcher in the Institute for Hereditary Biology and Racial Hygiene who had an unhealthy interest in genetics, particularly twins and promoted this obsession in his prodigy.

prisoners do not consider the work and money that has gone into the construction of these buildings and railways, the providing of their sleeping quarters and the infirmary to cater for their race specific diseases such as Noma.[37]"

"You mean malnutrition, dysentery and scurvy, not to mention food poisoning and gangrene all brought about by your brutal treatment?"

"The Final Solution has some unfortunate side-effects," Mengele said, his voice cold and emotionless. "You can't imagine the strict deadlines Himmler enforces, he demands results and there are more of these bastards arriving every day."

"I hope the Allies appreciate your hard efforts when they arrive," Cain sneered. "And of course your barbaric medical experiments in your own private torture chamber."

"Speaking of which, I would like to conduct various tests on your strength and incredible regenerative abilities, under heavy sedation of course to prevent any possibility of escape."

"And what makes you think I would submit to such treatment?" Cain asked. "I will rip the head from your shoulders in an instant."

"You risked everything to save those children," Mengele retorted. "If you reject my proposal, I will order not only their immediate deaths, but also the execution of every prisoner

---

[37] Mengele recruited Jewish paediatrician Berthold Epstein to investigate the origins of the disease which appeared to be confined to the children of the concentration camp. While their research proved inconclusive, it probably occurred due to severe malnutrition combined with measles, tuberculosis or chickenpox. Victims suffered from gruesome tissue degradation of the face, especially the nose, mouth and cheek which literally rotted away.

here. At least one quarter would have been selected for labour and maintenance of the camp and thus spared the gas chamber, however I will now send all of them and the Jews in the next ten trains to arrive straight to the showers. All of these unnecessary exterminations will be on your conscience."

Cain glared at the doctor in rage and contemplated killing him right there and then, but the guards would shoot him and clap him in chains before he had recovered to take care of them also. The fates of the prisoners would then be sealed in his absence. Cain looked around at the Jews who lined outside the train, all staring at him in silent terror, fearing their imminent deaths were upon them.

"Very well, I will do as you command," Cain said and Mengele smiled.

The White Angel motioned to the soldiers to remove the prisoner and put him in chains while the remainder of the stormtroopers began directing the Jews to their relative destinations, some to the camp interior, the rest to the gas chamber. Cain turned around and watched them leave, the man and woman he had conversed with earlier not among the doomed, their professions securing their place as slaves to the Third Reich.

Cain was led deep into the concentration camp, passing by various slum like buildings before finally arriving at a large brown house with barred windows and a steel door barring entry. The name Block 10 was imprinted on the metal looking out onto a wide pavement where a single tall leafless tree stood amongst trimmed rough grass. The vulgar stench of death was all around, and in the distance Cain could see a tall chimney spouting black smoke into the sky from an enormous structure he knew was the location of the gas chambers. Even though Cain knew whatever torture instruments lay inside could not kill him, he still felt apprehensive knowing pain would be visited upon his body the like of which he had never before experienced. He would be held captive until the mad doctor either tired of his gruesome experiments or the Allies liberated him.

Once inside, Cain was escorted into a large room where a polished marble table lay in the centre. Metal rings lay at either side and at the top and bottom, presumably to strap arms, feet and restrain the head. Several small holes were located around the surface leading down to a central funnel which fed into a round foot high bucket at the base which was nearly half full with what appeared to be blood. The stone structure was obviously a dissection table normally used in medical laboratories for post-mortem examinations.

The nazi butcher of Auschwitz however had a different purpose for this clinical instrument. Whilst compassionate doctors in the rest of the world used such a table to examine patients who had died after exhaustive attempts to save their life, in order to establish the cause of death and further the advancement of medicine, Mengele had the exact opposite intention; to perform unnecessary and horrific surgeries without anaesthetic on young patients who were starving yet otherwise healthy for his own sadistic pleasure.

Cain knew with dreadful certainty that he was now at the mercy of probably the most awful and evil human being yet to cross his path. Not even the Jewish leader Joshua, the Emperor Constantine or the gladiators of the Roman Coliseum in their worst moments could possibly conjure up such tortures.

As if needing no introduction, the Angel of Death entered and ordered the prisoner to be strapped to the table. Once he was confident there was no possibility of escape, he instructed the soldiers to leave.

"I would like to speak with you a while before we begin the tests," Josef Mengele said and Cain nodded. "Who and what exactly are you? Be warned, I have interrogated hundreds of cunning patients and will spot a lie instantly. Failure to answer my questions truthfully and twelve children will have their throats cut in front of you, and a dozen more every five minutes you distract from the subject."

Cain glared up at the doctor in fury, but knew it was pointless to disguise his origins. "I am Cain Kadmon, son of Adam and Eve, brother to Abel and Seth. I am immortal and cursed by God to live forever, to be spurned by society and friendship, to derive no growth from the ground and therefore survive on the kindness of strangers. However I have been blessed with great physical strength and self-healing talents so I may flee my enemies."

Mengele stared at him in astonishment. "That is extraordinary, you will be beyond doubt the most interesting and fascinating patient to ever enter this chamber. I will carefully document all my research for the Führer, this will secure my appointment as Chief Medical Officer of not only Auschwitz, but the entire Third Reich!"

"I am so glad I can be of assistance to the *monster race*," Cain sneered.

"Very amusing," the White Angel replied. "But you have been so dutiful to tell me who you are, so it is only right I tell you my story. I was born on the 16th March 1911 in a small quaint town called Günzburg in the Kingdom of Bavaria to Karl and Walburga Mengele. My father was a German pioneer of modern farm machinery specialising in milling and baling. This brought substantial wealth to our family which allowed me to study and become a doctor of Anthropology from the University of Munich in 1935. Two years later I joined the nazi party and the following year earned my degree in medicine. In 1940 I enlisted in the army in the special medical wing of the Waffen-Schutzstaffel[38] where I soon earned awards for bravery including the Iron Cross and a Medal for Care of the German People. In the winter of 1942 in Russia I pulled two soldiers from a burning tank and was promoted to the rank of SS Captain. However, I was wounded in the battle and removed from active military duties. Shortly afterwards I was assigned to Auschwitz-Birkenau as Chief Medical Officer[39] to the notorious 'gypsy camp' overseeing all inmates within that section of the concentration camp. I also became responsible for examining and selecting new arrivals for labour and those not strong or old enough for such work, therefore sent immediately to the gas chambers. I have strived to be efficient and diligent in my duties at all times, considering the conditions of the camp. I was once forced to send all seven hundred and fifty women inmates of a

---

[38] The *Armed SS*.

[39] Mengele's medical superior in the concentration camp was Auschwitz Garrison Doctor Eduard Wirths.

block to the death showers when it became infested with lice."

"That was a bit drastic a treatment for a few bugs, a case of killing the disease by murdering the patient," Cain said. "And what of your other victims, the children that entered these doors and had the misfortune to end up on this table?"

"Everything I did was to further the medical cause of the German people," Mengele declared. "I took no pleasure from the actions required. You have to understand, these creatures are sub-human, parasites upon Germany. They are not worthy of your concern or compassion, you would not regret standing on a rodent?"

"People are not rats," Cain retorted sharply. "The Roman Empire had the same viewpoint on the rest of the world, believing their sole destiny was to expand Caesar's domain. They made other nations slaves or fed them to wild animals in the arena, they were treated worse than pigs to slaughter."

"I understand," Josef said. "Do you then believe me to be mad or evil?"

"Only history will decide that," Cain replied. "But you are certainly delusional, and did not for a second remember your Hippocratic Oath; to harm or by your actions bring harm to another human being."

Mengele shook his head in contempt. "The Führer is creating an empire greater than the Romans or Alexander which the Allies said was impossible. If we were to stop because of American or English hypocrisy who preach their holy values to what they claim are inferior nations, but do not practice those same ideals themselves we would achieve nothing. You only have to examine how Britain has treated their colonies such as India and

Ireland, subjugating the populace and attempting to eradicate their unique culture and language. But to answer your earlier question about my experiments on children, this was done to further the advancement of science, those twins who manage to survive will live on to testify the sacrifices made were for the greater good of mankind.[40] I was particularly interested in physical deformities on new inmates, especially the Romanian Ovitz family of which seven of the ten members were dwarves. Prior to the war, they would tour around Europe as the 'Lilliput Troupe.' Why so many siblings within the one family were abnormal fascinated me."

"The Spartans had the same viewpoint, believing any child born that was not perfect should be thrown over a cliff." Cain said in a sarcastic tone.

Mengele smiled. "I think you are finally becoming aware of the nazi ideology, there might be hope for you yet. Besides, creatures like dwarfs have no place in society, they cannot do the same work as a proper man and lack the intelligence for any complicated task," the doctor said before returning to his earlier subject matter. "I am a pioneer performing groundbreaking work having the privilege of an inexhaustible patient base, no

---

[40] During Doctor Mengele's tenure at Auschwitz, he operated and carried out gruesome experiments on approximately three thousand twins, of which only about one hundred pairs survived. Whilst twins were segregated from the main concentration camp and better treated than their adult or non-twin counterparts, they went on to live a life of suffering and physical abnormalities because of the extreme surgeries and poisonous injections inflicted on them. However, because they were spared the gas chamber, ironically he would sometimes introduce himself to new child patients as "Uncle Mengele" or "Mengele the Protector." This testimony only furthered witnesses' claims that he was obviously insane.

matter how many died, there was always thousands more to replace them. I have attempted various operations and procedures including removing the eyeballs of one twin and sewing them to the back of the head of the other child to establish if they might fight better. I have changed the eye colour of patients by injecting the retinas with chemicals which unfortunately blinded them. I have performed sterilisation operations on young girls including removal of the labia and clitoris, and shocking them with electricity which again in most cases killed them. I took two Romanian children and made them Siamese twins by sewing them together, however infection set in causing gangrene in the veins of the arms. In one particular procedure, I placed fourteen pairs of gypsy twins here in this very room and injecting their hearts with chloroform killed them. I then removed all their organs to identify if they might match their counterparts in weight and appearance. I operated on all these patients without anaesthesia, sometimes severing limbs and removing hearts and parts of the stomach."

Cain was shocked by what he had heard and the cold emotionless manner in which he described the procedures as if he were cooking a meal or making coffee.

"Tell me Mr. Kadmon, did you meet any famous Jews on your travels down through the ages?" Mengele asked.

"I encountered Moses and his successor Joshua, a sociopath not unlike yourself, having no regard for human life who appeared to enjoy inflicting misery." Cain retorted.

"The Prince of Egypt?" The doctor gasped in amazement. "Now there is a sub-human I would have liked to interrogate. You say Joshua was a psychopath who adored violence, do you then believe the Jewish people brought this event they already call the Holocaust upon themselves, as if history was punishing them for the wrongdoing of ancient ancestors?"

"I once thought that way and expressed that very same viewpoint to Joshua himself," Cain said. "But I now believe you cannot judge an entire race by the actions of a few madmen, besides this genocide you enforce in the camps is more to do with Hitler and his cronies' interest in the occult than anything the Jews might have done in the past. The nazis are fervent followers of Christ, they believe they are doing God's work by killing the people who murdered the Saviour."

"You are very astute. One last question," Mengele enquired. "You allowed yourself to be captured, having been found in the Jewish quarter of Munich helping the sub-humans, you offered no resistance when it is obvious you could have easily killed the soldiers removing the families for deportation."

"I wanted to know if the rumours were true about what was going on here," Cain said. "I had to see it with my own eyes to believe it."

"And now you know, and I wager you now wished you had remained safe and sound in blissful ignorance," Mengele laughed. "Now then, let's begin!"

In the months that followed, the Angel of Death subjected his prisoner to many gruesome and bizarre surgeries, all committed without anaesthesia. These included amputations of limbs, removal of organs and even decapitation. In each case, within minutes, the severed body part reattached itself and healed without any sign of injury. The doctor carefully documented all his research and Cain's reaction to the different chemicals. He ascertained after exhaustive tests that his captive's strength was equal to that of approximately ten grown men.

The experiments continued right up until the morning of January 27th 1945 when the concentration camp was abandoned days before the Allies liberated Auschwitz. The shocked American soldiers found Cain, still strapped to the marbled table, a shell of his former self, gaunt and weak with hunger and driven nearly to insanity by the endless torture.

After brief questioning, he was sent to the United States and settled in Chicago. It took many long years for Cain to recover from his ordeal but never forgot his experiences at the hands of the mad doctor and swore revenge, not just for himself but for Mengele's many victims. He at first believed like so many others within the American government, that the Angel of Death had not survived the war. That was until the Israeli secret police Mossad discovered he was in hiding somewhere remote in the world living under an assumed name. Either way, Cain thought retribution would never come to pass until the door to his apartment suddenly opened and in walked two men in suits, operatives of the Central Intelligence Agency.

"Good evening, Mr. Kadmon," one of the agents said, a forty year old American dressed in an expensive suit. "Do not be surprised that we know your true identity. We know about your liberation from Auschwitz and the poverty you have been living under for the last few decades. We have the solution to both those problems, carry out errands for us in Cambodia and other 'hot spots', and not only will we set you up in a new profession and identity in America or Britain, but we will give you the information you desire to locate Doctor Josef Mengele. Mossad know where he is, but cannot touch him for sensitive political reasons, however that is not an issue for someone of your talents." The operative smiled. "He was in hiding in South America, in Buenos Aires where he continued to practice as a doctor carrying out illegal abortions under a new name. He had been arrested when a patient died during a botched operation but he was released, the police never realising who he really was. He spent many years in Argentina before fleeing to Paraguay after his friend the nazi Eichmann was kidnapped by Israel. However, Mossad could not apprehend him due to the dictator Alfredo Stroessner being in power and claiming to be of German blood. The despot was known to even recruit nazis with their stolen Jewish gold to help develop his nation. We now believe him to be in Brazil."

Cain smiled. "When do we start? The sooner we get finished the quicker I find that bastard."

The covert operations in Cambodia and other locations sanctioned by the CIA lasted until January 1979 before the spooks finally gave Cain the information he required. They told him that Doctor Mengele was living in Bertioga, Brazil under the name Wolfgang Gerhard, a neo-nazi who had given sanctuary to the White Angel and provided the physician with a certain degree of luxury.

Cain travelled to Brazil and arrived in the country on February 7th 1979 to find after talking to the locals a sixty-seven year old frail man walking along the beach, enjoying the cool breeze, safe in the knowledge that he had evaded capture by the Allies and Mossad for thirty-four years.

The Angel of Death spotted his former captive coming across the sand, but did not try to flee, knowing it was pointless in his failing health and against a much younger opponent.

"Astonishing," Mengele said as Cain approached his elderly torturer. "You have not aged in nearly forty years, it is as you declared all those years ago that you are immortal. If only we could have discovered the secret together and I would not be now suffering old age and ill health."

"That pain and discomfort you feel is small punishment for the crimes you committed," Cain snarled. "Are you still without remorse?"

Doctor Josef Mengele laughed. "Two years ago, Rolf the son who I had been estranged from all his life came here and asked me the same question. I told him as I tell you now; that I have never personally harmed anyone in my life."

Cain stared at him in disbelief and rage. "Very well, butcher of Auschwitz, then let this be some measure of retribution for your thousands of innocent victims."

Cain slapped the old man in the face and as the elderly physician lay in the sand, he stripped the doctor of his clothes in memory of how he had ordered so many to be removed of their garments and humiliated before sent to the gas chambers. Pulling Mengele to his feet, Cain proceeded to break all his fingers one by one, knowing the digits are precious to a surgeon even though it had been many years since he had practiced.

The White Angel screamed in agony as Cain pulled the fingers back and snapped them before dragging him down to the shoreline, the cold waters of the Atlantic Ocean lapping at their ankles. Mengele struggled to break free but Cain held him fast. He brought the naked surgeon into the frothy liquid until Cain was in the waters up to his waist. Cain then began ducking his head under the water, two minutes at a time, enough to terrify the White Angel, but not sufficient to drown him.

"We call this a form of water-boarding," Cain declared. "A little torture trick of my own taught to me by my friends of the Central Intelligence Agency as a means to interrogate terrorists. Do you not like the cruel treatment, Angel of Auschwitz, for a pioneer surgeon as you once claimed yourself to be, you should appreciate the irony of getting *a taste of one's own medicine?*"

Doctor Mengele could only gasp for air in response, the sea water running down his face and out of his nose. Cain glared at him in uncontrollable anger before shoving his head under the liquid and keeping it there for several minutes. Cain continued to hold him under the water long after the struggling had stopped and the White Angel was obviously dead. He finally let the body drift away in the waves before walking into the sand.

Cain left the beach and did not look back, his business with the mad doctor at last finished, his vengeance sated and content in the knowledge that the many victims of Auschwitz could finally find some measure of peace.[41]

---

[41] German police exhumed Josef Mengele's body on 6th June 1985 and DNA proved in 1992 that the corpse was indeed that of the White Angel. The Sao Paulo Institute of Medicine attempted to return the remains to the Mengele family but they refused to accept them. The bones of Doctor Mengele, the Angel of Death continue to be in the custody of Doctor Rubens Maluf.

CHAPTER SIXTEEN

Cambodian Secrets

Cain arrived in Cambodia in 1970, given the forged identity of an American journalist using the name Sam Philips. The Central Intelligence Agency decided since he had not developed a Chicago accent despite spending the last twenty-five years in the city he would blend into the populace quite easily, his darkish skin hiding the fact that he was an American spy.

Cain was met at the airport in the capital city Phnom Penh by two middle-aged men dressed in local clothes, complete with bad hairstyles and cheap jewellery.

"Welcome to the Kingdom of Cambodia, Mr. Philips," the spook said. "We have a car waiting outside to take you to a safe-house where you will be briefed with the terms of your assignment. Is this your first time in this part of the world?"

Cain nodded and the man smiled. "You will have to excuse the heat, summers in Chicago never got this humid," the American laughed. "Phnom Penh is the country's largest city, the centre of all political, commercial and industrial activities. Siem Reab, the main destination for tourism is the route to the Angkor region and Sihanoukville is the coastal settlement where all primary sea transportation takes place. In fact, it is this beach city that interests the CIA most especially and the communist policies of the nation's leader that concerns us."

"Just tell me what shitty task lies before me," Cain said sharply. "I have somewhere else to be and someone to kill."

"Yes, we were informed you seek the location of some nazi," the spook declared. "Your mindset does not differ that greatly from ours, we may have separate objectives but our methods are the same."

"I am nothing like you," Cain snarled. "The Central Intelligence Agency and the nazis are quite similar in how they treat races they consider inferior, the only difference between you is that the nazis carry out the torture themselves, whereas you simply export it as a 'legitimate method of interrogation' and prefer to not get your own hands dirty. This country's communist ideology does not concern you, the CIA and the Russian secret police the KGB have been known to have polite discussions over coffee and cake on many occasions. What troubles you and your superiors is Cambodia's neutrality in the Vietnam War under the leadership of Prince Norodom Sihanouk.[42]"

"You've got a big mouth," the spook sneered. "And principles you cannot afford to possess or throw around."

The agents approached the car and after placing his meagre belongings in the trunk, Cain was driven through the capital's congested roads until he reached the outskirts and a poorer part of the settlement. Escorted into a two-storey building, he was greeted by two more slightly older men

---

[42] Full title: Preah (sacred) Karuna (compassionate) Preah Bat (foot) Sâmdech (prince) Preah Norodom (quality among men) Sihanouk (lion, jaws) Preahmâhaviraksat (courageous).

sitting in a makeshift office containing two chairs and a battered wooden table on which stood a typewriter, several maps of Cambodia, Vietnam, Laos and China.

"Here are your employment records," the eldest spy announced, rising from the seat behind the desk and passing the folded document to Cain. "You are a reporter from Washington sent to interview cabinet members of the Norodom administration. But in reality I want you to liase directly with our counterpart in the government the Prime Minister General Lon Nol and Prince Sisowath Sirik Matak."

"So your goal is to overthrow the democratically elected people's choice Head of State?" Cain enquired.

"You are not here to offer opinions on matters that do not concern you," the spook growled. "You are here to follow orders like a good American soldier."

"You mean like those unfortunate troops drafted against their will to fight a dictator's war in a country far from home, to propagate the lie that this battle is for freedom; to suppress communism and protect the American way of life?"

The man turned to the company of spies in disbelief. "Jesus Christ," he said gruffly. "Where did Langley find this son of a bitch?"

Cain ignored the rhetorical question directed at the assembly of spooks. "Just tell me where this Lon Nol is now and how many balls I have to lick in order to go home?"

The elderly American stared at him. "He has a house just out of town," the spy said. "Inform Mr. Nol that we are prepared to transfer the money to him once he is ready to launch the military coup against Norodom Sihanouk. The Prince will be out of the country soon and that will be the perfect time to strike. Tell Lon that our agreement stands, remind him of promises made and commitments to be fulfilled when he attains power. The French made a mistake with Mr. Sihanouk[43], but it is now time to rectify that error."

"Surely one of these morons could have been messenger boy for you," Cain sneered. "Why exactly do you need me?"

"Lon Nol is deeply paranoid and has a tendency for violence," the leader of the spies replied. "He always has a dozen or more bodyguards with him at all times. Langley could only afford to send us few agents to monitor the situation in Cambodia and so little men would draw less attention. If events take a bad turn, it will be up to someone of your unique talents to convince Mr. Nol of his fragile allegiance with the United States."

"I am not comfortable with this foreign interference in another country's peaceful democracy, who after centuries of conflict and domination by tyrants like France only seek to remain an outsider in a battle not of their making or their concern." Cain said. "This Norodom Sihanouk is not only the people's elected head of state, but

---

[43] France held control over Cambodia from 1863. When the king died in 1904, the French government decided that the throne should pass to the monarch's brother Sisowath. However, when Sisowath's son Monivong died, France again decided to ignore the rightful heir; Monireth who was Monivong's son, and instead passed the throne to the maternal grandson of King Sisowath. France wrongly believed the eighteen year old Norodom Sihanouk would be easy to manipulate, but the new ruler gained independence from France on 9th November 1953.

their national hero for gaining independence and keeping his populace out of the Vietnam War."

"I am told by my superiors in Washington that you seek the location of the nazi butcher Doctor Josef Mengele," the spy declared. "The Angel of Death is known for staying in one place for only a short while, you would find it impossible to discover him on your own. You would be wise to remember that. Besides, your so called peaceful Cambodian ruler has made pacts with China allowing the communist nation to deliver supplies to North Vietnam through the port Sihanoukville. When the Cultural Revolution in China occurred coupled with the military bases of North Vietnam he sanctioned on Cambodian soil, this led to the Battambang Province revolt on the 11th March 1967 which instigated a civil war."

"And if these events had taken place in America," Cain interrupted. "Would you have found it morally or politically acceptable to have foreign powers interfere, attempting to install a despot with terrorist policies?"

The elderly spook glared at him. "This debate is over, do your job or perhaps we might inform Lon Nol that you are really an agent of Norodom Sihanouk with plans of assassination. A few decades in a Cambodian prison might soften your skull and silence your mouth."

Two of the spies led him out of the office and bundled him back into the car. A short journey later and they arrived at the house of Lon Nol. The incoming Prime Minister lived in opulent luxury, residing in a four storey mansion surrounded by several hundred acres of carefully maintained lawns. Cain guessed the Cambodian economy which was primarily agriculture afforded the majority of the rural population little wealth, and certainly nothing like the soon to be Prime Minister enjoyed inside the lavish building.

Cain was greeted at the gates by five men armed with AK-47s as his escort disappeared quickly back into their car and sped off into the distance. Cain was led into the huge mansion and did not have to wait long before Lon Nol approached him.

"I understand you are the new American representative," Lon said, opening a bottle of wine and offering a glass to his guest. "Please excuse the guards, I have many enemies within Norodom Sihanouk's administration. When the tyrant leaves the country soon to meet foreign leaders I will convene the National Assembly and remove him from power. Do not be concerned about the terms of my allegiance with the United States and the Central Intelligence Agency. I need America to recognise my leadership and the financial commitment they have promised to bring Cambodia away from a purely farming based economy. These are dangerous times, my friend. I fear Sihanouk will form an alliance with the minority extremist party the Khmer Rouge. They currently have an army of some six thousand in hiding, but those ranks could swell with Norodom's support considering his popularity with large sections of the population."[44]

---

[44] Upon being removed from power, Norodom Sihanouk formed an alliance with the Khmer Rouge allowing their ranks to swell to sixty thousand. Their extremist values and twisted ideology was instrumental in a countrywide policy of genocide which resulted in millions of deaths from starvation, torture and refusal to use modern medicine. They split families, believing parents were tainted with capitalism and encouraged children to practice torture methods on animals. The entire

"Does the CIA not consider the Khmer Rouge a threat, that this coup could destabilise the nation and polarise moderate members of this minority party?" Cain enquired.

"It's possible that outcome may be inevitable," Lon declared. "But Norodom Sihanouk is a threat to international peace, his collaboration with China will lead to civil war. We already got a taste of that with the Battambang Province revolution three years ago, but that was localised. Besides, an invasion by North Vietnam is purely a matter of time,[45] we need to end this supply trade operating on our soil to that country and prepare our army to repel their forces."

"I understand," Cain replied. "I am here to inform you that the Central Intelligence Agency and America are ready to support you both militarily and financially. I have carried out the orders given to me and will now return to my superiors."

Lon Nol nodded in agreement before escorting Cain to the door. The agents returned with the car and brought him back to the office where a strange sight greeted him. Strapped to a wooden chair with his hands bound at his back was a

---

population, irrespective of their profession, was forced to tillage the land for twelve hours a day without break.

[45] The Khmer Rouge were finally removed from power and their totalitarian regime dissolved in 1979 when the North Vietnamese army invaded with the military help of the United States. After nearly ten years of manipulating the country by the CIA and heavy bombing raids by America, the country was in ruins and the population decimated. Historians now believe this foreign influence and bombing by the United States drove large parts of the populace into the ranks of the Khmer Rouge, without which there probably would have been no civil war and millions would have not perished in nationwide genocide.

twenty-five year old man. The eldest spook who gave Cain the orders earlier was placing a square towel approximately twelve inches in length over the individual's face whilst pouring water from a jug over it. The man was spluttering and gasping for air and Cain was aware he was witnessing some bizarre method of torture where the suspect was forced to endure some type of drowning.

"You're just in time," one of the agents laughed. "We call this water-boarding. We used to shove the foreigner's head in a bucket of water or a bath in the past, but we find this much more appropriate. The suspect used to knock over the bucket and we don't have to worry about finding enough liquid to fill a bath. Besides it's much more comfortable for us, having him sitting and easy to interrogate. Isn't it amazing how someone can drown with a small hand-towel over their face? We used to teach this procedure to the Vietnamese until traitors within their ranks taught it to the Viet Cong and now unfortunately they use it against our troops."

"Who is this man?" Cain enquired.

"A spy from Norodom Sihanouk, somehow they have discovered our location. We need to know how much information they have on us before we eliminate him," the spook replied, smiling.

Cain ignored the Cambodian's plight, feeling he had enough of interference in matters not of his concern. "I did as you commanded," Cain said to the leader of the American spies. "I want to know where Mengele is."

The eldest spook glared at him in temper. "We are not finished with you, Mr. Philips. You will remain in Cambodia for the next few years, until your next assignment in Australia and then on to Angola. It will be nearly ten years before we are ready to release that information and relinquish you of your responsibilities to this agency. And if you are thinking of simply killing us now and walking away, rest assured you will never discover the nazi's location and twenty spies from Langley will replace us. The operation here and abroad will continue in our absence, as it says in the Bible when Jesus encountered the Devil in the possessed herd of pigs, we are Legion; we are many and insidious like rattlesnakes."

"Of that I have no doubt," Cain retorted. "I am beginning to regret this Faustian deal, but I will do as you command. I will carry out the operations in Australia and Angola without complaint, however if you try and screw me you will find I am like the mongoose; killer of cobras and rattlesnakes, and possess a terrible bite."

Cain remained in Cambodia for the next two years ferrying covert messages to Lon Nol until he was deposed by Pol Pot and the murderous Khmer Rouge who instigated a civil war and carried out a countrywide genocide on their own people, creating the infamous 'killing fields,' where millions of peasants were tortured and decapitated, their rotting bodies left unburied in the rice-fields throughout Cambodia. The Central Intelligence Agency operatives were forced to leave when the American Congress cancelled the funding for their secret war in Cambodia in 1972. However, the brutal war they had helped to create continued until 1979 when the North Vietnamese army invaded supported by American bombers.

Cain arrived in Australia in 1975, his assignment being that of personal bodyguard to the Governor-General John Kerr. The politician whose employment within the Australian government was purely ceremonial under the appointment of the English Queen, was secretly an operative of the Central Intelligence Agency. He received orders from his true masters to remove the democratically elected and popular Prime Minister Edward Whitlam using an archaic and never used law. The CIA fearing the liberal and left-wing policies of the ruling government used John Kerr to exercise his constitutional right and dissolve the Australian assembly. Shocked and angered by this decision, death threats were made against the Governor-General and Cain was forced to defend this puppet of the CIA, until he eventually fled the country.

Shortly afterwards in the same year, Cain was dispatched to Angola where he witnesses the greatest yet involvement of the Central Intelligence Agency in another nation's politics with tragic results. Furious with the defeat of the American army in Vietnam and frightening Congress with stories of communist threats, Henry Kissinger grossly exaggerates the political situation in Angola. He ordered the CIA to offer unconditional military and financial support to the dictator Jonas Savimbi. This results in the terrified and oppressed normally peace-loving people of Angola to seek help from communist countries Cuba and Russia. The American Congress concerned by the volatile situation cancelled the Central Intelligence Agency's funding a year later, hoping this would cease their illegal operation in the third world nation. However, with monies secured from drug-running and arms trades, the CIA continued the policies without this funding until 1984 when the support from Congress returned. When the dust had settled and the completely unnecessary war came to an end, over three hundred thousand Angolans were dead.

Cain, disgusted and aghast at his own involvement however passive in this horrific conflict, left Angola towards the end of 1978. Surviving countless assassination attempts by spooks determined to silence him and threatening to go public to American newspapers, the CIA decided to give him the information he desperately desired and revealed the location of the nazi doctor Josef Mengele. Furthermore, they set him up with a new forged employment record on condition he left America and never returned. Cain promised to settle in Britain and not partake in any actions of revenge against members of the Central Intelligence Agency. He also gave commitments to keep his mouth shut and never reveal his involvement with the spies or any of the Company's operations over the decades. The CIA knew only too well if they broke or interfered with this agreement, Cain would have seen them dead.

CHAPTER SEVENTEEN

"That is some story," Alice said in amazement. "Meeting the Romans and fighting in the Coliseum. Being witness to the destruction of Pompeii and conversing with the Emperor Constantine, but facing years of torture by the Angel of Death and forced to take part in terrible actions by the CIA."

"I very much regret my involvement with the Central Intelligence Agency, the atrocities I had to witness and provoke," Cain sighed. "But it was a necessary evil to find Doctor Josef Mengele and make him pay for his crimes. Even as an old man he still held steadfast to the twisted ideals of the nazi party. At the Nuremberg Trials the Gestapo officers insisted they were only following orders, but I learned that the nazis really believed in their hearts and souls that they were doing the right thing by not just the German people, but the whole world; in their bizarre viewpoint of adopting the Spartan method of selecting only the strong and the pure, and massacring the Jews because they were a convenient scapegoat for Germany's defeat at World War One and of their ancient tenuous link to the execution of Christ."

"It seems you encountered only religious hypocrites like Constantine and monsters like the Romans and Nazis," Alice said. "Perhaps God saw this as a way to redeem yourself, to be tortured mercilessly for nearly a year by the White Angel as a means to atone for the death of your brother."

"Maybe," Cain echoed. "But as much as I regret every day the crime of killing Abel, I have paid a terrible price, not so much the physical pain I endured at the scalpel of Mengele, but more so being a helpless witness to what he did to innocent children I could not protect or save from the gas chambers."

"None of that was your fault, if you had never been born these terrible acts would still have taken place," Alice declared. "Whether an individual lives for a hundred years or six thousand, a person can only do their best by their morals and upbringing and take every day as it comes. The sad fact is that free will is an illusion, we are captives to our fate, our destinies are predetermined by wealth, health and circumstance."

Cain smiled. "Did you learn this philosophy from your father, the fabled Grandmaster?"

"Contrary to what his cronies may think, I do have a mind of my own," Alice sneered.

Cain got up from the bed and went to the window. "It is nearly dawn, the officers stationed outside the hotel room door will be sure to knock soon to take us to the rendezvous."

Alice approached him and embraced him from behind, wrapping her arms around his stomach. "I am so afraid, Cain," she whispered.

He turned around to face her. "Your father needs you alive as coercion for me, to ensure my cooperation for he knows only too well that threats are useless against me."

"I wish I had your confidence," Alice Carson sighed. "Not to mention your physical strength and immortality."

There was a sudden rough knock on the door and she took a step back in apprehension. Cain grabbed hold of her hand and they both opened the door. Standing outside were three armed policemen carrying sub machineguns alongside the all too familiar New Scotland Yard Detectives Albert Maher and Sean Neilson.

"Have a pleasant nap?" Maher asked.

"Not really," Alice replied, stretching herself with fatigue. "Let's just get this over with."

Albert nodded in agreement. "Before we leave, I am curious about one thing, Mr. Philips or whatever your real name is which the CIA won't reveal," the detective said sharply. "Samuel Carson is prepared to risk everything to obtain you, the Illuminati which for centuries was a secret organisation which was unknown to everyone except historians and one fixated author of Vatican-based conspiracy books, now they have become public knowledge and international pariahs akin to Al Qaeda or the Irish Republican Army before the Good Friday Agreement. In short, except for certain Middle East countries that might give them sanctuary, there is nowhere on Earth they can hide or practice their questionable politics. However, now they are fully prepared to throw away not only their ancient heritage, but their very lives on the likely information that you possess. To get to the point, Mr. Philips, who the fuck are you and what do you know that is so damn important?"

"Perhaps it is my irresistible charm they seek," Cain laughed. "Did the American spooks not tell you all about me?"

"Those bastards need an escort taking a shit in case one of their operatives might be writing national secrets on soiled toilet paper," Maher growled. "They are the most paranoid, suspicious of outsiders and insular society I have ever encountered. The only language they understand are threats and their only concern is where their next funding cheque from Congress is coming."

Cain smiled. "I have no real love for authority but I actually like you, detective. However, there is some knowledge best left unknown and some history best forgotten."

Cain snatched hold of Alice's hand and they entered the corridor, closing the door behind them and silencing any further questions. Albert Maher glared after him briefly before ordering the armed cops to follow them out of the hotel and into a waiting van.

"Samuel Carson will likely order you to be stripped and remove all jewellery," Sean Neilson said. "Swallow this tablet, it contains a small transmitter so we can trace your location in case we lose your kidnappers."

Cain glanced at the large blue tube before putting it in his mouth and swallowing it. Sean looked at the policeman staring at a laptop and the cop nodded in return, indicating the bug was operating perfectly.

"We have just received new orders," Maher announced. "We are instructed to leave you on the corner of one of London's most busy streets. There you will be picked up by members of the Illuminati. Once your identity has been certified, they will call off the bombs."

Cain and Alice shook their heads to acknowledge that they understood the command. A short journey later through the capital's congested roads and they reached their destination. The detectives bid them farewell and the van sped off down the street and was soon out of sight. However, Cain knew police officers and probably even army snipers were already in position, this being no ordinary stakeout on small-time criminals. Nothing would be left to chance.

Barely ten minutes passed before a black jeep pulled up alongside them and the back left door swung open. Cain glanced inside and was surprised to see the driver was the only occupant, apparently the Illuminati were either short on operatives or believed only one man was required to ferry them to their real destination. Besides, Cain surmised if he simply killed the single mercenary inside the vehicle, thousands of innocent people would die somewhere in the country from an explosive device.

Cain and Alice got into the jeep and it raced off down the road with no obvious consideration for fellow drivers or pedestrians. Fifty minutes later they arrived at a run down warehouse in an industrial part of London. The mercenary told them to exit the vehicle and enter the large brown building. As soon as they removed themselves, the jeep once more sped off, leaving them standing alone in a dirty courtyard apparently completely deserted. Cain could see neither any people on the adjacent streets or policemen, though he knew they were probably nearby watching their every move and monitoring his location via the transmitter on computer.

They entered the warehouse through a single metal door and were instantly accosted by armed guards, a soldier pushing a revolver into Cain's face. He groaned as the familiar face of Samuel Carson appeared from amongst the assembly of mercenaries.

"I'll wager you hoped to never see me again Mr. Kadmon," the Grandmaster smiled. "And behold the beloved daughter my betrayer. I believe I made a mistake calling off the Muslim wedding with that sheik in Saudi Arabia, perhaps it is time to make a phone call and resume the marriage preparations. I still have the burka."

Alice sneered in defiance. "That old bastard will wake up some morning with his severed testicles served to him in a bowl of ice cream."

"Charming as ever, Alice," Samuel said before turning to one of the guards. "Take her away and for fuck's sake keep a close eye on her this time!"

"You know there is no chance of leaving the country alive," Cain announced.

"Do you take me for a complete fool, Mr. Kadmon?" The Grandmaster retorted. "I know the police and likely even the army are watching this building right now. I have no intention of dying soon or being arrested. Remove his clothes and my daughter's, including their shoes and watches. Examine carefully all buttons and even belt buckles. Drink this." Samuel Carson handed his captive a small vial containing an orange liquid. "Make sure Alice gets the same and give her a plastic bag for puking into."

Cain glanced at the tube. "I won't comply with your demands and I should point out I am used to torture."

"We know about your experiences in Auschwitz, Mr. Kadmon," the Illuminati leader replied and drew alongside a mercenary. "Soldier, remove my daughter's fingernails with a pliers and then proceed onto her toes."

The guard began to leave for the back room when Cain stopped him. "Wait," he said. "Alright, I'll drink it. Give me a bucket unless you want a mess on the floor."

The Grandmaster grinned in satisfaction. "You may be physically strong but you are weak in compassion, Mr. Kadmon. You should have held out, I would have only removed the nails and maybe broken a few fingers. No further violence other than that would have been necessary."

"It is as Alice declared, you really are a monster," Cain sneered. "However, none of you are prepared for what waits for you in Eden, the creatures deformed by dark magick, Lilith a goddess of great evil and the power source at the base of the Tree of Life. Mankind is supposed to exist for another four thousand years, but if you attempt to remove that device or whatever it is at the Tree you will bring the Apocalypse immediately."

"The Illuminati has existed for centuries for one purpose, to establish a world government with us at its head," Samuel said. "We will achieve our aims and it is you Cain that will be the instrument, we are ready for whatever lies at the Tree. And as for the demon Lilith and the animals in Eden, we have purchased weapons including machineguns and flamethrowers, a little twentieth-first century technology for ancient creatures."

Cain drank the blue liquid and promptly vomited into the bucket. Samuel looked into the container and smiled, removing from amongst the waste food the small tube. He placed it in a tissue and put the transmitter into his pocket.

"Aren't you going to destroy that? The police will know your every move while it still functions," Cain said in puzzlement.

"That's exactly what I intend, Mr. Kadmon," the Grandmaster smiled. "I am fully aware the British armed forces know about the boat tonight, we however have arranged different transport to take us to Iraq."

Cain stared at him in confusion and the Illuminati leader began to laugh loudly. Detectives Albert Maher and Sean Neilson were seated alone in a police car nearby listening to conversations between snipers on the rooftops through the radio.

"One of the men says he can see Carson laughing through his scope, he seems pleased to finally have Mr. Philips in his custody," Sean said.

"He won't be too happy tonight when we arrest him and his friends, terrorist offences against the Crown carry a mandatory life sentence," his partner replied. "We have to be careful with this Grandmaster, he's a slippery bastard. If he somehow manages to escape the operation at the docks, I intend to have another conversation with our friends from the Central Intelligence Agency, even if it means arresting them for obstruction and have MI5 carry out their own brand of interrogation on them. I want to know why this Sam Philips is so important to both the Illuminati and the Company."

"All we can do now is wait; time for bad takeaway coffee and stale doughnuts," Sean laughed. "In the meantime, I want to discuss something with you while we are alone of a personal nature. I finally plucked up the courage and left my wife."

"Well, it's about fucking time," Albert sighed. "My ears can at last rest from all the complaining, I know there were financial concerns to consider, particularly in relation to your two young boys, but in the long term it will be for the best. I warned you about the dangers of marrying an only child; such infants are worshipped by adoring parents who overlook their child's faults and exaggerate their achievements. No husband can ever attain the idolised position an only daughter has for her father, despite his barefaced lies and fantasies, and no son-in-law no matter his profession, family breeding or wealth can become worthy of dating their daughter. It is ironic to think that the emotional problems your wife has faced her entire adult life is of a direct consequence of bad parenting; your mother-in-law, the psycho hag from hell and the father-in-law; the delusional fantasist who denies to your face the accomplishments you have done for him, and whom consistently does not check his facts before making gross assumptions about your parenting skills!"

Sean nodded in agreement. "It's time to set the record straight once and for all, enough of the lies and half-truths; the he said and she said endless stories. At last perhaps I can sleep in a proper bed and not a mouldy sleeping bag in the spare room. I firmly believe a person can look back through their life and pinpoint almost the exact moment it all went wrong for them, when she denied me sex first in quality and then quantity, even before we got married. I naively thought it was simply a phase or something that could be worked through over time, but it only got worse to the stage where we were intimate if you could even call it that once a year. But most of all it is the supreme arrogance and refusal to even listen to another person's opinion, especially if it might contradict hers. I have had enough of being browbeaten with her college degrees and daily reminders of paying the mortgage, while ignoring the many bills I have paid and achievements I have accomplished. The primary problem is she does not understand the concept of compromise, only submission. The sad fact is after nearly ten years, I have forgotten what it is to be in love. I criticise others for their belief in marriage or plans for betrothal because I have lost my own faith in that emotion, at times doubting after so long that it ever existed. She allows her psychotic mother to assault or threaten me on a regular basis, even making vague threats in front of my children against me as if it were normal behaviour. My wife says one day my sons will see me for what I am and spit in my face to her amusement, but she should be more worried about what they will really think of someone like her. I now firmly believe that as a woman ages, they care less for handsomeness and sense of humour in a man, but favour instead a thick wallet and a willingness to listen to endless nagging; a husband in their eyes should be obedient without question. Every time she leaves the house my wife orders me to perform some mundane task so it will interfere with my work or any possibility of enjoyment in her absence, as if it were punishment for marrying her. What really irritates me is that she can smell a fifty pound note a mile away as if she were some kind of money bloodhound, and sees my wages as some type of free-for-all; in essence what is mine is hers, and what is her own is hers also. I am allowed no material possessions, the only reason she permits me the clothes I wear is simply because I cannot go to work naked. Every day she becomes more like her mentally unstable mother, the same bitterness with life; the same emotional and sexual deadness inside."

Maher stared at his friend. "I have a good relationship with my spouse because we respect each other's opinion, she doesn't view me as a doormat; a serf whose only purpose in life is to hand over all my money, and she does not see my hobbies and interests outside of my job as a distraction or inconvenience to doing endless housework. My wife is a reasonable person who realises while it is important to maintain a clean and presentable home for yourself and surprise visitors, it should never be considered your vocation in life; after all a hundred years from now someone else will be cleaning your house, in essence despite advances in technology hoovering and polishing will never end."

"The main problem here is that the girlfriend I fell in love with and the wife I married are complete opposites, it is as if something died inside her and never came back." Sean sighed. "Every day she becomes more like her volatile mother, consumed with bitterness that life and fate have dealt her a bad hand, that all of her problems are someone else's fault. She is obsessed with the 'grass being greener on the other side,' of the neighbours, her work colleagues and friends who have material goods seemingly denied her because of her parents' view that she married beneath her. Her mother believes her daughter being a high-earning professional should have a husband who is a doctor or an engineer. It would not matter if he was an asshole, as long as he was bringing in greater money than her so she could enjoy a better life. I have tried many times to be a good father and spouse before I eventually became a bad husband, withdrawing into my own separate interests of playing on the playstation and watching repeat movies into the early hours. We became 'strangers in the night,' at first fighting over everything and anything, obsessed with points scoring before finally ignoring each other. I became engrossed in my work and these activities, angry most of the time from sleep deprivation and the way she talked to me like as if I were scum."

"And yet you still remain in that house buying furniture and paying bills, doing voluntary housework without thanks and even going on holidays at your own expense," Albert said.

"I have been a fool with eyes open, somehow hoping things would get better, but the more I tried she still remained the same emotionless Ice Queen; a bully and a tyrant who tells her biased psycho mother about all the work she performs and bills she pays while steadfastly ignoring mine; it's all about what I didn't pay for and tasks I didn't do in the last five minutes, not what you did in the distant past; in essence she has a selective memory and even when she is confronted with the absolute truth she does not apologise believing I am not worthy of it. I know I am not perfect and am certainly no angel having committed many mistakes, but I am not the Devil she claims me to be while idolising herself as a saint with no flaws. My wife believes without a shred of doubt that she should be called Your Majesty, but the only things she is a Queen of is perpetual nagging and bitchiness where everything is a problem. The main issue here is that I married a wolf in sheep's clothing whom revealed its fangs when my flesh was at its weakest and most vulnerable; when she had hooked the fish."

"Just console yourself there are plenty more fish in the sea and not as many sharks," Albert laughed. "And don't worry for an instant about her finding a replacement husband after you have left for no man would put up with a fishwife like that for very long."

Sean smiled in response as they drank their coffee in silence awaiting the night and the police operation that would finally bring this terrorist activity to an end. Several hours passed and Detective Maher started the car upon hearing on the radio that masked men could be seen getting into two vans, the transmitter identifying that their suspect was being transported. They followed the vehicles from a safe distance, remaining out of sight and watched as the vans approached the docks. The Illuminati parked alongside a motor-powered large yacht and the men departed from the vehicles and began to board.

"Wait until they all aboard," Albert said over the radio to the two hundred policemen and MI5 operatives stationed nearby. "There are armed gunboats just outside the harbour preventing their escape, we will intercept them all and catch them red-handed together on the ship. The suspect Sam Philips and Alice Carson must not be harmed, the transmitter identifies they are on board."

His partner watched the same mercenary that had driven Cain to the warehouse depart from the yacht and get back into one of the vans, the rest of the twenty Illuminati members remaining on the ship.

"What is he up to?" Sean Neilson declared and watched the vehicle begin to leave the dock, the soldier removing a device from his pocket with an aerial attached. "What is that he has got there?" The detective shouted before realising in shock at what was about to happen. "Quick, everyone move on that van and arrest that man."

The mercenary slowed the vehicle to a halt and watched the thirty armed police officers including Albert Maher and Sean Neilson approach him. The detectives saw the man smile as he pressed a button on the device. At first nothing happened and the soldier stared down at the machine in confusion before suddenly an explosion occurred on the dock. The yacht still apparently containing the twenty Illuminati members exploded in a huge plume of fire and smoke. The policemen gazed as their prime suspects including Sam Philips, Alice and most importantly Samuel Carson died, helpless to intervene and knowing it was too late to save their lives. The ship began to sink and the detectives could only stand by as observers.

Albert Maher opened the van door and pulled the mercenary to the ground. "Why did you do that? Why did you kill your master?"

The soldier laughed in reply and Sean Neilson picked him up and shoved him against the bonnet of the vehicle. "It doesn't make sense," the detective said and then his mouth dropped in realisation. "Samuel Carson wasn't on board, was he? He sacrificed those people including all those that knew too much, so he could escape with his daughter and Sam Philips."

"You're too late cop," the mercenary smiled. "We planted your transmitter with the Illuminati members who no longer were necessary including the Chief Constable and the Lord Mayor. They were unaware of their true fate, I would have loved to see their smug faces as their flesh was burnt from their bones. My employer including his brat and Cain are on their way via private jet at a secluded airport outside of London, being transported to Iraq."

Albert Maher ran back to the police car and radioed the Home Office. He returned several minutes later, his face contorted in rage.

"This bastard speaks the truth, they left two hours ago on a private airplane registered to some Saudi Arabian sheik, they are now over international waters and beyond our jurisdiction," the detective growled. "The jet will likely refuel at Morocco and pass through Syria before entering Iraq. They will be careful to keep to flying over water and not enter any country, ensuring we cannot call on any nation to intercept them. The American army may have completely withdrawn from Iraq, but I'll wager the Central Intelligence Agency still has agents operating inside the troubled country. It's about time we paid the spooks a call and see what they know about this Sam Philips or Cain."

"Throw this piece of shit into a police car and have MI5 interview him," Sean said. "Time for suntan oil and shorts for a hot summer in Iraq."

His partner shook his head in dismay and smiled. "I don't know which will be worse, Al Qaeda militants or your hairy tree trunk legs."

CHAPTER EIGHTEEN

"I hope those chains don't chafe too much, Mr. Kadmon," Samuel Carson grinned. "I wouldn't want you to get too uncomfortable. I spared no expense in getting that titanium steel to ensure no further escapes. Don't look so glum, after all you're going home."

Cain stared at the Grandmaster in anger but did not respond. He watched the thirty mercenaries assemble their weapons in preparation for Iraq to defend against rogue elements of the Taliban operating well beyond Helmand Province and Afghanistan, the terrorists flexing their muscles to show they can strike at foreigners anywhere. But the guns' primary function was for the Zagros Mountains and Eden where all manner of creatures driven mad by dark magick awaited them.

"We'll land at Baghdad International Airport, the Russian army vacating some time ago in favour of local militia," Carson declared. "We have contacts within the Iraqi government sympathetic to our cause and especially our American dollars. They will provide armoured transport to the northern mountains in a few days. Let's enjoy the hospitality of our friends in the meantime, of course your accommodation will be less than comfortable, Mr. Kadmon."

"I was born in the desert, I am used to hardship," Cain sneered. "But be aware, once I am certain of Alice's safety and she is far from your reach, first available opportunity I am going to feed you your own entrails."

The mercenaries burst into laughter, no stranger to threats from bound captives.

"You will find those chains unbreakable, Mr. Kadmon," Samuel smirked. "And you will remain in them until we are at the Tree. To think we will soon be entering Paradise, the cradle of civilisation where no person has been in six thousand years, the birthplace of the first human. Perhaps we might bump into your father there?"

"Adam vowed to leave this planet once he founded Babylon,[46] my parents are long gone with no possibility of ever seeing them again."

"That's truly sad," one of the mercenaries remarked in a sarcastic tone. "I never met my father and my mother was turning tricks just to make ends meet, spending all her whoring money on booze. I was raised by the State in a foster home, beaten every day by a vicious drunk and left home at sixteen to join the army. However, I am grateful for the bruises and broken bones for it made me the man I am today, as mean a bastard as any hard soldier should be."

"And a free education it was too," another mercenary said and they all laughed.

The pilot peaked around the door leading to the cockpit to announce they were approaching the Iraqi main airport and that they should fasten their seatbelts. Twenty minutes later they had touched down and were greeted by government officials, their pockets lined with American dollars. Six armoured jeeps lay on the tarmac awaiting their inspection. Samuel Carson nodded his approval and the Iraqis saluted him.

"We have secluded accommodation for you in Baghdad," one of the officials declared. "You should leave immediately, this country is crawling

---

[46] *Baghdad.*

with American spies. The forces of Occupation may have departed, but their insidious spooks remain and are always watching."

"How soon before you can guarantee the road to the Zagros Mountains?" The Grandmaster enquired. "We have urgent plans there and every minute only draws suspicious eyes to armed foreigners."

"We will have removed all landmines and homemade bombs from the path within the next forty-eight hours," the Iraqi replied. "Although the Taliban and Al Qaeda's focus is on southern Afghanistan and the invading American army, you should be aware that they have operatives and suicide bombers everywhere."

"Hence the need for speed, the longer we stay the greater the risk of detection and having a captive in our possession who bears Middle Eastern features only adds to the danger," Samuel said sharply.

The company left the plane and entering the jeeps were soon on the road to the Iraqi capital. Cain watched through the window at the poverty and destroyed buildings on their approach to the safe-house, the consequences of an illegal war to remove a CIA puppet who no longer obeyed his former masters, but who committed in their eyes the greatest error of irritating neo-conservatives seeking new oil fields and weapons traders, and especially a gullible president already angry at an assassination attempt on his overbearing father.

"What a waste of human life," Cain remarked. "Over one hundred and fifty thousand civilians dead to remove a dictator."

"A despot they could have easily eliminated with no loss of life to their own troops had they only supported the rebellion in Basra a few years earlier. The Iraqi rebels, like so many other nations were deceived by the Central Intelligence Agency who promised in words the moon and stars but when it came to the crunch offered only peanuts, the Iraqi patriots and the northern tribes the Kurds were decimated as the spooks stood by; an ancient culture eradicated simply because if the Iraqis had determined their own future without foreign intervention they would have secured the oil fields for their own civilians and not be forced to hand them freely to international unscrupulous investors," Samuel added.

"I wonder if they believe they are better off without Saddam Hussein?" Cain asked. "At least there was very little crime and the state services like electricity and water worked."

"In the long run with elected democracy they will have opportunities they could only dream of under the Hussein regime, like Russia after the fall of the Soviet Union which at first was virtually bankrupt but now is on the verge of once again returning to being a superpower," the Grandmaster said. "Government corruption on every level will be prevalent for decades, like Ireland who after removing themselves from the English Empire suffers even now after nearly a century political bribes and backhanders. In time these will be exorcised from a society whom no longer accepts such behaviour as the norm."

"You speak eloquently of injustices," Cain remarked. "Such comments do not usually arise from the mouth of someone from the Illuminati. Be careful, I might for a second almost believe you had principles."

"My father believed in a classical education derived from many cultures, not just western colleges in America but also the Middle East and China," Samuel stated. "People often say travel broadens the mind, but it is experiencing different thought processes from learned professors who sometimes have opposing viewpoints that gives your mind focus. Don't confuse this extensive experience and education I possess with principles; that has no place in the Illuminati."

Cain stared at the Grandmaster, knowing now without a doubt that he was conversing with the most intelligent and dangerous individual he had ever met in six thousand years. He remembered Adam warning him how devious and manipulative his first wife Lilith was, always fidgeting at her fingernails, barely able to keep under control her violent outbursts, often sating this rage on a passing animal and tearing the creature to shreds. But the clinical and cold emotionless manner of Samuel Carson was a far greater threat, and Cain now knew he would have to stop the Grandmaster even if it meant his own life, for in Eden he would be vulnerable and susceptible to a mortal injury like an ordinary human. Nevertheless, it was a risk he would have to take if it became necessary.

"One last question," Cain enquired. "You had that Detective Inspector Richard Bellings assassinated when he was captured in order to ensure his silence, and yet you freely allowed the police to detain the mercenary at the dock who blew up the yacht and killed the other Illuminati members."

Samuel smiled. "I am not concerned. That soldier volunteered for the task, he has mere weeks to live as he was recently diagnosed with advanced terminal cancer. I promised his wife and children would be well cared for in the way of a lump sum after his death. He has nothing to lose by being arrested but everything to forfeit if he talks, besides his military training will make him resistant to interrogation."

They arrived at the safe-house on the outskirts of the city, far from prying eyes. The mercenaries placed Cain in the basement which contained no furniture or windows. Two armed soldiers stood guard a few feet away from him, their eyes never leaving their captive and would be relieved every twelve hours by another two guards. They had been given orders to shoot the chained prisoner in the feet if he even tried to sit up, ensuring he would not escape a second time.

Cain attempted to push the thick metal rings to establish with his great strength if it had a breaking point, but quickly found it was a useless waste of energy, the layers of titanium steel wrapped around his lying body was unbreakable in his constrictive position. If his arms were free he might have some possibility of pulling the rings apart, one link at a time with his superior strength, but with the limbs bound in several layers of titanium it was pointless to consider. The Grandmaster appeared and smiled down at his captive.

"Hope the accommodation is to your liking," Samuel laughed. "You will remain here until we are ready to travel to the Zagros Mountains. However, I am not a complete monster, I have a visitor for you to wish you goodnight."

Three mercenaries escorted a bound Alice Carson down the flight of stairs and Cain noticed she had been crying.

"You son of a bitch, if you have harmed her you will have to find another guide to take you to Eden," Cain snarled.

"Relax Mr. Kadmon," the Grandmaster said. "I only inflict violence when it is necessary. I am not Doctor Mengele or the Roman lanista in the Coliseum, I do not worship bloodshed and pain, but neither am I afraid to use it."

"Don't worry Alice, we will get through this," Cain said to the weeping female. "Once I get out of these chains, we will leave this place and never return. If I get free, rest assured I will come back for you."

The soldiers and Samuel Carson laughed. "There is no escape this time and Alice will not return to this basement," the Grandmaster declared. "The Iraqi officials have been well bribed, giving me absolute licence to do what I want. Even if you managed to free yourself which is impossible, I have the authority to round up a hundred civilians from nearby buildings and shoot them, no questions asked and no retribution given. Their deaths will be on your conscience as punishment for escape."

The Grandmaster, Alice and all the mercenaries bar the two at the bottom of the stairs left, leaving Cain to his solitude. He stared at the soldiers in rage and attempted to sit himself up. One of the guards approached their prisoner in response. He knelt down and revealing a large syringe, injected the strange liquid into Cain's arm.

"This is horse tranquilliser," the mercenary said. "We are unsure how much to give someone of your strength, so it is best to be over-cautious and inject you with enough tranquilliser to put an entire herd of stallions to sleep for a month."

Cain grimaced with the pain as the poison travelled through his system. He began to feel drowsy, but did not fall completely asleep. Instead he started to see shadows everywhere and mysterious coloured lights all over the basement. The faces of the two soldiers appeared strange and contorted, and he realised he was hallucinating.

He shook his head, trying to focus his mind as he watched what seemed to be a lone figure appear near the top of the stairs. The hooded person jumped the entire long flight of steps in a single bound which Cain knew was impossible. The peculiar nightmarish individual grabbed one of the mercenaries from behind, putting the arm around the soldier's neck and with a quick tug, broke the guard's neck. The person then punched the other soldier in the face with a sickening crunch, killing him instantly. Cain began to drift in and out of conscious, but could just barely distinguish the mysterious figure remove the layers of titanium steel and heaving Cain over it's cloaked shoulder, travelled back up the stairs and out of the building. Cain could see through his zombie like haze three more mercenaries near the entrance, their bodies lying at odd angles, obviously dead.

The strange individual brought the barely awake Cain through several streets before stopping outside a ruined house. The figure placed the prisoner on the ground and shoved a blue liquid into his mouth. Cain coughed but managed to swallow it, his senses slowly returning. However, he was still too drugged to see the person's face to identify his rescuer. The hooded figure stood up to leave, but Cain grabbed hold of the sleeve, fearing this individual would always remain a mystery.

"Who are you?" Cain asked. "Why did you free me from the basement and risk your life with the guards? I have been too long from this place; my home country to have any friends."

"You have little time son of Adam," the hooded individual said in a voice Cain thought seemed familiar. "Recover your strength quickly and leave this city, your jailers will be looking for you. Your long life journey is nearing an end, but events have to yet unfold to discover your redemption."

Cain watched the figure leave and disappear into the street. He slowly raised himself to his feet and thought he could hear what seemed like Samuel Carson screaming in rage not far away. He began to stumble into the crowd going about their daily business, his skin colour and Arab appearance not looking out of place, ensuring he could blend easily amongst the people.

"How is this possible?" The Grandmaster shouted, gazing out into the road, hoping to see their captive. "That metal was unbreakable, and yet the titanium rings are stretched completely out of shape as if they were cardboard."

"I don't know sir," one of the mercenaries replied. "An industrial pliers the like of which firemen use at car accidents to cut trapped drivers from their vehicles would not be able to sever the metal easily, and yet this intruder broke the chains in mere seconds, considering the time from when we heard the first commotion of the guards being killed and us reaching the cellar."

"And this individual was fast enough to carry Cain out of the house and into the crowd before we got downstairs, extraordinary." Samuel declared. "I would very much like to establish the identity of this bastard. In the meantime, round up the hundred civilians from the adjacent buildings and the street, we need to keep to the commitment I made in the basement and give a warning to Mr. Kadmon, that the longer he remains in hiding, the more innocent people will die. Let his conscience be the guide that leads him back to our door."

The soldier nodded and ordered the remaining company of twenty-five guards to kick in doors and drag the residents including women and children into the road and lined them up against the nearby wall to be shot. Alice Carson appeared at the door to the safe-house, still bound and escorted by a mercenary who pushed her out of the building.

She stared at the events unfolding in shock. "Father please stop this," she said fearfully. "This madness has to come to an end. At what point is enough?"

Samuel snarled. "I'll say when it is enough. We have come too far to turn back, the Illuminati are now an illegal organisation in America and Europe. We have to find Eden or die trying, there is no other choice left open to me."

"What has happened to you?" Alice asked. "Consider what you inherited from grandfather Walter Carson; your own father who once ruled the Illuminati world council and whom hoped you would possess the wisdom to govern after his death. There has to be another way."

"That coward never understood me since the day I was born," Samuel retorted sharply. "I will be strong where he was weak. I'll show you what it means to be ruthless and without compassion."

The Grandmaster nodded to the soldiers who stood with weapons raised to the trembling and frightened civilians lined up against the dirty wall.

As the hundreds of shots rang out, Samuel Carson closed his eyes and began to remember the events from his earlier life which formed the tapestry that brought him to this place.

CHAPTER NINETEEN

A Grandmaster's Tale

Walter Carson stood at the bottom of the grandiose staircase, losing patience with his only son, fifteen year old Samuel. "Christ boy, where are you?" The sixty year old shouted. "It is the year 1970, but it will be the millennium before I get you to school. I have a meeting with the sheik; the nephew of the ruler of Saudi Arabia within the hour. Don't you know these Arabs have no tolerance for lack of punctuality?"

"Apologies, father," Samuel finally said as he appeared at the top of the stairs. "It's bad enough to wear this ridiculous uniform, but those dark-skinned classmates of mine mock my blond hair, pale skin and not to mention my American accent."

"Unfortunately we both still carry the Chicago taint in our voices, but I find it useful in business with the Arabs as they respect Americans," his father retorted.

"They respect American dollars as the United States is the single biggest purchaser of petrol, but deep down they despise us. You only have to listen to my arrogant school colleagues to appreciate the hostility they bear," Samuel said. "It may take thirty years but that hatred will be visited upon America, whether it be terrorist bombs or driving commercial airplanes into skyscrapers. However, a war with Saudi Arabia will never come, their oil fields will secure that false peace between our two countries, and presidents will find convenient scapegoats in less wealthy nations."

Walter Carson shook his head in shock. "What are they teaching you in that private school? They promised a classical education from the writings of Alexander, the Roman Petronius and many others, but next they will be teaching Oscar Wilde."

Samuel laughed. "I very much doubt that, you know how much the Saudi Arabians loathe homosexuality. They would consider such books subversive, and would decapitate you in the street for less. You only have to examine what they do to so-called adulterous women to understand their hypocrisy, beating females for looking at another man sideways while they frequently visit prostitutes by night. They deprive women of the vote, higher education and any chance of independence; subjugating half of the population by enforcing the full dress burka. Saudi Arabia is only one step above Iran where they stone women on rumour after forcing them to dig their own unmarked grave."

"It's comments and views like that which get you into so much trouble at school," Walter said. "I don't wish to receive another phone call while I am in a business meeting about a bullying incident involving an older classmate who may have mocked your accent. The Arabs do not tolerate interruptions."

"Those sheiks are too scared of you to pass judgements," Samuel retorted. "The sitting head of the Illuminati World Council controls every situation, those Arabs take a breath and silence their chatter when you enter the room, knowing a single phone call could destroy their precious reputation and even their life."

Walter Carson glared at his son in anger. "I told you never to speak about such things, loose talk sinks ships as they said in the billboards for the great war. Perhaps one day you might inherit the title, but if you throw your weight around, the Council will decide you should rule a smaller part of the organisation instead, maybe South Africa or even England where all they do is take bribes and self-congratulate themselves on how fucking brilliant they are. That is the difference between a simple Grandmaster of a country or region, or the Supreme Grandmaster who governs the entire globe."

"Since as you once declared that I am incapable of taking orders, I had better achieve the latter," Samuel sneered.

"If arrogance was a prerequisite qualification for membership into the Illuminati, you would be ruling the Council alone and not needing any subordinates." Walter stated sharply. "Excessive violence is not a trait appreciated either, I heard what you did to the last bully in school who crossed your path, was it really necessary to deliberately break his arm?"

Samuel smiled. "It was a warning to the others, shatter the limb of the superior bully and his lesser cronies will leave you alone; it was an exercise in power."

His father sighed. "You are destined for great things my son, but all you will do is create enemies who do not respect you and every day plot your downfall."

"Your subordinates in the Illuminati do not respect you either father, a Brutus wearing the clothes of a friend lurks in the shadows waiting for your demise and his moment to shine. Absolute fear is a far more powerful and useful weapon than meaningless adoration, the person who licks your arse every day is the individual who plans your death."

"Funny you should that," Walter smiled. "The World Council which resides in New York has requested my presence. It appears the Vice-Supreme Grandmaster has begun to question my leadership and wishes a new vote on my ability to rule. An assembly has been called for next week. A successful election would silence this creep called William Masterson and finally put the subject to rest."

"Is he a threat?" Samuel enquired. "If he wins the vote, does that mean you will be demoted to Grandmaster of a region or country, or worse a bullet to the back of the head?"

"Contrary to what you might have read, the Illuminati is not the Italian Mafia," his father laughed. "We don't take failed members to a cliff and push them over, I would like to believe we are more civilised than that."

"So why do you sound so worried?" Samuel replied.

"You should be more concerned with getting to school on time," Walter Carson declared. "Leave the problems of adults to their own affairs."

Samuel sighed in reply and running down the stairs, went out of the door and into the waiting car. They left the mansion behind and entered the busy streets, Rolls Royces and similar expensive vehicles passing by them, sheiks being chauffeur driven to skyscrapers in the oil obsessed city Riyadh. Samuel was astonished by the sheer wealth of the country, even though he travelled this same route every day; it never ceased to amaze him. Incredible luxury abounded everywhere, from the many gold heavy chains which adorned the Arab's necks to the five-star hotels catering to celebrities and American businessmen with thick wallets.

Walter Carson dropped his son to school and swiftly departed for an urgent meeting. Samuel groaned, the all too familiar bullies from a class senior to his were waiting at the entrance, their arms folded in smug satisfaction of their superiority in physical strength and numbers.

"Well, if it isn't the blond yank," the leader of the Arabian gang grinned. "Our friend is still in hospital with the broken arm, care to try your chances with me and my pals, you will find us a harder and tougher target."

"You obviously are stupid that you didn't heed the warning I gave. I was too soft on your comrade, he got away easy," Samuel sneered.

The eldest boy ran at Samuel, but the American managed to sidestep out of the way and at the same time, tripped the Arab up. The bully fell on his face, slapping his nose off the ground, the blood splattering across the playground. Samuel could hear the familiar "Hey everyone, a fight" nearby, but did not take his focus off the remaining three boys who advanced on him.

A rather fat Arab dressed in a white silken pants and short-sleeved top, complete with traditional headband approached the young American, waddling like a duck out of water, his enormous body mass swinging from side to side. Samuel punched him in the stomach, but to no obvious effect, the obese schoolboy laughing at the feeble strike. The American looked in puzzlement at this ridiculous bully before him before slapping him across the face. The fat Arab stared at his opponent in momentary shock before bursting into tears, the liquid streaming down his face. Samuel could only watch in amusement as the boy ran off, trying his best to keep the back of his pants up and prevent his tremendous bum-cleavage being displayed to the now gathered audience.

Samuel did not wait for the two remaining boys to approach, jumping up the steps towards them. The burst of speed took the bullies by surprise and the young American grabbed the taller schoolboy by the testicles, holding his balls in a tight grip. The Arab screamed in pain and fright and placing his hands on Samuel's shoulders, pleaded with him to stop. The other boy took a few steps back, shocked by the ferocity of the attack and not wishing the same treatment.

"You must be jerking off every hour if it hurts that much, I thought masturbation was against your code of conduct, or is it just girls that are forbidden from touching themselves?" Samuel snarled. "I don't enjoy violence, but I understand its necessity and I am not afraid to use it. I believe this time the warning will be understood and heeded?"

The two boys nodded and the American released his grip, the Arab clutching his crotch in agony. They picked up their leader from the ground, still nursing his shattered nose but glad the assault was over. The crowd of assembled schoolboys began to shout and cheer in applause, the bullies long been a terror and nuisance in the play-yard.

Samuel smiled, knowing it was as he had told his father earlier, fear is always greater than respect. Phoney friends would now gravitate towards him, but would be less likely to betray him. Craving respect was akin to cowardice and bravery alike to stupidity. This Samuel knew with certainty, the clear differences between him and his father. Secret handshakes mingled with cash favours to buy false respect from devious Illuminati subordinates, in the naïve belief that a confrontation or betrayal in the future would be less probable; this was cowardice by another name and this Samuel knew was his father's crime and would surely be his downfall. The young American also believed bravery; sticking your neck out in situations that were unwise just to gain favouritism and impress Grandmasters who saw you as inferior was stupidity in disguise. Samuel vowed to himself a different path; the road less travelled where he would secure a following of powerful politicians and businessmen, but always keep them at arm's length and consider them expendable when their usefulness expired.

The bell for classes rang out and Samuel left the gathering which already had begun to disperse, proud and satisfied this matter was finally put to rest. The remainder of the day and the week went without any further problems and his father notified the school that Samuel would be absent the following ten days as they departed on the Saturday morning for Riyadh airport and transport to the United States. They arrived several hours later in New York where an escort awaited their presence at the terminal. The two Americans were delivered to a five star hotel in the centre of the city.

Walter Carson and his son had just entered their huge room boasting a leather suite of sofas, chairs and two king-size beds when the telephone in the chamber rang. Walter picked up the receiver and sighed as he heard the familiar voice of his former friend and now challenger William Masterson.

"Good evening my old friend," the forty-two year old Vice-Supreme Grandmaster of the Illuminati said down the line. "I hope you are not too jet-lagged for tomorrow's debate and vote, I would hate to see you not at your best and be forced to step down, being found lacking in rhetoric."

"Don't worry for me, old friend," Walter retorted sharply. "You should be burning the midnight oil brushing up on your own wordplay, rather than ringing and trying your intimating skills on your betters."

William Masterson growled down the phone in rage. "See you in the morning, old man. When we are through I'll make you Grandmaster for Siberia."

"Still think the Illuminati are not like the Mafia?" Samuel smiled.

"Get some sleep, it will be a long day tomorrow," his father replied, placing the telephone back into its receiver. "Because of my rank I have special privileges, one of which includes being able to name my assistant for such a crucial debate. This person has to be an Illuminati member, sworn in before the World Council, I guess there is no better time for you to take a front row seat at the Coliseum."

Samuel's mouth dropped open in shock. "I am to be a member of the Illuminati? I'll wager not many fifteen year olds can claim that title."

"Well, you are nearly sixteen and in Saudi Arabia you would be considered a man at that age, having the right to marry and vote." Walter said. "However, they will require you to be disciplined in the knowledge of the order; including history, the writings of former members of high renown and secret sciences especially the occult before taking your rank and seat in the lower council. You will be twenty-five years old by the time that happens, but your title and rights will be waiting for you when you graduate."

Samuel Carson laughed in delight and went straight to bed, dreaming of ruling the world as only a teenager could. His father on the other hand started to improve on his speech, knowing the following morning would bring heated debate and the loser risk losing his seat and in certain cases, even his life.

The two Americans woke early, Walter Carson tossing throughout the night in apprehension, his young son awake at dawn from excitement as if it were Christmas morning and his presents awaited. They dressed quickly and after a brief breakfast left the hotel and entered the waiting chauffeur-driven Mercedes.

Samuel Carson watched the busy traffic from the back window, mothers bringing their children to school, fathers hurrying to work. Although this was the liberal seventies after the wild sex and rock-n-roll of the sixties, times had moved very slowly; the men were still the breadwinners and the women the stay at home housewives, content with watching daytime soap-operas while fantasising about the main characters. Their bored husbands carried out worse tasks, enduring shouting and derogatory insults from jumped-up bullies half their age while bonus-craving two-a-penny secretaries gave them blowjobs from under the table. This was the American Dream, his father told him; cleaning up other people's shit, hoping one day while mopping up vomit, piss and semen stains on the floors of café-toilets they would be spotted by some grubby slob Hollywood agent desperate for the next face on the top shelf porno video cover. Samuel knew without even experiencing this mundane life that so many millions of illegal immigrants and high-school dropouts throughout the United States lived every day without cessation and hope, that the only way to truly succeed in America was to either be born of wealthy parents or be a member of a powerful and influential organisation like the Freemasons or the Illuminati, where bribes and backhanders were handed out like coffee and biscuits, keeping the subordinates content to wash your car and fetch the newspaper; as loyal as a dog so long as you keep feeding it, otherwise it will have ambitions on your throat.

They arrived at a magnificent mansion situated on the outskirts of New York in the centre of large grounds surrounded by twenty-foot walls. Samuel guessed the isolation was necessary to ensure secluded privacy, armed guards at the entrance and several more wandering through the grass guaranteeing no intruders or nosey journalists. A single man dressed in a red uniform including a multi-coloured tie which Samuel believed must have been picked out by his grandmother approached and opened the back door. Walter Carson got out and his son swiftly followed. The young American noticed many more chauffeur-driven cars pull up and their occupants leave and enter the mansion quickly, eager to hear the promised debate.

Waiters and subordinates immediately ran to greet the Supreme Grandmaster and his heir apparent offering glasses of champagne and their support prior to the crucial vote later in the evening. Samuel had heard his father declare these cowardly Council wannabes and lackeys would kiss the arse of the Devil if they believed for a moment it might give them a second's audience with God. Brief pleasant hypocrisies passed between Walter and the cronies before a bell rang out, signalling the higher and lower Council to the backroom chamber to be assembled for the debate. Walter Carson caught sight of his one-time friend and now sworn enemy William Masterson as he rushed to be first into the room, as if this eagerness for battle would increase his chances of success.

The members of the Illuminati gathered into their seats, the windowless chamber having the atmosphere of a Coliseum, the wooden chairs situated in a circle three deep on an incline, the debaters separated from their colleagues by a four foot oak wall which surrounded them. Before them on a raised platform sat the eight remaining members of the High Council, two seats vacant belonging to the debaters; the challenger and the defender.

Standing next to William Masterson was his younger brother John acting as his assistant, carrying a bottle of water and his notes. Walter Carson stepped forward and beckoned to his son to come into the light of the arena.

"I present Samuel my only child and heir as my assistant," the Supreme Grandmaster declared. "Though he is only fifteen, I believe he has adequate knowledge and understanding to fulfil the duties required of him. It is my wish that one day he succeeds me in my role and leads this society into the millennium and the twenty-first century."

"High Council, I must protest," Masterson interrupted. "We are assembled here tonight to vote on the worthiness and ability of Walter Carson to continue as our leader, and he has the sheer arrogance to defile these proceedings by forcing his child barely out of nappies onto us and attempt to proclaim him as our future ruler. You must object on reasons of sanity and justice and throw this impudent infant out of this chamber which is designated strictly for members of the Illuminati only."

"Vice-Supreme Grandmaster Masterson," the oldest council member said and leaned forward. "By challenging your superior in open debate and requesting a vote of confidence, you have placed a question over your own abilities as leader in waiting of this society. It is up to us and not you that decides the fate of Samuel Carson. It is our judgement that the boy be accepted as a novice member and be sent for training in the arts and knowledge of the order, perhaps one day with proper guidance and accomplishments he can stand before a future council and proclaim his abilities, in hope of securing the position of leader. In the meantime, he will fulfil the role of assistant to his accused father. If Walter Carson is declared unable to continue as head of this organisation, the ruling will stand and his son will be accepted into the order; the sins of the father do not pass onto the child. As regards matters of justice, Mr. Masterson, you once held the position of Grandmaster of the African continent and sanctioned Illuminati help in the Apartheid government of South Africa, supporting the army in their persecution of the landless blacks in return for gold; money this society has yet to see. You went behind the backs of this council and had dealings with a totalitarian regime; the pariahs of the free world and jeopardised this organisation, risking our involvement in that political chaos and potentially exposing our existence to the governments of the world."

William Masterson bit his lip in frustration but did not respond as Walter Carson smiled to himself in satisfaction. Samuel gingerly stepped forward and one of the High Council members leaned forward, placing a blue ribbon over his shoulder, signifying his introduction into the order. The young American turned around and grinned at his father in delight as Walter nodded his approval.

"Let us begin before we are all too old and deaf to hear," growled the Vice-Supreme Grandmaster, snatching his notes from his brother in growing temper. "It is my contention that our esteemed leader has lost sight of the aims of this society. Blinded by the recent death of his wife from cancer and secluded from the centre of the organisation by long periods in self-imposed isolation in the Middle-East, he has forgotten his brothers; the members of the society from whom he has run away like a coward and hid in the comforts of his Arab friends, his new order of heathens."

Walter Carson laughed. "That is pretty weak, even from you William," the father of Samuel announced. "I have worked tirelessly in Jordan and Saudi Arabia to further the interests and coffers of the Illuminati, taking only a modest wage for myself, the rest of the profits from my business dealings going straight to the society. While the air of corruption hangs over your head and your questionable dealings in Africa, my conscience is clear."

"Any further statements to make, Mr. Masterson?" The oldest of the High Council asked. "If not these debates are at an end and we vote."

The Vice-Supreme Grandmaster shook his head, signalling he had no more questions or allegations of guilt to make, the declaration of the oldest member of the Illuminati on the platform earlier taking the wind out of his sails.

"This should be brief," Walter whispered to his son and smiled.

A large bucket was passed around the chamber as all the members wrote their choice on a small piece of paper, a society based on bribes emphasising the need for a secret ballot. However, the decision was clear and without doubt as after several minutes of counting the eight men of the High Council read out the verdict; Walter Carson was to continue as head of the order, while William Masterson was to now face in one week a debate on his confidence and ability to continue in the position of Vice-Supreme Grandmaster; a title he would hold with all rights attached until his own vote.

"This is not the end of the matter, old man," Masterson snarled, as he drew alongside his former friend.

"You should be gracious in defeat," Walter grinned. "And put your energies into your defence notes for next week, you're going to need all your rhetoric skills."

The Vice-Supreme Grandmaster turned and left the chamber, his two enormous bodyguards following close behind. The congregation descended onto the floor of the central room and began to congratulate their leader, patting him on the back and murmuring abuse about his failed challenger. Several members hugged Samuel, welcoming him as a novice and telling him how much they looked forward to his own debating skills one day.

After nearly half an hour, Walter Carson and his son bid the assembly farewell and prepared to leave the building. The Supreme Grandmaster tapped his son on the shoulder and motioned for him to move towards the toilet, instructing they should use the lavatory before they make the long journey back to their hotel in the centre of New York City.

The Americans entered the large toilet area and were immediately accosted and separated by two huge men dressed in expensive suits that seemed three sizes too small for their enormous frames, their bulging muscles stretching the arms of the jacket to bursting point. One of the guards pinned Samuel against the door, keeping him motionless and stopping any intruders from entering and helping them. The other man pushed Walter Carson across the chamber and picking him up, held the Supreme Grandmaster against the far wall.

"This is outrageous, do you have any idea who I am?" Walter shouted. "I will have you posted to the Sahara Desert for this assault where the nomads will feed your entrails to the camels."

"They know exactly who you are, and who their real master is," a voice announced from behind a closed toilet door as out walked William Masterson. "I told you earlier this matter was unresolved. You may have bested me in the debating chamber, but my youth and two large friends will seal your doom."

The Vice-Supreme Grandmaster revealed from his inside pocket a syringe with six-inch needle attached, however the contents seemed absent; the tube to all intents and purposes appearing empty.

"I have here a syringe with nothing but air inside, once injected into your bloodstream the bubble will travel through your system until it reaches your heart and cause a cardiac arrest,"

Masterson said. "The coroner could carry out a hundred post-mortems and never identify a different death result other than a massive heart attack, which would not be uncommon for a sixty year old in a stressful job. I will insert the needle somewhere the pinprick would be difficult to detect, like the roof of the mouth."

"Let my son live and I will not fight the procedure," Walter stated.

"This is not the time to be a coward, father," Samuel interjected. "They will have to inject me in the arse, no way am I going to willingly open my mouth."

William Masterson nodded to his former friend and placing the needle past his teeth, inserted the contents into Walter Carson's top palette. Within a few seconds, the Supreme Grandmaster clutched his chest in agony and let out a brief groan before slipping lifeless to the tiled floor.

"You bastard," Samuel snarled. "When I leave this toilet I will see you burn for this treachery."

Masterson laughed. "No-one is going to believe a fifteen year old boy in grief against the word of the now Supreme Grandmaster of the Illuminati. My advice to you is to keep silence, inherit your father's substantial wealth and leave this society forever. If not, you will never see the end of your training that I promise you. However one final mention, your life was never in danger. I may be ruthless but I am not stupid. The police and Illuminati may believe the sudden death of a sixty year old, but the untimely demise of his only child would be impossible to ignore. So it is as you said, your father was a coward."

The two henchmen smiled and left the boy go. Samuel walked over and stood at the corpse of his parent while his murderers departed. The young American stared down at Walter Carson in silence but did not lean down or approach the body. Instead he looked on in morbid fascination, the first time he had seen somebody die. He had loved his father mostly, but theirs was a difficult relationship based on frequent disagreement from choice of breakfast cereal to greater intellectual debates. He had never understood his parent's interest in the Illuminati until recently, but was glad for his membership into the order that Walter had endorsed, knowing this would be his father's greatest legacy to his only son.

Samuel did not hear one of the waiters open the bathroom door and swiftly run off in shock, reporting the collapse of the society's leader to the congregation back in the main lobby of the mansion, eating sandwiches and drinking champagne. Within two minutes the toilet area filled up with twenty senior Illuminati members, one of whom escorted Samuel out of the bathroom while others inspected the corpse.

The young American was interviewed by three New York detectives, nervous that this was a potential murder investigation and they would be compelled to question other guests, some of whom were Congressional Senators and high-ranking superiors of the police force. Samuel however allayed their fears when he told them his father collapsed without a word in the bathroom and there were no other witnesses or persons present at the time. The officers soon departed and the boy was chauffeured back to the hotel. Samuel declined any help from police counsellors or Illuminati members to stay with him for the night, instructing he would prefer to be alone in his grief.

The teenager began searching his father's luggage once they had left, hoping to discover his address book and the residence of William Masterson. He had just located the notebook in delight when the doorbell rang. Samuel ran to the door, expecting to see more detectives or do-gooders but was surprised to see the eldest High Council member standing alone in the hallway.

"May I come in, Mr. Carson?" The seventy year old enquired and the boy nodded, allowing the judge who had presided over the crucial debate enter the hotel room. "I see you have found your father's address book, no doubt you intend to go after his killer, that being of course William Masterson."

Samuel stared at him in shock and dropped the book on the carpet. "You knew that bastard murdered my father, and yet you and your cronies are going to do nothing?"

"Walter Carson and I were long time friends, becoming novices of the order when he was just nineteen, I being ten years older. He looked up to me as an elder brother and I was instrumental in his election to be Supreme Grandmaster of the Illuminati. There was an unbreakable bond between us, greater than blood family. But I cannot accuse the now leader of the society without proof of his crimes, despite how much I loathe him even prior to this event. I always knew William Masterson was an ambitious ruthless son of a bitch, but even I am surprised he would stoop to murder. However he and the rest of the order would never suspect a teenager committing vengeance and killing one of the most powerful people in the world. I will drive you near to the home of the Supreme Grandmaster where he resides alone, he always dismisses his bodyguards for the night at one am, preferring to either work on his computer into the early hours or sometimes invite prostitutes to entertain him until dawn."

"So there will be no interruptions?" Samuel asked. "And what about afterwards, when I will be interviewed by the police?"

"Considering the lies you told those frightened officers at the mansion, I believe you will have no trouble with any others that turn up," the elderly man smiled. "I will drop you back here after you are done. I am the Grandmaster for the United States of America, the third most powerful position in the Illuminati. I am going to leave instructions in my will that after my death you are to be promoted to Vice-Grandmaster of America once your training ends and you are twenty-five years old. This is my legacy to an old friend; your father whom I promised I would look after his only child should anything happen to Walter. I would strongly suggest you move back to Chicago and stay away from New York City as William Masterson has many allies here. Use this blade and not a gun as the order will believe the traitor was mugged on his doorstep, no assassin would use a knife on such a normally well-protected target."

Samuel accepted the seven-inch dagger from the elderly gentleman and they both left the hotel for his car parked nearby, the Grandmaster leaving his chauffeur at home and therefore minimising any potential witnesses.

"I never asked your name," Samuel said. "Especially as you are now both my sponsor and the facilitator of my vengeance."

"David," the man declared. "My surname is unimportant as are any titles other than what you carry in the Illuminati. Your life before this night is over, forget your friends, acquaintances and even girlfriends. They matter not, only your brothers in the order who will both protect and guide you in your new destiny. This is the gift and the curse of the society; the sacrifices we make for the greater good so the aims of the Illuminati may one day be fulfilled. However, at the same time you will hold sway over entire governments and nations; decide the fates of presidents and prime ministers and have in your pocket senators and assassins, ready at a single phone call to do your bidding at a moment's notice."

David parked in a narrow dark side-street where Samuel could see rows of mansions on both sides of the adjacent road, this obviously being the location of one of the wealthier parts of New York. He pointed to the large house across the street.

"Keep to the bushes until you get to the front door," the Grandmaster said and then grabbed hold of Samuel's sleeve. "Are you certain you are up to this task? It's not easy killing a man, even one that deserves it."

The boy smiled. "I am used to dealing with bullies. They are all the same, no matter their age and position, in fact in my experience they tend to get more sour and abusive as years pass like vinegar knowing their challengers die or retire." Samuel announced and turned to his elderly sponsor with a stern look. "I know you haven't said anything, but I am certain this is a test, to see if I have the courage; the balls to not only take a man's life, but to assassinate a dangerous and powerful person like William Masterson."

David laughed. "You are most astute. I did not declare that this was part of the mission, but it is true. We need to establish if you have the guts to carry out such a task; if you have the makings of a future Grandmaster."

"Who is 'we'?" Samuel retorted. "I thought you were alone in this, that no-one else was involved. Who are these shadows hiding in the darkness?"

"This is the Illuminati, my dear boy," David said sharply. "We are a society of equals, people of privilege who have come together having mutual ideals willing to make sacrifices for the greater good. Nothing goes on in the order without at least twenty men having intimate knowledge of it, especially something as monumental as murder. Many in the organisation were shocked by what happened to your father, he had won that vote fairly and that usurper comes along and kills him like a spoilt brat."

"Why send a boy to execute a leader?" Samuel shouted. "Why not send an assassin; a professional killer for hire?"

"Nobody would suspect a teenager of assassination, especially of someone like William Masterson." David retorted. "Virtually everyone at that convention would expect you to be crying into your cocoa tonight. In the morning when the shit hits the fan, you will be the suspect on the bottom of the list."

Samuel hid the dagger under his fleece jacket as he watched the bodyguards depart from the mansion across the road. He got out of the car and ran into the bushes. A few minutes later and he was at the large brown wooden door. Samuel rang the doorbell, but there was no response. He continued to push the buzzer until he could hear someone curse loudly in the hallway. The door opened and William Masterson stared out, dressed in blue pyjamas and matching dressing gown. The forty-two year old was holding a mug of coffee in his right hand. He looked at the schoolboy in momentary confusion, before the realisation of who this young intruder was.

"Jesus Christ," the man declared. "How did you find my house? What the fuck are you doing on my property ringing my doorbell at this ungodly hour?"

Samuel revealed the blade but the Grandmaster laughed in response.

"Who do you think you are, coming here waving that knife?" Masterson sneered. "Are you seriously intending revenge for that pathetic father of yours? You should go back to the Middle East and spend that large inheritance on some Arabian prostitutes, alcohol and cocaine."

"Walter should have fought you, despite your two henchmen," Samuel snarled. "He was a coward and in some ways he got what he deserved."

Masterson stared at him in shock. "So you actually despised your parent, that's certainly the right requirements for entrance into the Illuminati. But if you are not here to seek retribution for your father, then why are you really here?" The Grandmaster said sharply before the realisation dawned, as he glanced all around the road, expecting to see a crowd of Illuminati members waiting in the shadows. "You were escorted here by someone in the order. Who was it, was it David?"

Samuel smiled. "That is not important. When the police find your rodent eaten body on the doorstep, I will never be considered a serious suspect. While you rot in the ground I will rise through the organisation and one day ascend to the position of my father."

Masterson grinned. "That will never happen. The High Council want someone they can manipulate, that is why they want me dead. If you don't play ball, you will never get the crown. But why worry, a little twerp like you will not have the courage to kill someone, especially the Supreme Grandmaster of the Illuminati."

"Everyone dies no matter their importance, and anyone can be killed, even the son of God," Samuel stated flatly as he moved closer to his target. "I don't enjoy violence…"

William Masterson interrupted him. "Get off my property, you little creep."

Samuel shoved the dagger into the Grandmaster's crotch, impaling a testicle as the blade ascended four inches into his body. Masterson stared at him in disbelief and fell back onto the wooden floor of the hallway. Samuel removed the knife and bending over him, shoved the dagger into his left eye socket, severing the eyeball and driving the weapon into his brain. The Grandmaster let out a scream as the blood jetted into the air and onto the floor. Samuel removed the blade and watched in silent fascination as Masterson's life ebbed away, the hallway rapidly filling with dark liquid. Once he was satisfied the killer of his parent was dead he left, carefully wiping the buzzer to remove any trance of fingerprints. He got back to the car where David was waiting patiently. Samuel handed him the weapon and he put it into a plastic bag. He ordered the teenager to remove his shoes and gave him a pair of slippers instead. Once they returned to the hotel, he asked the schoolboy to place all the clothes he was wearing into the bag also for incineration.

"Well done," the elderly man said. "You have a bright future ahead of you in the order. Get some sleep for detectives will be at your door in the morning. Although they will not consider you a likely suspect, they still have to carry out proper procedure."

"Thank you for all you have given me," Samuel said softly.

"And gratitude for the gift you have bestowed on me," David replied. "I am now Supreme Grandmaster thanks to you."

The young American looked at him in shock. "I never considered that, with the deaths of my father and Masterson, all other challengers to your leadership have been removed."

"Would it have made a difference? Would you have walked away from vengeance?" David retorted. "And now you have a powerful sponsor to ensure your future. Welcome to the Illuminati," he said and laughed.

Samuel watched him leave down the hallway before closing the door and going to bed. As the elderly man said, policemen arrived early in the morning to inform him that one of the main suspects in the death of his father had been murdered. They had been afraid to question William Masterson about the sudden demise of Walter Carson, despite Samuel insisting no other people had been present at his father's death, suspicious bruising had been discovered by the coroner on Walter's body and warranted further interviewing of guests at the mansion. Samuel noticed the men were actually relieved this burden had been removed of them, William Masterson would not be missed or grieved over.

Many years passed and when Samuel reached twenty-five and his education in the history and occult matters of the order had been attained, the now eighty year old Supreme Grandmaster kept to his word and made the young man Vice-Grandmaster for America. When the current Grandmaster of the United States died, Samuel Carson would ascend to that title. The grown up schoolboy returned to his father's home in Chicago where he met a young and beautiful red-haired woman and married her shortly afterwards. Samuel's wife gave birth to a daughter who he called Alice, but his spouse died in childbirth, the now Grandmaster of America being forced to raise the infant alone.

When Samuel heard of his sponsor David's death, he knew his safety might be in question. Reports within the Illuminati over the years mentioned a man of Iraqi origin living in Britain under the name Sam Philips who might know the location of the fabled Eden. Samuel believed this information would kill two birds with one stone; he could guarantee his future by leaving the United States, and launch a coup against the current leader of the order if he found the legendary Garden and the power source rumoured to exist in the Tree of Life.

CHAPTER TWENTY

Cain struggled to get to his feet, the drugs in his system still leaving him quite weak. He stumbled out into the main street, hoping to see his mysterious helper somewhere and ascertain his identity. Cain started to bump into people going about their business, mothers wearing full burkas dragging their reluctant children to the market, their fathers talking gossip on the nearby corner ranging from who was seen breaking Muslim law of consuming alcohol, to who they suspected was a collaborator of the recently departed coalition occupational forces.

Cain collapsed into two women, bringing them also to the ground. The adjacent men which included their husbands ran towards him, strict Islamic law in Iraq allowing them to defend their wife's dignity and honour, not to mention any possibility of interference or suggestion of adultery. They picked Cain up and threw his body across the street. He rolled several times before coming to rest on the kerbside. The men advanced on him, intending further harm when a middle-aged bearded individual appeared and they abruptly halted. The husbands quickly turned around and went back to their favourite street corner.

"You are most fortunate I was here," the man declared as he waved at a dozen armed insurgents which passed by and continued with their mission. "My soldiers are investigating what appears to be gunfire coming from down the street. Although this is nothing new in Baghdad, I have a duty to my people to determine its origin. My name is Al Hussein, no relation of course to that bastard dead president and his psychotic sons who raped this country for their own means. I cheered with my family as we watched his execution on television. I am a commander in the Sunni Militia who oversee security in this section of the city, although the Shia dominated Iraqi government does not approve of our actions. However, they did not argue when we drove Al Qaeda from Baghdad after the Americans failed to locate their cells."

"I thank you for your assistance, but I require only a few minutes rest before I return to where I was held captive and sort out unfinished business," Cain said.

"So you were held prisoner, this makes sense given the bruising on your wrists and ankles where bonds were placed," Hussein replied sharply. "Was it in the building where the gunfire came from?"

"You would be wise to leave this matter alone, these are dangerous people." Cain whispered to the man who burst into laughter.

"My dear friend, I am no stranger to violence. This city is one of the most volatile settlements on the planet," the Sunni commander said. "In 1988 we were fighting Iran, then we hid from Saddam Hussein and his secret police until the Americans came in 2003, and we fought against them until we turned on our former colleagues Al Qaeda, who suddenly decided we weren't militant and psychotic enough to be in their murderous brotherhood. Look around, every man and woman here expected every day to be either shot or blown up. It was simply a matter of 'wrong place, wrong time' when a suicidal bomber had you in their sights."

One of the insurgents carrying an AK-47 machinegun returned and drew up alongside them. "No sign of them, just a hundred civilians shot dead against a wall. Witnesses said they just grabbed people from houses and killed them for no reason," the Iraqi said, out of breath. "However, they declared the person giving the orders appeared to be American; a blond man in his mid fifties and a red-haired young woman not wearing a hijab."

"That's all we need," Hussein growled. "Another CIA assassin and his friends gone rogue, or worse paid off by Iran to incite a fresh war with the United States."

"It's not what you think," Cain announced. "They are a separate group of mercenaries not affiliated with any insurgency. Their leader seeks a place in the Zagros Mountains near to Bakhtaran."

Hussein looked at him in shock. "That town is deep into Iranian soil and close to a training ground for foreign insurgents. I have buried enough of my friends and relatives in the War of Occupation, I do not wish to contemplate terrorists starting fresh battles on our borders. The United States are gone from this nation now, not that I particularly miss them, but their marines and technology kept Iran at bay."

"American and coalition forces have suffered enough also, it is not only your countrymen that lost loved ones or have to care for relatives with missing limbs and disfigured features; they also paid a heavy price for Saddam Hussein and President Bush."

"And where were the United States in Basra[47] when we attempted a coup against the Iraqi despot?" The commander shouted in rage. "The Central Intelligence Agency promised us air support and special forces to back up our armed civilians, but instead they let them be butchered."

"I have seen firsthand the treachery of the CIA and their dirty tricks," Cain retorted. "You cannot blame an entire nation for the deceit of a few men who rarely act in the best interests of their own population. The same applies for Iraq, just because your country is going through great upheaval on their fragile road to democracy and are plagued with several different and separate insurgent organisations, you as a nation should not be held accountable for the evil deeds of a few thousand."

Al Hussein smiled. "You are most wise, whether you be Iraqi or foreigner, which brings us to the point at hand. Why did those men hold you captive?"

"They believe ancient treasure can be found in the Zagros Mountains and that I alone possess the knowledge of its location."

The commander laughed. "The only money to be found in that wilderness is the bounty they place on American or British heads, these individuals who seek you must be stupid or insane.

---

[47] The 1991 Basra revolt was in response to local civilians falsely believing that Saddam Hussein was vulnerable and a coup supported by promised American troops from nearby Kuwait, already stationed there during the first Gulf War would ensure victory. However, President George Bush Senior had vowed to liberate only the oil-rich nation Kuwait, and was not prepared politically for a full-scale invasion of Iraq. This view was supported by Central Intelligence Agency operatives on the ground, meaning that thousands of poorly armed Basra civilians were butchered by the Iraqi Republican Guard.

However, that does not concern me, what troubles me is why they would murder a hundred innocent civilians."

"It was a warning to ensure I return should I ever escape, I must leave this region lest more Iraqi women and children be killed in my name. I would not have their deaths on my conscience."

Hussein stared at him in curiosity. "You are an interesting individual, most people in this country are so focused on daily survival they care little for the lives of their neighbours. I will strike a deal with you stranger, I will spread the word that you have left Iraq so these soldiers will no longer seek you out or murder more civilians, and I will give you the location of their new hiding place once I ascertain it. In return you will help me destroy an Al Qaeda nest that has troubled us for some days now and which the official army are too afraid to attack."

"What makes you believe I have the experience to assault a terrorist base?" Cain enquired. "What difference will my presence make to the battle?"

"True, I know nothing of your background in specialist army training," Hussein replied. "However, anyone who could escape alone unarmed from so many guards, not to mention the five mercenaries we found dead at the building who suffered horrific injuries apparently inflicted without any sign of a visible weapon, must be capable of extraordinary things."

Cain grinned. "Very well, I will help you. Besides, considering the stories I have heard about Al Qaeda, their deaths will not trouble my conscience. Their elimination will be a blessing to humanity. My name is Sam Philips by the way, I am originally of Iraqi descent, but have spent many years living in the United States."

"So you possess the blood of one of my countrymen, but the heritage of our former occupier," Hussein smiled. "I suppose nobody's perfect."

The Sunni commander instructed his troops who had returned, to follow him through the streets until barely fifteen minutes later they spotted a large rundown building situated down a side road. Ruined houses destroyed by tank-fire surrounded the structure and Cain could see shadows passing by the paneless windows.

"How many are in there?" Cain asked.

"Cannot say for sure, but probably at least twenty," Hussein replied. "They have been seen going out at night to recruit teenage boys, homeless and starving; easy prey for an extremist. This is why we sided with the coalition forces against our former Al Qaeda brothers, their insight into Islam has become so twisted they regard Osama Bin Laden as Mohammed reborn. This is blasphemy and their poisonous propaganda must be exterminated."

One of the Sunni soldiers handed Cain an AK-47, but he refused it.

"I never had a liking for firearms," Cain stated. "Give me that curved sword you carry instead. There's nothing like getting up and personal with your quarry, see the fear and agony in their eyes in the last moments of life."

The men looked at Cain in astonishment and Hussein burst into laughter. "Now I know for sure you are an Iraqi," he smiled. "I am prepared to go out on a limb here and pass command decision to you. What do you have in mind?"

"There's no need for any of your troops to die," Cain replied. "Create a diversion by using suppressing fire on the main front of the building. That will keep them occupied while I go in the back."

"You plan to go in alone and confront twenty heavily armed terrorists with nothing but a sword?" The commander said in shock. "You must have a death wish."

"Trust me," Cain retorted flatly. "Remember I escaped the prison basement where the American mercenaries were holding me captive. I possess certain extraordinary abilities that will give me an edge over the soldiers inside the building, but I am afraid I cannot allow you to witness these talents. This ignorance is for your own good, some knowledge brings deadly danger with it."

Hussein gazed at him in amusement. "Very well, I will allow you go in alone," the commander said. "But you get only ten minutes, after that we will use rocket propelled grenade launchers against the house, and no special abilities will save your life."

Cain nodded in agreement and ran across the street. As he prepared to leave their sight and travel to the back of the building, he signalled Hussein to begin launching their attack on the front face of the house. The Sunni commander held up his hand to wave the crazy stranger off before he ordered his soldiers to starting firing on the structure with their machineguns. True to what Cain declared, the Al Qaeda insurgents rushed to the front half of the building and sticking their firearms out broken windows and holes in the wall, began to rain bullets down on their former brothers in arms.

Cain smashed in what remained of the already shattered door and entered the house. The noise of gunfire inside the structure was deafening. The terrorists did not appear to notice his intrusion, such was the focus of their attention on the Sunnis on the street. He passed close to what once seemed to be the downstairs kitchen area of the building, pieces of a sink and taps lay on the floor amidst dirty tiles littered with rat faeces. A masked Al Qaeda individual stood inside, busy shoving rounds into an AK-47 machinegun clip, his frantic fingers occasionally letting the bullets fall to the ground. He looked up and saw Cain, his brain at first not registering the stranger for what he was. He dropped the metal clip and reaching to his side belt, removed a ten inch dagger. The terrorist raised the blade and ran at him, but Cain was too fast, striking the insurgent across the chest with the sabre. The man let out a scream and fell to his knees, blood quickly staining his brown shirt and pouring down onto the tiles. Cain then shoved the sword into his exposed throat. The terrorist gurgled before dropping to the floor.

Cain searched the body, hoping to find grenades but the insurgent had none. He contemplated taking the AK-47, but gunfire originating inside the house and behind them without draw all the terrorists immediately to his position. Although he could not be killed, their continuous suppressing fire on his body would prevent him completing his mission and place the Sunnis outside on the street in further danger. Cain left the kitchen area and noticed three more soldiers in the living room of the structure, their machineguns pointed through gaping holes in the wall, shooting at the Iraqis on the road. Cain saw one of them had several grenades in a box near his feet. Cain crept up behind the nearest terrorist and shoved the blade through his back, the sword piercing his liver and stomach before appearing out the other side of his body. The two other men instantly turned, wondering why their comrade had ceased his gunfire. Cain threw the sword at one of the insurgents and it pierced him in the middle of the chest, severing a large section of his heart, the tip protruding from out of his back. The terrorist fell to the floor as the remaining soldier began to turn his weapon towards this intruder.

Cain picked up the first insurgent he had killed and holding him up by the back of his shirt, advanced on the last terrorist. The man began to fire on Cain and his dead friend, hoping the bullets would travel through his former comrade and into Cain. Dozens of rounds ripped into the corpse and Cain nearly fell back, such was the ferocity of the attack. However, he managed to keep his balance and the bullets failed to pass through the man's body. Once Cain had moved to within a few feet of the remaining insurgent, he let the cadaver fall to the ground and punched the terrorist in the face, breaking his jaw and left cheekbone. The soldier dropped the gun in shock and agony and Cain threw him against the far wall, shattering his spine. The man fell to the floor and stared at his killer in silent pain, the last minutes of his life ebbing away.

Cain picked up the box of grenades which appeared to contain ten explosives in all. He slowly crept up the wooden stairs and standing a few steps from the top, peered around the upstairs landing and into the two bedrooms. He could see at least four more insurgents in each room, their AK-47s pointed out the shattered windows and shooting onto the street. Cain could hear Hussein call his name faintly over the gunfire, meaning that was the signal signifying that he was about to launch the rockets at the building and put an abrupt end to the fighting. Cain removed the pin from one of the grenades and placing it back into the box with the rest of the explosives, shoved the container against the far wall. Although it was in the landing and some distance from the adjacent bedrooms, the blast would most likely destroy the entire structure.

Cain ran down the stairs and out the back door. He jumped over a nearby wall and laid flat on the ground. The earth beneath his body shuddered as an explosion ripped through the region. An enormous plume of black smoke descended over the area and pieces of mortar hit the wall with a great thud next to him. After some minutes Cain finally rose to his feet and saw the entire top half of the building had disappeared, the lower section in ruins. He walked onto the street and smiled as he approached Hussein. However, the Sunni commander did not appear to share his congratulations. Cain noticed that he and his men standing alongside him were all unarmed.

"I am sorry my friend," Hussein sighed. "They arrived a few minutes ago and disarmed us."

Cain began to see through the cloud over a hundred Iraqi army personnel, standing adjacent their armoured jeeps, a soldier on the back of each vehicle where an M-16 lay mounted and pointed in his direction. A man dressed in full combat uniform drew up next to him, bearing the rank of Colonel.

"This man is our guest," Hussein shouted to the leader of the army. "He is under our protection."

The official turned quickly at this intrusion. "I do not answer to Sunni vigilantes. You and your group of insurgents have been instructed many times before to lay down your guns. This city and country is under the control of the elected Shia government."

"CIA bought traitors," Hussein snarled. "Those Al Qaeda scum have been operating in this street for weeks, converting our young to their twisted cause and selling heroin to our children while you have stood idly by. It took a stranger to our land to remove these bastards."

"Enough," the official retorted sharply. "This man is an escaped prisoner from an American military company not far from here. He is to be handed over forthwith. Stay out of matters that do not concern you," the Iraqi commander retorted. "Go back to your homes and be grateful your families are still alive and waiting for you. Al Qaeda dissidents will be dealt with by the official army of Iraq and not trigger-happy insurgents."

Cain walked over and shook Hussein's hand. "We have done some good today, my friend. Let us always remember that. International media may report only bad things about the Middle East and Iraq, but I know there are fine people here with strong principles which no bomb can shatter."

The Sunni smiled in response and watched him being led away to be returned to his prison. Cain stared up at the sky as he was placed in the jeep, ready to be transported back to the mercenaries and Samuel Carson.

"It's time to finally come home," Cain said to himself. "Time for this long journey to end at last."

CHAPTER TWENTY-ONE

Cain was escorted through the streets of Baghdad until he arrived at the new safe-house. He groaned in frustration when the Illuminati leader approached the vehicle. The mercenaries dragged Cain out of the jeep and placed fresh titanium steel chains around him. Samuel Carson stared down at his knelt prisoner, before punching his captive in the face, splitting Cain's lip.

"Welcome back, Mr. Kadmon," the Grandmaster snarled. "That's for escaping me a second time, I promise however there will not be a third. We leave immediately for the Zagros Mountains, and interventions of your new friend will not save you this time."

"Was it really necessary to kill all those people?" Cain asked. "What purpose did it serve?"

"I warned you of the consequences of your actions; the effect your selfish principles had on innocent civilians. Their deaths are on your conscience, not mine."

"How much did it cost for Iraqi officials to turn their backs while you murdered a hundred women and children?" Cain shouted as they bundled him back into the jeep.

Samuel laughed. "You have no concept of the poverty and desperation in this country, there are Sunni and Shia alike that would sell their mothers for twenty dollars. Imagine how much twisted loyalty a hundred thousand buys you."

Cain watched as the mercenaries gathered their weapons and got into four more vehicles and prepared to depart, Alice pushed into the front jeep.

The Grandmaster got into the same vehicle as his prisoner.

"Tell me about your mysterious helper who killed five of my men with his bare hands, no bullet or blade injuries were found on any part of their bodies," Samuel said, leaning close to his captive.

"I know nothing of him," Cain replied flatly. "His face was obscured by a mask. He disappeared into the crowd, it was the insurgents who offered me support and promised me retribution for your crimes."

"We will see, Mr. Kadmon," the Grandmaster said sharply. "We will see."

Several hours passed before they sighted the base of the Zagros, a vast mountain region stretching fifteen hundred kilometres across the entire length of the plateau of Iran, from the north-western point of the country to the Straits of Hormuz. Continuously on the move due to stresses of the Eurasian and Arabian tectonic plates, the region was host to several ecosystems of which a great forest dominated a large section of the hills. Cain instructed they should leave the vehicles behind which were not suitable for the steep terrain as they would be travelling in the direction of the second largest mountain in the Zagros range, that being Dena having a height of fourteen thousand, three hundred and one feet.

Cain saw Alice pass near him and she gave the fellow prisoner a frightened look. Samuel Carson noticed the gaze and he drew up alongside his guide.

"One thing puzzles me, Mr. Kadmon," the Grandmaster declared. "In all the thousands of years and nations you visited, you never remarried and had any more children. The daughter of Nok the

Elder died in childbirth due to malnutrition, another infant might have survived the curse and lived. Seth after all is rumoured to be the founding father of the fabled Menes and the earliest Egyptian pharaohs including the legendary Scorpion King."

"True, it is possible a child might have survived the hex," Cain echoed. "But I did not wish any son of mine inheriting the sins of the father. The infant would be infamous because of his divine link and bear my immortal stain; sins he would have passed onto his child. Better to sever any possible chance of repugnant history and inheritance at the source."

"You don't have a high opinion of yourself, despite the great accomplishments you have achieved," Samuel said. "And especially the momentous events yet to unfold in a matter of hours."

"My entire life has been dedicated to fulfilling redemption for killing Abel," Cain responded. "And as regards Eden, the Garden should never be discovered by man, its secrets are too dangerous even for the Illuminati. Be warned Samuel Carson, you thread on grass sown by God himself, there will be a high price for ultimate knowledge. My father Adam can testify to that."

The Grandmaster looked at him in curiosity but said nothing further. The group began to climb the rocky steep surface and had been travelling for nearly two hours when the lead soldier abruptly halted his ascent. He motioned for the assembly to stop and keep silence. Four more mercenaries quickly climbed up next to him and they glanced over the edge of a nearby crop of boulders and into the clearing beyond. Samuel stared at them for a few moments before ascending also. They waved their hands at him to drop to the ground and he placed his stomach on the rocks. Looking over the edge he cursed under his breath as he saw a dozen men dressed in rough clothing and all carrying AK-47s, one appeared to be holding a rocket launcher. Three tents lay in the centre of the clearing and they appeared to be training, waving their weapons about in the air, but not discharging them.

"Fuckit," the Grandmaster said. "What are they, Iranian insurgents?"

"Worse I fear," the captain replied. "Al Qaeda terrorists performing military exercises in preparation for an assault into Iraq."

"Can we go around them?" Samuel enquired.

"It would add days to our journey and we do not have provisions for that," the officer replied. "Besides, you did not hire me and my men for our charming personalities. No one is going to miss Al Qaeda insurgents, these monsters have been ostracised from their home countries and even their families. Putting rats like these out of commission would be a good deed for humanity, they should give us a medal."

The mercenaries laughed and the captain waved at them to separate into divisions of five men each, two snipers taking position at different locations around the clearing.

Samuel pushed Cain who was still bound in chains of titanium and Alice who was handcuffed further down the mountain and beyond the boundaries of the battle. The captain instructed the snipers to open fire, removing the terrorist with the rocket launcher and the insurgent who was most likely the leader of the cell. Shots rang out and the officer smiled as the Iranians fell, bullets ripping into their unprotected skulls, splattering blood and brain matter to the ground. The remaining ten insurgents glanced around in surprise, knowing Iraqi army would never enter Iranian soil and their sponsors in Tehran had guaranteed their safety in the Zagros Mountains. Also their main enemy the American marines had left Iraq and moved their forces instead to Afghanistan and Helmand Province to combat the Taliban. They considered perhaps it was a rogue Sunni group with thoughts of revenge. However, whatever nationality the fighters were or their real motives, this was unimportant at this moment. They began to fire wildly around the clearing and the outcrop of rocks where the soldiers were hidden.

The captain ordered the rest of the mercenaries to 'go loud;' signifying they should open up on the terrorists with everything at their disposal. Hundreds of shots were heard and Alice placed her hands over her ears such was the noise. The Al Qaeda insurgents swiftly collapsed onto the ground, their bodies torn apart by large calibre rounds delivered by machineguns and sniper rifles.

The captain shouted to the Grandmaster that it was now safe to proceed and he dragged the prisoners back up the hill to where the mercenaries lay. Alice let out a scream of fright when she witnessed the battle scene, bloody corpses littered the clearing, some missing limbs and heads. Samuel Carson nodded to the officer in satisfaction of a job well done.

"How much further?" The Grandmaster asked.

"Dena Mountain is directly ahead, there is a cave to the left a short distance up the side of the hill, that is where Eden lies," Cain replied.

"I hope so for your sake, Mr. Kadmon," Samuel snarled. "I would hate to hurt someone close to you."

Alice stared at her father in shock. "You bastard, threatening me like that," she declared. "I sincerely wish you never leave this place alive."

The company approached Dena Mountain and the captain spotted the cave entrance just as Cain had said. They climbed slowly up and entered the cavern. After a short distance through the rocky hallway they suddenly came to a massive solid golden door, inscribed with various markings the like of which the mercenaries had never seen. Samuel Carson pushed past them to reach the sealed portal.

"Extraordinary," he said softly. "Behold, we are at the entrance to Eden; the fabled Garden and birth-place of mankind, a kingdom personally forged by God."

"Look," announced the captain. "In the centre lies an impression for an outstretched hand. That must be how it opens, as there appears to be no handle."

The officer placed his digits into the carving but nothing happened. Samuel grabbed hold of Cain by the scruff of his shirt shoulder and threw him against the door. However, he stood at the portal motionless and did not make any attempt to move his limbs.

The Grandmaster glared at his prisoner in rage. "I understand your trepidation, this being the murder scene of your brother and where you were banished by your father, never to see them again. But know this, do my bidding or else something terrible will happen. I will not be denied my prize after a lifetime's quest, especially as it stands just beyond my reach before me."

Cain stared at him in silent anger, trying to flex his muscles and break the chains, knowing only too well once the portal to Eden was opened he would be stripped of his powers, and become mortal having ordinary human strength and not be able to heal himself. However, the bonds of reinforced steel were too tough to shatter, so he relaxed and waved his hand at his waist to indicate the limb would have to be freed of the titanium in order to reach the impression in the door.

"I am not that stupid," Samuel declared. "Even with one hand free you could kill the men here and escape the mountain. Once inside the Garden, I will order those chains removed as you will be weak and easy to eliminate; you will become a complacent prisoner."

The Grandmaster motioned to the soldiers to hoist the captive up so the hand held fast to his waist could just barely fit into the impression. Five mercenaries lifted Cain up and turning himself he shoved his hand into the carving. The soldiers dropped him to the floor and he landed with a grunt. Samuel Carson stepped forward, barely able to contain his excitement. The company of mercenaries looked at him in puzzlement, not knowing what to expect. A tremendous creaking could be heard and the door began to open. A rush of bad air filled the hallway and the men coughed with the stench, thousands of years of carbon monoxide escaping from the mountain.

The portal opened fully and the company expected darkness, but instead they were greeted by bright sunlight. The intruders stared at the ceiling of the giant cavern before them and saw the sealed rock seemed to be exuding light.

"That's not possible," the captain stuttered in awe. "It is as if we were back in the desert in the open air, but instead we are witnessing a fully enclosed miniature world; a microcosm created by ancient magick."

"You are very astute," Samuel said. "Let us descend into the cavern and find the Tree of Life."

As the company left the outside world behind and ventured into the deformed forest, they noticed the trees around them appeared dead, their leaves black and withered and they seemed to be making a groaning sound. Throughout the woodland they could hear strange noises of creatures that almost appeared to be in agony or filled with terrible rage.

"This is what happens when a deity turns his back on his creation, the world becomes dead and consumed with anguish. Perhaps this is a small mirror representation of what Hell might be like; a place forever cursed by God." Samuel declared. "Stay alert, animals twisted by dark magick roam this forest and have not tasted fresh meat in many millenniums."

The captain ordered his men to remove the safeties from their weapons and also instructed two soldiers to make ready the flamethrowers, the mercenaries placing the petrol tanks on their backs with the hoses attached in preparation for whatever horrors awaited them. Their fears were realised as out of a nearby bush leapt a bear. The soldiers gasped in surprise for the creature was at least twice the size of a normal bear, its eyes red with rage and revealing fangs the size of a man's outstretched hand.

"Christ Almighty," the officer whispered in shock. "He is colossal."

The mercenaries opened fire and over a hundred rounds hit the beast in the head and chest. It collapsed to the ground and the men breathed a sigh of relief. This however was brief as several more gigantic bears, two tigers and a lion, all twice the average size of their counterparts in any zoo or in Africa rushed out of the bushes and attacked them. These were followed by four elephants the size of woolly mammoths, their three metre tusks protruding in a horizontal line to their open mouths.

Samuel and his two prisoners fell to the grass as the soldiers opened fire wildly at the beasts. The Grandmaster watched helplessly as his men were torn apart by enormous tigers, their severed limbs and skulls rolling into the undergrowth. He looked on as one mercenary was pinned to a tree by the tusk of one of the elephants, the ivory jutting out of the other side of the wood. It attempted to shake itself free when the captain shot it point blank in the head with his machinegun and the creature collapsed, its tusks still trapped in the tree.

"You can get up," the officer gasped. "They are dead."

Samuel got to his feet and saw a bloody battleground of soldiers and beasts. "How many did you lose?"

"Besides you and your two captives, there is only me and one other soldier with a flamethrower still alive," the captain announced. "That combat was fierce, you never warned me I could be facing creatures like that."

"I could not be certain of their existence, and if you knew you would have never come along on the mission," the Grandmaster said.

"I live for adventure and I am not scared of death," the officer replied. "But I would have asked for three times the payment."

Samuel smiled. "Further ahead is our reward. Time to play your part, Mr. Kadmon."

"I have gone far enough with these chains," Cain snarled. "Release them or I go no further. Besides, you do not need them, I am mortal here and possess only normal strength."

"Very well," the Grandmaster declared and revealing a set of keys, removed the handcuffs from Alice and shoving a key into several locks, threw the titanium steel rings to the ground.

"What the fuck is that?" The captain said suddenly as a human like shape rushed through the trees near them. "There can't be anyone alive in here, especially with the exit sealed for six thousand years."

"Welcome home, son of Adam; child of my betrayer husband," the female voice said from out of the shadows in a tone that seemed almost musical.

"You can't trust her, she's not human and no friend of mankind," Cain declared. "She is also a cannibal."

The two remaining soldiers raised their weapons at the last remark and watched in transfixed fascination as the six foot woman approached them. Lilith had an African appearance, possessing dark skin and jet black straight hair which ran all the way down her back. She was voluptuous having large breasts and hips and was very beautiful. Her lips were full and she had piercing blue eyes, a gaze which the men found uncomfortable. Samuel remembered in the Old Testament Lilith was likened to the Devil; the ancient serpent who tempted Adam to eat the forbidden fruit. What was most startling was not only her naked appearance, but the fact that she seemed to rejoice in the freedom of not wearing clothes and the movement of her body was seductive. The Grandmaster noticed her fingernails were quite long, at least two inches and ending in a triangular point, as if they were miniature knives to tear flesh.

"Is my father also here?" Cain asked her in both excitement and apprehension. "Have you seen him?"

"Your parents left this planet not long after you murdered your brother Abel," Lilith said, moving closer to Cain. "Although I remained in Eden after Adam deserted me for the human female you call mother, I could still feel his presence out in the wilderness. But suddenly one day the sensation of his existence left me and I knew with certainty he had departed this world."

Cain's head bowed down in shame and regret and she laughed at his misery. She placed the left side of her face against his cheek and held it there for several moments before removing it.

"Strange thing tears," she said softly. "So much pain in such little liquid. My tears however dried up six thousand years ago when God created for Adam a more appropriate wife. But I was the succubus; I was the monster he still dreamed about every night he made love to Eve, in essence I am your true mother."

"You are a beast of evil intent," Cain snarled. "That is why you were never permitted to leave the Garden; that is your punishment for your crimes and the nightmares you wished to inflict on humankind."

Lilith abruptly turned and struck Cain across the face, a thin red line appearing on his cheek which did not heal, much to Samuel's interest. She stared in fascination at the single drop of blood on her fingernail and ran the finger across her tongue, savouring the taste. Alice noticed Lilith's tongue was unusually long, at least nine inches and was forked like a snake, giving truth to the stories of the demon being associated with the ancient serpent mentioned in Genesis in the Bible.

"I had almost forgotten the sweet taste of man-flesh," Lilith remarked with a sly smile. "Adam often gave me a few drops now and then in return for sexual favours. I am so bored and tired of feasting on the rotten meat of these twisted creatures of which you created."

"Show us the way to the Tree of Life," the captain shouted and pointed his machinegun at her head.

"Use your eyes human," she growled. "It is hard to miss. Your weapons are useless against me, unlike Cain I cannot be killed as long as Eden exists, I am immortal and can survive on the power of the Tree for all eternity."

"But I am guessing you can still experience pain," the other soldier with the flamethrower announced. "Ever imagine what it would be like to be on fire?"

Lilith glanced at him in amusement before leaping at the captain, her sharp fingernails tearing out his throat in an instant. The officer dropped his machinegun and clutched at his neck, blood jetting out of the deep wound onto the grass. The mercenary with the flamethrower turned the weapon and shot orange fire across the region. Samuel and his captives ran and threw themselves to the ground as the captain and Lilith were engulfed in flames. The demon screamed in agony and rushed towards the soldier. She tore at the mercenary with her nails, tearing his neck and face to shreds, before running off into the forest, her entire body ablaze. Cain watched her flee into the woods, a distant shape of orange flame disappearing into the bushes. He approached the fallen soldiers but it was obvious they were dead.

"That was incredible," Samuel declared as he revealed a semi-automatic handgun from beneath his jacket. "However, I still have a quest to fulfil. Lead me to the Tree."

Alice stared at him in astonishment. "Father be reasonable, your men are dead," she said. "You cannot continue in this mad mission, we must abandon this ridiculous quest and return to Iraq to get replacements for these mercenaries."

"There will be no reinforcements," Samuel said sharply. "I burned my bridges with the High Council in America, they have already named my successor for Britain and placed a death warrant on my head."

"Murdering all the Illuminati members of England probably sealed your fate," Cain interjected.

The Grandmaster moved forward and pointed the gun straight at Cain's skull. "Remember you are mortal here," Samuel sneered. "Are you prepared to leave your beloved Alice to die alone in this terrible kingdom ruled by monsters?"

Cain looked at him in silent anger and saw Alice's fear. He turned around and began to walk towards the centre of Eden. A short distance later they entered a huge clearing and Samuel gasped in amazement. Standing in the middle of the grassland was an enormous Tree, its bright orange leaves the antithesis to the rest of the Garden, its branches aglow and full of life. The Tree was at least three hundred feet high and stretched far into the clearing.

Alice stared at the object in astonishment. "Never could I have imagined anything so magnificent."

Samuel pointed the handgun at his captives, motioning for them to approach the Tree. They arrived at its base and Cain looked at the wood in apprehension, expecting to still see the blood and battered body of Abel lying there, but knowing Adam had long since removed the corpse and carried it out of Eden.

"Get digging," Samuel snarled, removing two trowels from his jacket and throwing them on the ground. "I want to see the roots."

"You can't be serious," Alice replied. "This could take hours and Cain no longer possesses superhuman strength."

"You got somewhere you need to be?" The Grandmaster growled.

Hours passed as the prisoners dug at the soil, slowly revealing the deep buried roots of the Tree. Cain could see a strange blue glow beneath the mud which got brighter the more he dug. Finally he unearthed a small perfectly rounded crystal ball the size of a football. As Cain removed the glass orb he saw the Tree above him begin to groan and the leaves grow dark, as if the plant was dying. Samuel's eyes opened wide when he saw the crystal ball.

Cain handed it to him and the Grandmaster noticed the orb had a faint warmth to it. He could not see into its interior but could certainly feel great magickal power exuding from the ball.

"Now will you let Alice leave this place?" Cain asked. "I care not for my own life, but I wish her to be safe, you can promise this for your own daughter."

Samuel gave his captive a stern glance. "I can't afford anyone coming after me, not even my own child."

The Grandmaster raised the weapon and prepared to fire. Alice cried out in terror and placed her arms around Cain. Just as they expected to die Samuel abruptly fell forward and dropped the crystal orb onto the grass. Standing behind him was the familiar hooded stranger who had saved Cain in Baghdad. He removed the cloth from his head and Cain gasped in astonishment.

"I told you once we would meet again, brother," Seth declared. "Six thousand years I held vigil in that city from whence it was a small village called Babylon which I helped found with father until it was named Baghdad. Many friends and wives I have buried in the centuries past while I waited."

Seth grabbed Cain's hand and pulled him to his feet and the brothers embraced.

"Is it true what Lilith said?" Cain enquired. "Have our parents left this planet?"

Seth nodded. "When the town Babylon reached a population of two thousand, Adam felt his task was at an end. He and mother prayed to be released of immorality and God heard their pleas. They travelled one morning into the wilderness and I never saw them again. I promised father I would wait and protect you when you returned."

"Well this is touching," Samuel said, getting to his feet and once again pointing the weapon in their direction. "Another son of Adam reunited with his brother, I should have guessed only an immortal could have killed five of my mercenaries unarmed."

"It is over father, let us go," Alice pleaded.

"Nobody is going anywhere," the Grandmaster declared, picking the blue orb from the ground. Samuel cursed when he noticed a deep crack in the surface of the ball.

"What have you done?" Seth asked in anger. "The magick will become unstable and destroy the world. You have doomed this planet to the Apocalypse, the explosion that will erupt from that orb will rip the Earth apart."

"I am taking this power source and leaving Eden," Samuel stated flatly as he grabbed hold of Alice and placed the gun to her temple.

"You son of a bitch," Cain said and moved towards him. "Let her go and I will take her place; my life in exchange for hers."

"A noble gesture," Samuel remarked with a smile. "I have a better arrangement for you."

The Grandmaster turned the weapon and a shot rang out. Alice screamed in fright and Cain fell to his knees as blood began to stain his shirt from the bullet wound to his chest. Seth stared at the injury in shock, knowing in the Garden his brother's self-healing abilities were nullified and such a wound would be fatal. Alice elbowed her father in the face and he fell back, dropping the blue ball. She picked up the crystal orb and handed it to Seth.

"The Tree of Life might contain the blast and prevent it from reaching outside the cavern," Seth said and shoved the orb back into the ground beneath the roots of the Tree and placing soil back over it, concealing the ball. "However, Eden will be utterly destroyed and disappear forever. You must leave this place immediately."

"What about Cain?" She enquired. "He will die unless we get him out of here and bring him back into the wilderness."

"If I try to move him now the injury will surely kill him," Seth declared. "I will remain and take care of my sibling. Do not worry for Cain, I can hear the Tree whispering to me like it did so long ago to my brothers when they made their offering and ended the ancient famine. Cain has achieved worthy redemption by giving his life in exchange for yours, only in the Garden was he mortal and such a sacrifice would have true meaning. It is time to go home and meet our parents."

Cain extended his hand and Alice grabbed hold of it. "I am sorry," he said. "I would have liked to spend the rest of your life with you. Go now and find your destiny."

Alice turned and saw her father lying on the ground, still dazed from the blow she had delivered. She watched in amazement as the tall grass and roots of the Tree began to come to life and wrap themselves around his legs.

He stared at her in fear. "Daughter, please help me. I cannot get loose."

Alice shook her head. "This is your fate father," she retorted. "Many opportunities had you to change; you have freely accepted this death before you by your choices."

She turned and ran into the forest, heading for the exit. The animals ignored her, more afraid of the approaching explosion and began tearing at the trees in their terror. Samuel watched the two brothers as a bright orange light engulfed them and they disappeared. The Grandmaster of the Illuminati screamed in frustration as the grass and roots covered his face and entered his mouth, his cry echoing throughout the Garden.

Alice looked back as she reached the exit and saw the forest begin to shake violently, the shudders ripping into the very cavern itself, the ceiling falling apart as giant rocks smashed into trees and the beasts below. She ran down the stone hallway and breathed a sigh of relief as the outside daylight struck her face. However, Alice knew her life was still in danger, as the imminent explosion threatened to not only destroy Eden, but Dena Mountain and the surrounding region.

Alice began to cry in fear, the tears streaming down her face; to survive the events in the Garden, but now lose her life because her escape proved too far. She suddenly looked skywards as she heard what sounded like the faint noise of helicopter blades. Alice let out a shout of delight and surprise as she saw the faces of Albert Maher and his partner Sean Neilson appear from the opened door of a helicopter. The detectives extended a rope ladder and she quickly climbed up.

"How is this possible?" Alice asked. "How did you know I was here?"

Albert smiled and pointed to the other passenger, a middle-aged man in an expensive suit. "Courtesy of our friends from the CIA," the policeman laughed. "They have been monitoring your father and the mercenaries for days by satellite. They were kind enough to loan us the helicopter. Where is Samuel Carson and his group of soldiers, not to mention Sam Philips?"

"Hold on," the pilot interrupted them. "I think the mountain is about to blow, grab onto something secure."

Tremendous violent shaking rocked the airborne vehicle and the pilot had to take evasive actions to keep it in the sky. All the passengers glanced back and gasped in awe as the sight of Dena Mountain disappeared from view. An enormous mushroom cloud of dense black smoke exploded into the atmosphere and began to cover the entire region.

"Christ," Albert declared. "It is akin to Hiroshima out there, did Carson have a nuclear device on him? Iran is going to love this."

But Alice did not reply. She sat near the edge of the door and looked out at the fiery ash cloud in dismay, knowing she would never see her father or the sons of Adam again, but content in the knowledge that Cain had finally found redemption and could go home. However, she still wished to see him one last time if just to say how much she loved him, her best friend and lover Cain, the man, the myth; the legend.

www.ingramcontent.com/pod-product-compliance
Lightning Source LLC
Chambersburg PA
CBHW061021120726
47910CB00006B/2042